"WE HAVE NOTHING TO HIDE, MARNIE."

Ian's voice was soft but determined.

"We're going to make love in the daylight, in the sunshine.... No inhibitions, no secrets are going to stand in our way." He drew her to him, making her tremble with sweet surrender.

"I'm innocent, too, Marnie," he declared, slowly and sensually stroking her sun-bathed body. "I didn't break your heart, but by God I'm going to do my best to mend it," he vowed, stepping into the cool, cool water.

She gasped as they immersed, her arms draping around his neck as he clamped her tightly against his swollen manhood.

"Marnie..." he choked. "You feel so damned right. How can this be wrong?"

"Who says it is, counselor?" she whispered seductively.

From that moment on, Ian Dunn was lost....

ABOUT THE AUTHOR

Ruth Alana Smith is an award-winning author from Texas. As Eileen Bryan, she won the 1983 Gold Medallion Award for her Dell Ecstasy, *Memory and Desire*. Ruth surrounds herself with the things she loves—her husband of twenty years, her two children, her calico cat and, of course, her writing. At present she is working on an idea for her second Superromance.

Ruth Alana Smith

THE WILD ROSE

Harlequin Books

TORONTO • NEW YORK • LONDON
AMSTERDAM • PARIS • SYDNEY • HAMBURG
STOCKHOLM • ATHENS • TOKYO • MILAN

Published April 1985

First printing February 1985

ISBN 0-373-70158-6

Printed in Canada

This story is dedicated with inexpressible love and esteem to a remarkable lady who personifies the spirit of the "wild rose." A vivid imagination invented the legend, but it was through her inexhaustible and sensitive guidance that the essence of the fictitious tale was instilled into the author and eventually spilled onto paper.

To most, she's affectionately known as Mif. Only three young women are privileged to call her Mom. I'm proud to say I'm *one*.

Here's hoping the book does you justice, Mif! And for all the times I failed to give you credit in the past, I'm making amends now, Mom!

PROLOGUE

DEEP IN THE HEART OF KENTUCKY, in a region located somewhere beyond the Pine Mountains' shadows and miles inland from the great Ohio River, there exist a few precious acres where only God has tread. Even the trailblazer Daniel Boone never glimpsed this majestic spot. Miraculously it still remains unsullied by a pillaging and disbelieving world.

The Indians thought the land to be sacred. For nearly two centuries, they'd chanted the legend of the "everlasting valley." Their praises told of a vast and brilliant rainbow that perpetually arched above the hallowed ground. According to the legend, the rainbow's splendid colors changed with each of the four seasons and the glow it cast competed with the moon and stars as well as the sun.

And beneath this bow of dazzling hues, the land was fertile beyond compare—the earth so rich that it gave eternal life to the vegetation; the waters so pristine that the animals that drank at the shale banks were granted immortality. All that was encompassed by the rainbow was immune to exterior elements. The plant life and animals did not succumb even during the great drought of 1736 or the winter blizzard that all but annihilated the Delaware tribes.

Amid this fertile land bloomed a flower—a rare and

hearty flower whose fragrance and color was unlike any other. It was stronger and sweeter, its essence uncommonly pure. As Indian folklore would have it, the intoxicating fragrance, once inhaled, lingered forever in one's soul. It sustained through drought and blizzard, rendering strength when weakness threatened, giving hope when despair prevailed. Only a privileged few had ever been chosen to be touched by the opiate essence of the valley flower. The Great Spirit guided the wind that carried the fragrance. Those who had been chosen to experience it, though perhaps sorely tested, would eventually be blessed with an embosoming peace. They would know a union of faith, of love—a love that was protected by the mythical rainbow and born of the incomparable wild rose.

CHAPTER ONE

AT THE ROSEHILL ESTATE outside Lexington, Kentucky, weary domestics tidied up after an elaborate dinner party. The hour was late and a thunderstorm waged as they grumbled through their chores.

"I don't know why these high-society folks can't eat at a decent hour," one tired and impudent maid complained. "I guess they figure the hired help don't need no sleep." She sampled a leftover canopé, then smacked her lips.

"If Miz Mimms catches you snitching food and whining, she'll retire you permanently," a more seasoned employee warned. "She don't tolerate...."

At the appearance of the stoic-faced Nadine Mimms in the doorway, the conversation instantly terminated. Predictably the black head housekeeper of Rosehill had come to observe the progress of her subordinates. Her reputation for being a perfectionist, with a tongue as sharp as her ebony eyes, snapped the servants into double time. One disapproving cluck escaping from her fleshy lips and virile menservants and cocky maids alike were known to quake in their shoes.

As Nadine Mimms silently directed with an authoritative nod or censorious point of her finger, the sound of Senator Hill's voice carried down the winding staircase. His words were indistinguishable, but his tone was

unmistakably angry. Covert glances were exchanged
among the domestics. This wasn't an unusual occur-
rence; they'd heard such arguments before. It was becoming a way of life, a repetitive cycle—the senator and
mistress attending or hosting a social function, retiring
to the bedroom, then quarreling behind closed doors.
Always it was the senator's voice that grew harsh and
loud, hurling to the perked ears below partially heard
accusations that would become elaborated gossip whispered the following morning.

Nadine's eyes flashed a formidable warning—mind
your own affairs. The staff knew her meaning. For if
she discovered one word of this being discussed within
or repeated outside Rosehill, it would be cause for immediate dismissal. Loyalty was her first command-
ment.

Yet tonight the upstairs battle was nearly impossible
to ignore. Mr. Seth and Miss Marnie were making no attempt to hide their marital discord. Their words were
muffled, but everyone present was painfully aware that
the scene taking place upstairs was as intense as the
static lightning slashing the groaning sky. Those in the
parlor below grew apprehensive, including the ever-
disciplined Nadine.

She drew her proud, spare frame even more erect, a
furrow of concern nestling between her arched brows.
For her thirty years in the Hills' employ, of all the secret
joys and sorrows she'd witnessed and kept confidential
from a prying world, the situation lately was by far the
most disturbing, the most exposed. The fact upset her
greatly. She'd taken secret delight in young Mr. Seth's
courage when he'd rebelled against the old judge's
wishes and married Miss Marnie. She'd taken heart in

the newlyweds' devotion and spunk as they'd overcome the odds. She'd rejoiced at the birth of their girl child and swelled with pride at each personal and political victory they claimed. But now...during the past year and a half she'd watched the union wither, losing faith, losing life.

As a young girl she'd once heard the Indian legend of a rose that grew wild under a magic rainbow in an enchanted valley. No adversity could destroy the delicate flower. She'd never forgotten the tale. When Mr. Seth first presented his bride at Rosehill, Nadine had been reminded of the childhood lore. There was a quality about Miss Marnie—pure and sweet, strong and resilient—an essence as remarkable as the wild rose. Mr. Seth was a man deprived of love. Miss Marnie was a woman with an abundance to share. Nadine had sensed her goodness and strength of character upon first contact, nearly ten years ago.

Nadine's head jerked toward the staircase at the boom of the senator's voice. This time his words were not only loud but excruciatingly clear.

"I can't live like this anymore. Damn you! I can't!"

A silver tea service rattled on a tray clutched in a skittish maid's hands. A vicious clap of thunder tinkled the chandelier overhead. And Miss Marnie's reply, if there was one, became lost in the tumult.

"Pay no attention," Nadine Mimms instructed in a detached tone. "Continue with your tasks." They obeyed in anxious silence, moving like industrious ants about the room.

"It's over...." Mr. Seth's hard words induced Nadine's heart to palpitate. "Understand that, Marnie, and...." The last of his threat was inaudible. It was then, a split second later, when an ominous gust of storm winds seemed to rattle the very foundation of Rosehill, that it happened—the terrifying reverberation of a gun blast.

Panic swept the downstairs household. Only Nadine reacted with assertiveness, racing up the stairs and charging into her employers' private chambers.

Prickles of sheer alarm ran along her spine as she stood braced in the doorway. Her noble features grew tense as she stared at Mr. Seth's body sprawled on the floor, a pool of crimson blood seeping from beneath him onto the Persian carpet. Her stricken eyes moved to Miss Marnie poised above him, staring dazedly at her fallen husband, a gun dangling from her visibly trembling hands.

Nadine rushed to the senator's aid, kneeling beside him and gently turning him over to lie in her sinewy arms. She placed a hand to the wound at his chest, praying to feel a heartbeat. Nothing. She blinked against the scalding tears blurring her vision as she then checked Mr. Seth's pulse. Again, not a flicker of life registered under her searching fingertips. A wet track of anguish began to spill down her black cheeks as she looked up and met her mistress's blank gaze. She, too, was silently weeping, her angel face contorted with unimaginable pain.

Nadine began to rock to and fro, still cradling the dead senator in her arms. Her choked words became a litany, echoing the same agony as the Negro spirituals she'd sung each and every religious Sunday since she was a girl. "Lord, Lord, Miss Marnie," she grieved. "What have you done?"

CHAPTER TWO

DETECTIVE JAMISON GLANCED AT THE CLOCK on the squad-room wall. It was now four-twenty in the morning and his sleep-starved brain was functioning at half power. He'd been interrogating the dead senator's wife for nearly two and a half hours, and still he had more questions than answers. He studied the woman seated across the desk from him. Dressed in a chic evening gown, simply but elegantly adorned in eighteen-karat gold, a lace shawl draped over her bare shoulders, she looked ridiculously out of place in these dismal surroundings. But what struck the detective most about the flaxen-haired beauty before him was that she seemed to be removed from the reality about her.

Ever since taking the suspect, Marnie Hastings Hill, into custody for questioning, she had appeared totally dissociated from the grave set of circumstances that necessitated this wee-small-hour interrogation. It occurred to the detective that the glamorous socialite was in shock. She had all the symptoms—a glazed look in her light blue eyes, zombielike movements, slow and detached responses to his questions. But then, of course, he'd dealt with icy and unremorseful types many times in his professional career. He wondered which category Mrs. Hill fell into—unaware or uncaring? With a perplexed grunt, he searched for his missing pack of cigarettes amid the clutter upon his desk.

"Care for a smoke?" he asked, extending the emaciated pack.

Startled by his question, Marnie glanced up at the hollow-eyed detective, then silently accepted a cigarette and light. It wasn't until she'd inhaled the pungent menthol that she remembered: she hadn't had a cigarette in over ten years. She'd given up the smoking habit at Seth's request. Marnie exhaled, her eyes drifting with the lazy whiff of smoke as disconnected thoughts sifted in and out of her head. No more would Seth praise her abstinence from tobacco. No more would she take pleasure in pleasing him. The senator was dead, his widow once again smoking.

"I think they've brewed some fresh coffee. Want a cup?" The detective's voice tinkled in Marnie's head like faraway wind chimes.

"Yes..." she responded in a vague tone. Then remembering herself, the suspect at last looked to her interrogator, amending her tactlessness with a softly spoken, "Thank you."

As the detective weaved his way between the empty metal desks to the coffee maker in the corner, her gaze trailed him. Insensibly, her mind cataloged trivial things. Sergeant Jamison's suit pants needed a pressing, his shirt bleaching and his shoes resoling. Worst of all, he slouched. Tall men such as he should carry themselves with dignity. Seth always walked tall. She glanced away the instant the detective turned to retrace his steps.

"It's stout," he warned, setting a chipped mug on the desk, then resuming his seat. The chair creaked under his considerable weight. "Drink up, Mrs. Hill. It's been a long night."

She nodded absently, then brought the steaming liquid to her lips, sipping and thinking. Tonight had been the longest night of her life. If she lived to be a hundred it would never end.

Once more, Jamison analyzed her, stealing glimpses beneath drowsy lids and over the edge of his cup. The lady was in big trouble—first-degree kind of trouble. And though she wasn't exactly uncooperative, she wasn't helping her cause, either. No, not at all. Her version of what had transpired in the master bedroom had more holes than his socks. An accidental shooting, she claimed. But she refused to fully disclose the details that led to the fatal incident. Something was amuck, and this whole affair was too damn "hot" for a mere homicide detective to assume. And yet, for some inexplicable reason, he had reservations about this woman's so obvious guilt. He'd hoped during the past few hours to convince her to confide in him the real facts behind the shooting. Only two people knew for certain what had preceded the .38 Special's discharging—one of whom was beyond telling; the other was deliberately withholding the vital information. He couldn't stall much longer. Soon he'd have to contact the D.A.

"Okay, Mrs. Hill," he said, putting down his mug and raking his fingers through his hair. "I want to go over this a final time. You have got to be more explicit. The servants heard you and your husband arguing prior to the gunshot blast. It's important that I know what prompted the quarrel," he probed.

Marnie stared blankly into her coffee mug. Detective Jamison observed the slight tremor of her hand on the handle as she hesitated. He prayed she was relenting. It would make things infinitely easier on them both.

"I've told you before, Sergeant Jamison..." she replied resignedly, at which he expelled a defeated sigh. "It was personal. I'd prefer to leave it as such."

"I'm afraid you haven't a choice, Mrs. Hill," he all but groaned. "If you persist in being vague in your answer, it'll only cast more suspicion. Speaking frankly and circumstantially, of course, none of this is looking very good for you. Witnesses heard you arguing with your husband, then a gunshot; the housekeeper finds the senator dead and you standing over him, weapon in hand. You can't explain why your husband had the Smith & Wesson out of the nightstand drawer and you refuse to discuss what led you to believe he intended to use it."

Unconsciously Marnie rubbed her throbbing temple as she spoke. "Believe me, Sergeant. The argument wasn't especially vicious, nor was it a catalyst for what followed. It was an effect, not a cause."

"You're losing me, Mrs. Hill. You see, I'm just a simple fella. In my nineteen years on the force, I've probably worked on over a hundred domestic disturbances. Generally, in cases where one of the spouses ended up being a victim of violence, the actual act was incited by a heated argument. Sometimes there's no other cause but angry words. So I find your unwillingness to discuss the matter almost incriminating in itself. You say the shooting was accidental. Then convince me. Tell me the truth of what occurred between you and your husband prior to the firing of the shot."

"I am telling you the truth," she replied, her voice husky with despair and, weariness. "Seth had been under a great deal of stress. He wasn't himself. Anything he said to me at that moment was impulsive and personal, and I don't wish our private disagreements to be made public. Didn't you advise me earlier that anything I might say could be used as evidence against me? Then whatever I admit to you could conceivably be a matter of public record. You can't guarantee me confidentiality, can you?" For the first time, her distant blue eyes engaged his, demanding a candid answer.

"No, I can't," he reluctantly conceded. "But I can promise you that though your silence may ensure privacy, it will also only serve to implicate you further." The seasoned detective waited for a response. None came. He fidgeted in his chair, muttering, "Do yourself and me a favor, will you, Mrs. Hill?"

She acknowledged his request with a guarded look.

"Don't persist in waiving your right to legal counsel any longer. Whatever your reasons for declining representation, I strongly recommend that you reconsider."

"You say you're a simple man. Well, my reasons are just as straightforward. Surely you can understand?"

"I understand that you're risking a charge of first-degree murder without benefit of expert advice, Mrs. Hill," he warned. "I'm going to have to make a phone call to my superiors. I urge you to exercise your right and make one, too. Don't say any more without an attorney present." He scooted the phone toward her, jerking up the receiver and holding it out.

She shook her blond head, saying only, "Make your

call, Sergeant. I'll wait. Perhaps it won't be necessary for me to make mine.''

Looking deeply into her intelligent eyes, he knew she understood that the phone call for legal aid would, in all likelihood, have to be made. Yet she held out a slim hope that his superiors might offer a reprieve. Her chances were next to nil. Detective Jamison knew that the Hill name alone would drag District Attorney Sutter Cane out from his sleep-warm bed. This case had sensationalism stamped all over it. Cane was up for reelection. Sensationalism could very well gain him another term, not to mention Judge Aubrey Hill's support if he should later decide to make a bid for the state's attorney general post. The lady would not find compassion in Sutter Cane. Only ambition. He turned the phone around and started to dial, then paused and hung up. For some absurd reason, her nearness as he initiated the damning call bothered him.

''Excuse me,'' he said in a tight voice while abruptly standing up from his chair. ''Help yourself to the coffee. I'll be back shortly.''

''Sergeant?'' she called after him.

He halted dead in his tracks, turning to face her with urgent expectancy.

''May I trouble you for another cigarette?'' came the disappointing request.

''The pack and lighter are on the desk,'' he muttered. His shoulders slumped a bit more as a crazy thought seized him—the condemned was having a last smoke before facing the firing squad. Perhaps he ought to ask Mrs. Hill if she wanted a blindfold, too? He refrained from giving in to the impulse, leaving her, as he vacated the room, the privacy she so fiercely protected.

Once Detective Jamison was out of sight, Marnie placed a cigarette between her wan lips and picked up the lighter. Her hand shook so violently that she was forced to brace it with the other when lighting up. She inhaled and tried to steady herself, leaning her forehead against a clammy palm and closing her eyes. In the chambers of her mind a gun blast exploded, sounding a death knell that sent an icy ripple along her spine. Once again, she relived the instant of her husband's death—seeing him wince, then crumple, feeling the clutch of his hand on her arm before he fell to the floor. A grievous scream threatened to tear from her throat. She sprang from the chair and began to pace, inhaling, exhaling, trying not to remember, attempting to focus on the immediate ordeal before her.

Mustn't fall apart. Not now! Be strong, Marnie. Make it through this night. So much depends on. . . .

Her chin quivered. Her legs quaked. She groped for the ashtray on the desk, managing to extinguish the cigarette before collapsing into a chair. She felt nauseated. Clutching her queasy midsection, she rocked to and fro while taking several deep breaths.

Hold on! Don't dare give in. Don't tell! Silently, desperately, Marnie reached for the inner strength that had sustained her over the past few years. Too often of late, mind over matter seemed the only device standing between her and an impending crisis. Never in her life was it more imperative that she smother her private panic and maintain the "together" image.

Sunny! Above all else, she must protect her daughter. God! Why did this have to happen? How could she explain without jeopardizing Sunny's future? Her rocking motion ceased and a resolute glint crystalized

in her pale blue eyes. She couldn't! It was that com-
plexly simple. Suddenly Marnie felt as deserted, as
ostracized as when her mother had turned her back on
her some ten years ago.

She had only just told her mother of her intention to
marry Seth Hill. The matriarch of the Hastings clan
had blanched at the announcement. Throughout the
courtship she'd made no attempt to hide her fierce objections to the match. She believed the social gap was
too great, the bloodlines and backgrounds too distinct
ever to be mingled. As clearly as yesterday Marnie recalled the implacable look on her mother's face, the
finality in her tone. "Then you've chosen your place,
Marnie," she'd said. "You're borrowing heartache,
and I'll not be a witness to your misery." Her mother
had stared at her for a pronounced moment, then
slowly stood up, turned her back and begun to walk
from the room. Marnie had been too devastated to
speak. Yet her mother had added an afterthought,
never glancing around, only dismally shaking her
head. "Some bridges are not meant to be crossed.
What you envision on the far side is only an illusion.
The gap between you and Seth Hill is too wide, girl.
That's a fact you should have known from the first. I
won't give my blessing, and I won't be attending the
wedding." And with those farewell words, her mother
had not only disappeared from view, but vanished
from the forefront of her life. A year later she died
unexpectedly, still not forgiving Marnie for loving a
man on the far side of an invisible bridge.

Oh, mama, she silently groaned. *Is this your prediction come true? I feel as if the bridge is about to give
way beneath me.*

Marnie sat lost in soul-searching memories as time ticked by on the white-faced clock. Nearly thirty minutes had passed before Detective Jamison's approaching footsteps alerted the widow. The same as a chameleon, she altered her appearance, a composed mask descending over her delicate features. She looked the part she played—assured and reserved. Marnie Hastings Hill was about to give the performance of her life. She knew her role, her lines: a bereaved widow who emphatically disclaimed any guilt; the shooting was accidental; the argument preceding the fatal shot inconsequential. Marnie favored the detective with a glance at the exaggerated clearing of his throat.

"I'm afraid we'll have to detain you a while longer, Mrs. Hill," he said in a flat voice, loosening his tie and scratching his throat. Marnie had become quite proficient at reading body language. She was sensitive to his acute discomfort. His uneasiness gave her something to focus on, a blessed diversion from dwelling on her own precarious situation.

"Could I impose on you for another cup of coffee while we wait?" came the unruffled request.

He shrugged his stooped shoulders, then collected their mugs and efficiently went about getting them a refill. After resituating himself in his chair, he sat mutely studying his coffee for a few moments. His subdued and resigned manner heightened the sensation of doom mounting within Marnie. She tried to counteract the tension with idle chitchat.

"Would it be presumptuous to ask who'll be questioning me next?"

"District Attorney Sutter Cane," was all he answered, gulping his coffee.

Marnie tried to hide her anxiety, merely saying, "I'm surprised that the district attorney should take such a personal interest."

"You shouldn't be, Mrs. Hill," he grunted. "VIP cases get preferential treatment."

"Yes, I suppose you're right." She cast him a caustic smile. "It's just that I never considered myself a member of the elite."

"The point is, Cane perceives the late senator important enough to put in an appearance." Obvious disapproval colored the detective's voice. He had no doubt that the illustrious district attorney was driving at break-neck speed to the station house. Whenever glory beckoned, Sutter Cane was prompt.

"Yes, of course," she murmured, lowering her eyes and sampling the unpalatably bitter liquid. "I sometimes tend to underestimate the effect the Hill name has on most people."

Detective Jamison couldn't help but note the ever-so-slight play of emotion on the widow's cameo face. He suspected that Mrs. Hill was much more disturbed than she let on, but his suspicion was only based on instinct. This gentle-mannered lady was either very clever or semitraumatized.

"Is the press converging outside?" Her expression was as bland as her tone.

"Yes, ma'am. It's hard to keep something of this nature under wraps for very long."

She smiled sadly, saying, "You may become a celebrity by mere association, Sergeant."

"I'd prefer to remain anonymous," he replied, sensing the aura of reluctance that clung to her.

"So would've I," she said softly, bowing her head and once more sipping the coffee.

Detective Jamison felt compelled to make a last plea for her willing cooperation. "Please, Mrs. Hill, won't you reconsider and—"

"Did you know I have a daughter?" she interrupted, her words staccato, a flush creeping up her slim neck.

"Ah, yes," he stammered, becoming befuddled by her abrupt switching of topics.

Marnie knew she had to keep talking. She was attuned to the sergeant's purpose and feared she might succumb to any sympathetic overture at this highly emotional moment.

"Her name is Sunny. She's seven." She kept up the irrelevant chatter.

"I know. It's in the report." He sighed, intently analyzing her as he sipped.

"Have you any children, Sergeant?"

"No, ma'am. I'm a bachelor."

She nodded, then resumed the smoke-screen conversation. "That's a pity. You've missed a great deal."

Rubbing his red-rimmed eyes, Jamison yawned an appropriate response. "So I've been told. I guess it's a little late to regret the fact, though. I'm nearly fifty-one."

"You look younger," she managed with experienced finesse.

"Yeah?" He perked up in his chair, then practically catapulted from it at the stern boom of Sutter Cane's voice from the doorway.

"I hate to intrude upon this amiable chat, Sergeant. But since I dragged myself out before dawn at your insistence, I'm certain you won't mind if I steal a few minutes of Mrs. Hill's time.''

At the sarcastic remark, the sergeant bristled but acceded. ''Not at all,'' he muttered with equal disdain. As he relinquished his chair he made a motion to retrieve the pack of cigarettes from the desk, but then reconsidered with a poignant gesture. He left the pack, tossing the lighter in front of Marnie.

Her head jerked up in time to catch his sympathetic smile. ''Perhaps it's time to make that call, Mrs. Hill,'' he advised in a grave voice before grabbing his jacket from the back of the chair and lumbering toward the squad-room door.

''The lady's all yours, Mr. Cane,'' he declared, brushing past the impatient D.A. Before Marnie could recover from Jamison's swift exit, the door banged shut and a challenge was issued from Sutter Cane's lips.

''Shall we dispense with the pleasantries and discuss the reason that we're both being deprived of sleep, Mrs. Hill?''

''If you like,'' she answered coolly. Her eyes traveled up the prosecutor assessingly. The man she beheld was no more, no less than she'd expected—fortyish; conservative (probably Republican); New England with a jogger's physique; neutral coloring; thinning hair; clipped style of speech and a mind probably as sharp as his steel gray eyes.

''What I would like is some straight answers to a few pertinent questions,'' was his curt response. Sutter Cane was a man in a hurry—a man of colossal ambition with little time to waste. Through the years Marnie had encountered his type many times. It wasn't difficult to recognize the fame-greedy look, the eager passion he exuded. She'd known her share of men like Sutter Cane—men whose grand aspirations made his seem petty in comparison. She did not underestimate the shrewd D.A. Yesterday her power and status had been superior; today she was under his jurisdiction.

"I've already given a statement, Mr. Cane." Her frosted-bronze polished nails tapped the cellophaned cigarette pack.

He moved closer, perching on the edge of the desk, legs crossed at the ankles, arms folded over his chest. "Your version of what transpired in the bedroom is brief, to say the least. I believe you're being purposely vague. I also am convinced that you intentionally shot your husband, Mrs. Hill." To say that Sutter Cane was brutally direct would be an understatement. His steely eyes fixed on her, watching, waiting for a break in her imperturbable facade.

As much as Cane was analyzing the witness, he was also appreciating the woman. Mrs. Hill was classically beautiful. There was an undefinable grace about her. And something more...something carnal and taboo. Was it her sultry mouth? Or perhaps the contrast between her ethereal features and earthy voice or the sensuality she projected with each minute movement. She was a looker! The kind of woman that made a man aware of her provocative perfume, the sheen on her lips, the silky, almost undetectable but highly erotic brush of one nyloned leg against the other. As much as he hated to admit it, Sutter Cane found the widow undeniably distracting and absolutely voluptuous—an understatement that was almost a declaration and stimulating as hell. And he was stimulated by the widow. On a scale from one to ten, she was a twelve and a half. Undoubtedly she was also the biggest challenge of his career!

"You're wrong," was her only reply as Marnie leaned back in the chair.

"I don't think so," he said firmly. "It's established that your husband and you were engaged in a bitter argument. Witnesses heard him tell you—" he picked up a typed document, quoting " '—I can't live like this anymore. Damn you! I can't.' My theory is that your husband wanted a divorce. He was through with you and a marriage on the rocks. But you weren't having it. You knew you'd lose everything—position, security, face. According to Washington rumors, the senator may even have had ample grounds for gaining custody of your daughter. A divorce would be a nasty affair. The darling of Washington society would be smeared in every scandal sheet from coast to coast. You couldn't risk that. You were desperate, and 'hell hath no fury like a woman scorned.' "

"An imaginative but totally incorrect theory, Mr. Cane," she interjected, stubbornly resisting the racing of her heart. She mustn't let him see how hard she fought to conceal her panic.

"Who's to say, Mrs. Hill? Certainly not your dead husband. He probably didn't realize your intent until it was too late—only after you'd removed the Smith & Wesson from the nightstand drawer and aimed it at him. Did you even give him an option before pulling the trigger? Maybe the scenario went something like, 'There'll be no divorce or scandal. I'll see you dead first.' "

"This is absurd," she scoffed as she sprang from the chair. "You have a flair for melodrama, Mr. Cane. If

ever politics bore you, perhaps you ought to consider
script writing for afternoon soaps.'' She crossed to the
window, hardly aware that dawn had broken on the
Lexington skyline as she focused on nothing in particular.

''You're finding it difficult to sit still. Could it be that
my casting of you as a murderess struck a nerve? You
might think me smug, Mrs. Hill, but I believe I've captured your character remarkably well.''

His goading worked. She spun on him, frustration
and ire sparking in her blue eyes. ''How could you
presume to know my character or what truly happened
between me and my husband? I'm not impressed with
you or your assumptions, Mr. Cane.''

A subtle smirk twisted his lips. Finally the suspect,
Marnie Hastings Hill, was reacting to stress and
fatigue. If he pressed a little harder, he might have a
confession before breakfast. The notion was tempting.
But then another more enticing thought occurred to
Sutter Cane. Mrs. Hill's admitting to intentionally killing her husband would reap some major publicity, but
the coverage would be nothing in comparison to the national media attention a sensational murder trial would
draw. Weeks' worth of headlines and vote-getting men-
tions would be given to the prosecutor. And Sutter
Cane had not the slightest doubt about the identity of
the fortunate fellow who'd inherit the Hill case. He
would, of course. So instead of badgering Mrs. Hill into
admitting her guilt, the politically ambitious D.A.
elected to ensure a lengthy trial and his future.

''I'm not seeking your endorsement, only the truth,
Mrs. Hill. For the last time, I urge you to tell me the
unembellished and complete story of the shooting from

beginning to end, including the details of the argument between yourself and your husband.'' He leaned back on his palms, awaiting her refusal. Sutter Cane prided himself on being a keen judge of human nature, and he was convinced of her guilt. Mrs. Hill suffered from the rich-and-famous syndrome—her fragile ego was dependent on an image that under no circumstances did she want tarnished. Shallow types like her would go to great lengths, resort to any drastic measures, in order to preserve that image, even lying, cheating, killing.

Marnie wasn't a fool. She realized the D.A.'s ulterior motives. She was numb but hardly stupid. She knew there wasn't the faintest hope she could walk out of this police station a vindicated woman. From the moment of Seth's dying breath, she'd known it would come to this.

"I can only repeat what I've already stated, Mr. Cane." Her words came slowly and with no inflection whatsoever. "The shooting was a tragic accident. Yes, we were arguing. Yes, in the midst of the squabble, Seth took the gun from the drawer. Yes, Mr. Cane, Seth produced the gun, not me. I have no idea why he wanted it but it shocked me. I tried to retrieve the gun from him. It went off.'' Her voice drifted, as did her attention. No longer did Marnie see Sutter Cane; she was envisioning the disbelief on her husband's ashen face a second after a deafening gun blast resounded. "Contrary to what you may believe, I am not a heartless murderess. I'm guilty of a grievous error in judgment and I'll have to live with that tragic mistake for the rest of my life. But that's all I feel obligated to tell you."

"You're a very stubborn and foolhardy woman. I

can prove you had opportunity and motive. Surely you don't expect me to—''

"I expect you'll do what you intended to from the first. I really never thought that my plea of innocence would make the slightest difference," she retorted, clashing with his hard eyes as she turned to face him.

"I'm charging you with first-degree murder, Mrs. Hill," he responded without so much as a blink.

Her heart stilled in her chest, and it took every ounce of self-control she possessed not to flinch at the stinging words.

"I believe I'm entitled to one phone call," she said, easing toward the chair. She felt faint. His face dimmed, then came back into focus as she reseated herself.

"Certainly," came the monosyllabic reply. "A suggestion, Mrs. Hill—" Cane smirked as he pushed the telephone toward her "—opt for the very best. You can afford it and, believe me, you're going to need it."

If she hadn't been so weary, so drained, she would have slapped Sutter Cane's arrogant face. Visibly shaking, Marnie dialed her sister, Grace.

CHAPTER THREE

"A SKETCHY REPORT of the fatal shooting of Senator Seth Hill at his family estate this morning has been confirmed. The statesman from Kentucky was mortally wounded during what is being described as 'a domestic quarrel.' Senator Hill had been mentioned as a possible democratic presidential candidate.

"Our sources disclose that Marnie Hastings Hill, wife of the renowned senator, is being questioned about the tragic events leading to her husband's death. District Attorney Sutter Cane has scheduled a news conference for eleven this morning, at which time he is expected to announce formally charging Mrs. Hill. Further details to follow."

Grace Morgan snapped off the car radio in disgust. No matter what station she'd tuned in during her drive to the legal offices of Connery and Dunn, the result was the same—some newscaster randomly breaking into the regular programming to exploit her sister's troubles. Being a very conservative person of modest means, Grace had never quite grown accustomed to the media ballyhoo surrounding Marnie. For years she'd heard or read the half truths and malicious innuendos circulated about her younger sister, wishing the world could know the true character of Marnie and hating the liberties the hounding press took. But this was ridiculous! Not only had they blithely suggested that her sister was a "scarlet woman," now they were branding her with the letter *M* for murderess. My God! Was no one going to give her a chance? Because she was beautiful and enviable, did she automatically deserve public condemnation? How ironic that the very same people who had made Marnie a celebrity against her wishes now denounced their beloved idol as false and wicked.

With a worried sigh, Grace shut off the engine of her economical Toyota, exited and crossed the street to the law offices. A melodious chime announced her entrance, causing the receptionist to come alert behind the desk.

"May I help you?" she asked in a pleasant tone.

Grace clutched her handbag tighter. "I called earlier. My name is Grace Morgan," came the rehearsed introduction. "It's very important that I speak with Mr. Dunn."

With practiced poise, the receptionist responded, "I'm sorry, Mrs. Morgan. As I told you on the phone, Mr. Dunn is in court this morning and has a full agenda the entire afternoon." As she spoke, the prim and proper woman nonchalantly glanced at a calendar pad on her desk. "Let's see..." she began. "I could schedule you for an appointment a week from Thursday.'"

Unbridled alarm registered on the plain face of Grace Morgan. "Please," she beseeched. "I must see Mr. Dunn today." Her fingers kneaded the imitation leather of her purse. "My sister is being held at the police station, and I promised to—"

"There are many excellent and more available attorneys in town. Let me refer you,'' the receptionist coolly interrupted.

"No!" Grace blurted. "Mr. Dunn came highly recommended. Marnie needs someone with his experience. Can't I wait and speak with him myself? It won't take long. I'll just sit over here, quiet like, and catch him when he comes in, if it's all the same to you." With uncommon assertiveness, Grace retreated to the couch, her chin squaring stubbornly as she perched upon the cushions.

The receptionist tried once more to dissuade her. "I can't guarantee that Mr. Dunn can spare the time, Mrs. Morgan."

"I understand," was all the persistent lady answered as she picked up a copy of *Time* and began to browse through the pages.

The receptionist gave up with a shrug, then picked up the pen she'd discarded at the chime and resumed the paperwork Grace had interrupted.

To the sound of rustling pages and the soft scrape of a fountain pen, time crept by on the clock.

During the slow wait, a series of thoughts preoccupied Grace. She recalled Marnie's apathetic tone when describing her plight. Grace attributed her strange inflection to delayed trauma over the tragic circumstances of Seth's death. For in her heart Grace believed her sister totally innocent in the regrettable incident. But Marnie's voice had given Grace a nagging and unsettling feeling. Oddly she found herself remembering Marnie's guarded behavior whenever trouble threatened them when they were kids. Whether the crisis resulted from her baby sister's mischief or she was merely implicated by default, she'd withdraw into an impenetrable shell like a tortoise—never tattling, always avoiding the aftermath. Grace strongly suspected Marnie was resorting to the evasive tactic at this, the most painful moment of her life. It wasn't that her younger sister was cowardly. Marnie was acutely sensitive, not just when sensing danger directed at herself but also toward those whom she loved.

Phrases from the startling phone conversation she'd had with Marnie several hours ago surged through Grace's anxious mind like a tidal wave. "I can't believe I'm living this nightmare," her sister had said. "Seth's dead and I'm partially to blame. It was an accident. I never meant for this to happen." Grace had tried to impress upon her the seriousness of what she was saying. She'd begged Marnie not to say another incriminating word until she could retain legal counsel for her, but her sister was too distracted to listen to reason. She didn't sound hysterical, more like resigned. There wasn't a shred of emotion in her voice. And it was that very passivity that disturbed Grace most. She knew she had to act swiftly if she was to have any chance at all. At best, her sister would be charged with manslaughter; at worst.... Grace stiffened, rejecting the unthinkable possibility.

Instead, she relived the frantic phone calls she'd placed on Marnie's behalf in search of an attorney willing to represent her. The few who'd actually taken her calls tactfully declined once the connection had been made to the Hills. The influential family's name carried power and political clout throughout the state. No one she contacted was eager to challenge that power or take on a case that most certainly would draw nationwide media attention and might very well be lost. After all, they had their precious reputations and professional futures to protect. Only one lawyer was even courteous enough to offer a referral, giving her the name of Ian Dunn, who, according to his colleague, was shrewd and unintimidated by controversial cases. He sounded like the perfect person to champion Marnie's cause. And if ever a lady was in distress and needed a defender, it was her sister. Her situation grew darker each passing moment.

Grace didn't realize she'd sighed aloud. The unread periodical rattled in her hands when the receptionist broke into her thoughts with a misinterpretation. "I know you must be tired of waiting. There's a fairly decent diner across the street if you'd care to have lunch," she suggested.

"Thank you, no," Grace declined. "I wouldn't want to chance missing Mr. Dunn."

The receptionist cast her a wan smile while trying to ignore the growl of her own stomach. In her five years with the firm, she'd dealt with a variety of perspective clients, but none more anxiously persistent than Mrs. Morgan. She began to fear the lady might elect to camp out overnight on the doorstep, should Mr. Dunn fail to return as expected.

Grace glanced at her watch. Twelve-ten. By now the district attorney had held his promised news conference. A goodly portion of the citizens of Lexington knew her sister's fate, and here she sat ignorant of the final charges against Marnie. If only Marnie had been more explicit over the phone. "They plan to bring charges, and I need an attorney, Grace," she'd said. "I hate to burden you with this, but I'm afraid it'll take time to locate someone daring enough to take my case. Since they seem inclined to get on with it, time isn't something I have very much of at the moment.''

"Don't worry, Marnie," Grace had told her. "I'll find a lawyer. A really good one. We'll have you out of that awful place soon.'' Well, soon was now nearly six hours later, and Marnie had every right to be anxious. Grace had yet to locate an attorney willing to represent her, and Mr. Dunn, the best candidate thus far, could very well refuse on the grounds of professional preservation, also. Panic began to overtake Grace. Maybe she shouldn't waste another precious minute dawdling in a plush reception room awaiting a man whom she had no guarantee would even consider becoming involved? Perhaps Mr. Dunn was a phantom who didn't exist at all?

A chime sounded. Grace's eyes snapped toward the door. The phantom had materialized. And, oh, but he was an impressive figure—standing well over six feet tall, dressed in a fashionable, double-breasted silk suit and exuding a masterful air as he addressed the receptionist in passing. "Any messages, Carol?" a resonant baritone voice inquired.

The pert lady behind the desk held up several for his inspection. Grace stood and cleared her throat, at which the gentleman deigned to glance in her direction.

"Ah, this lady's been waiting quite a while to see you, Mr. Dunn," the receptionist informed him. He looked back to her quizzically, wishing clarification. Had he forgotten an appointment? "Mrs. Grace Morgan hasn't an appointment, but she insisted on speaking with you. She says it's urgent," the receptionist explained in a purely businesslike tone.

The attorney's hazel gaze lighted upon Grace once more. His carefully controlled expression softened slightly as he noted her obvious distress.

Quite unintentionally Grace discovered herself dangerously close to out-and-out gawking at the striking individual before her. He had to possess the most magnetic pair of eyes, the most masculine yet incredibly sensitive face she'd ever encountered. His skin was bronzed from massive doses of sun, the character lines etched at the corners of his eyes inscribing his nature like a bold signature. *He* was a man who enjoyed life with gusto. His smile was unblemished by subterfuge, his chin square, strong and cleft. And he moved with the assurance, the contained energy of a mountain lion—lithe and territorial. Never before and never again would Grace consign such innate power to a mere mortal man.

He stepped forward, offering his hand. It was a standard gesture, not especially significant, but it meant the world to her—it meant he wasn't opposed to sparing her a moment or two of his invaluable time.

"I'm Ian Dunn," he said in a warm voice. "How may I help you, Mrs. Morgan?" His hand fused with hers—steady and compelling. The simple act of his handshake caused grateful tears to suddenly violate Grace's composure.

"It's not me who needs your help, Mr. Dunn," she replied. "It's my sister. She's in terrible trouble." Her throat filled with the same emotion as her eyes, causing him to grip her hand a bit more reassuringly.

"Why don't we step into my office and discuss the matter, Mrs. Morgan?" Before Grace could respond, he released her hand, gesturing to a door on the right side of a narrow hallway.

She nodded, then silently proceeded down the hall. The spacious office was expensively furnished, full of character and amber noon daylight filtering through smoke-tinted windows. One wall was covered by a full-length bookshelf containing legal texts and reference books, and another was paneled in redwood and adorned with framed honors. Displayed throughout the room were art treasures, hunting trophies, mementos of special occasions, all set off by the lush greenery of potted plants. But what impressed Grace most about the private haven was the curious mingling of individual scents—lemon furniture polish, musky leather tinged with a vague whiff of spicy cologne.

She seated herself in one of the two overstuffed chairs arranged in front of a mahogany desk and watched the attorney's every move as he placed his suit coat on a hook in a closet, then took his place opposite her.

"I realize you're a very busy man, Mr. Dunn, but by reputation you're also one of the best criminal attorneys in this town," she began, her eyes averted to her lap, her fingers twiddling with the clasp on her purse. "My sister truly needs someone of your caliber to represent her," she declared, raising her entreating gaze to his.

"What kind of trouble is your sister in?" was all he answered, leaning forward in his chair and steepling his fingertips pensively.

"Maybe all this would be more simply explained if I ask you a question." She sighed, ignoring the look of puzzlement her remark produced on his tanned face. "Did you happen to listen to or hear about the district attorney's news conference this morning?"

Without the least change in expression, he repeated

her sister's name. "Marnie...Marnie Hill," he
elaborated. "She's accused of murdering her husband."

Grace's chin quivered at the remark. Unaware of the
D.A.'s statement, she hadn't known until this moment
that Marnie had been charged with first-degree
murder. "My God!" she gasped, paling. "I was hoping...." At a loss for words, she collapsed weakly
against the soft cushion of the chair.

"You didn't know?" he asked, his voice filled with
surprise and apology as he sprang to his feet, pouring
and passing to Grace a cool glass of water.

She shook her head and took a needy gulp. "I've
been trying to find someone to secure her release from
jail since six this morning. Marnie never told me the
charge. She only said that Seth's death was accidental
and kept insisting that somehow she felt partially to
blame," came the dazed response. "I was praying it
would be less—involuntary manslaughter or something like that." A deafening silence descended upon
the room as Ian considered the naive and shaken
woman before him. He wondered if he should even
bother to mention that the term "involuntary manslaughter" was more prevalent in Hollywood than in a
courtroom. Compassion won out over logic, and he
curbed the impulse.

Grace became aware he was studying her. She
fumbled in her purse for a tissue, then swiped at her
nose. "I'm sorry to fall to pieces like this. I'm afraid
it's typical though," she said, sniffing. "In her own
quiet way, Marnie's always been the strongest in the
family."

He cast her a kind smile, saying, "It took no small

measure of fortitude to endure the long wait to see me, Grace.'' Her head lurched up at his casual address. ''May I call you by your first name?'' he smoothly inserted while sitting down.

She nodded, the taut tension lines between her brows beginning to relax. ''It wasn't fortitude that brought me here, Mr. Dunn. It was desperation. I've met a wall of resistance trying to secure legal aid for my sister. No one wants to go up against the Hills. I think everyone believes that the old judge will undoubtedly be out for blood—Marnie's and that of anyone who dares to defend her.''

A barely discernible glimmer of defiance lit Ian's green-and-gold-flecked eyes. ''Do you concur with the assumption?''

Reluctantly she nodded again. ''Aubrey Hill hates my sister with a passion. He always has. Seth was all that ever stood between Marnie and the old man's ruthlessness. He'll go after her, all right. He'll hold her responsible for Seth's death, and nothing short of execution will satisfy him.'' Realizing the possibility she'd voiced, Grace was alarmed. ''Dear God! Is that possible? Could Marnie receive the death penalty?'' Stark terror shook her voice.

''Don't borrow trouble, Grace. She's hasn't been convicted, only charged,'' he assured her. ''Rather than hypothesize about the future, I'd prefer to discuss the past and present. Why don't you tell me a little something about your sister and the senator?''

Seizing on the fact that the capable attorney was even remotely interested, Grace was more than willing to supply him with a brief biography. ''Marnie is the youngest of six children. Being the baby of the family, she might easily have been spoiled, but just the opposite was true. Daddy died when she was only three, and mama was bone weary from hard work and raising a tribe of kids. The rest of us were several years older and mostly involved in going our separate ways. So Marnie was sort of left to fend for herself. I guess you could say she was a bit of a loner.''

"There's usually a big difference between being a loner and being lonely. It doesn't sound as if she had much choice.''

"Probably not,'' she agreed. "Marnie was lucky in one way though: she was by far the prettiest of the bunch. She grew into a beautiful woman, and all the attention she once lacked became hers for the asking. Men adored her; women were envious. It's no wonder that the media capitalized on her—she's a born cover girl. She never sought the acclaim, but once her life was linked with the Hills, she became an overnight celebrity. . . American royalty, if you will.''

"She's most definitely photogenic,'' Ian reflected, much more interested in the woman's character than her image.

"The magazine photos don't do her justice. She's even lovelier in person,'' Grace went on. "I suppose Seth Hill was as struck as everybody else when he first met her. They were introduced at one of those fundraising barbecues. He wasn't a senator yet, but campaigning hard. Of course, everybody knew that with his daddy backing him, the man was almost a shoe-in. But I guess that's neither here nor there. The point is,'' she continued, "he was absolutely taken with Marnie from that day on. I don't think a man ever pursued a woman more devotedly. By the time he'd claimed victory in the senatorial race, he'd also won my sister's heart. They married shortly after he took office."

"So you believe your sister loved him?" came the direct question from a man seeking understanding and the truth.

Grace met his bluntness with candor. "In spite of what you may have read to the contrary, my sister truly cared for and was deeply committed to her husband, Mr. Dunn. Theirs wasn't an easy marriage, especially considering all the outside factors. But it was nonetheless, until recently, a good match. Seth was very generous and kind; my sister extremely grateful and loyal."

Ian noted her choice of words but made no comment—"until recently...grateful, loyal." "You mentioned outside factors," he probed. "Could you be more specific?"

Grace took another sip of water, then answered. "Well, at first there were both the judge's and my mama's strong objections to the marriage. The two of them did everything in their power to discourage it." A distant look crept into her eyes as she spoke. "I remember mama once saying to Marnie that if you marry into money, you'll be obliged to earn the privilege every day of your life. Mama was so bitterly opposed to the wedding that she refused to attend. She firmly believed that the mingling of such different backgrounds would only bring heartbreak. Who knows? Perhaps she was right." She sighed, her attention drifting.

Ian mentally recorded her every word, every significant but unintentional fact she divulged. For though he was not yet aware, the charisma and intrigue surrounding Marnie Hastings Hill and the senator were slowly drawing Ian Dunn in. He wished to know more about the lonely beauty who aroused such contradictory opinions. "I'm interested to hear your thoughts. Do you think their different backgrounds played a part in what occurred last night?"

"No!" came the emphatic reply. "Gradually things changed between Seth and Marnie, but it had nothing to do with her being the poor waif from the wrong side of the tracks. Marnie always had class. Seth recognized it from the first and would've cut down to size anyone who said otherwise."

"Then what caused the violent situation your sister was involved in?" he persisted.

"I don't know," Grace groaned. "Something was very wrong between them. Whatever it was had been festering for nearly two years. Marnie's a very private person. She doesn't confide in anyone. People like her are easy prey for the press. Those damn celebrity hunters can speculate, insinuate, even assassinate the character of an introvert like my sister. They've stalked her for years. But I'm telling you, Mr. Dunn, my sister is not guilty of cold-blooded murder. I don't know what preceded the tragedy that happened in that master bedroom last night. I only know that Marnie is innocent yet somehow feels responsible. You've got to help her. Someone besides me has to believe in her." The panic she'd contained began to consume Grace once more. "Please, Mr. Dunn. I don't know where else to turn. How can I convince you that my sister's a warm, sensitive person incapable of the crime they accuse her of?"

Her plea was unnecessary. Ian had long since made

his decision, though he had not made it lightly. He was well aware of the Hill name and the power it represented. Even more, he realized the adverse publicity his defense of the socialite might reap. His conservative partner would be adamantly opposed. But rebellious Irish blood flowed through his veins. He never could forsake a challenge.

Reaching out and patting Grace's hand, he consented with a wordless nod, then pressed the direct line to the receptionist, confirming his commitment with a simple request. "Reschedule my afternoon as best you can, Carol. Then get me District Attorney Cane on the line and have Hoss Jorgenson of Guaranteed Bonding Service holding, will you, please?"

"Certainly," came the affirmative reply before he released the intercom and settled back with an easy smile. "Can I offer you some coffee while we arrange for your sister's release, Mrs. Morgan?" he said with assurance.

Grace had to suppress an urge to vault from her chair and kiss the handsome face of this timely savior. "That's the second best thing you could've offered, Mr. Dunn," she said, grinning.

He understood her meaning and appreciated the genuine gratitude she conveyed.

The intercom buzzed. "Mr. Cane's on the line and Mr. Jorgenson is holding," the efficient receptionist informed him.

And so it began—a binding of two strangers who were not only destined to share the most intense and passionate chapter of their entire lives, but the eventual fulfilling of a bittersweet legacy.

CHAPTER FOUR

"NOT HUNGRY, HUH?" the female guard grunted as she retrieved the untouched lunch tray through a slot in the cell door.

Marnie answered with a mute shake of her head. She was too humiliated to meet the eyes of her jailer. Instead she stared straight ahead at the whitewashed wall.

"Maybe some company will perk your appetite? Selma Garrett will be joining you soon. She's a real character...a regular around here," the custodian remarked as she sauntered down the aisle, then disappeared from view. The clank of a steel door echoed, and the lone prisoner shuddered at its sound. Marnie didn't know which was worse—the utter silence or the thought of some stranger seeing her as she was now— stripped of her personal belongings and pride. The degrading reality brought tears to her eyes. Instinctively, she wiped away the telltale misery with the back of her hand and swallowed the embarrassment collecting in her throat.

She stood and paced the small quarters, her gaze taking in the iron bars, sterile cot, indiscreet toilet facilities. The dismal accommodation was hardly the sort to which she'd been accustomed. Incarceration wasn't exactly luxury. She shivered in repulsion.

Could it have been just twenty-four short hours ago that she'd lunched at an exclusive restaurant, then attended an "invitation only" fashion show being held at an exclusive boutique? She hugged her midsection tighter, terrified by the prospect of losing more than just her sense of time. Suddenly everything seemed distorted, unreal.

Moments passed before she dared to release the tight grip she held on herself. Hesitantly she unlocked her arms and stood staring at her barren ring finger. They'd even confiscated her wedding band. Never, since Seth had slipped the jade-and-gold symbol of his devotion onto her hand, had the ring been off her finger. Now only a glaring white strip of flesh marked the place on her ivory skin where once an inscription of love had rested. "Forever" it had read. Her eyes squeezed shut as she remembered. "Forever!"

Vivid memories assailed her. She denied them, snapping open her eyes, then turning her hands palm up to examine the traces of black ink on her fingertips. She clenched her teeth and rubbed fanatically. The stain from the booking procedure would not come off, no matter how hard she tried. A soft, wretched moan escaped from her lips as she covered her face with tainted fingers. *Forever!* her mind screamed. *The stain is forever.*

She sank upon the rigid cot and buried her head in her hands, envisioning herself as she would appear in the mug shot—a demoralizing number dangling from her neck. Funny! She didn't even know her number. She only remembered the mortifying experience, an anonymous voice saying, "Try not to blink. Okay. Turn left. Turn right." The whole ordeal was an exercise in shame. Nothing was left her—not even dignity.

Mustn't wallow in self-pity, she told herself, lifting her head with a deep, rejuvenating breath. But where was Grace? Where was respite from this nightmare?

The steel door resounded again, croaking the arrival of another inmate. A female voice screeched a string of curses.

"Dammit! This is a mistake, I tell ya. How was I to know he was robbing the joint? You gotta believe me. He said he was going in after a bottle of wine. I ain't no accessory! All I was doing was waiting in the car! Dammit! I'm innocent."

"Pipe down, Selma. You'll have your day in court," the matron ordered, unlocking the cell and brusquely shoving the brassy prisoner inside.

"This is a frame," the indignant prisoner bellowed, gripping the bars and giving a futile tug. "I wanna see my mouthpiece as soon as the lazy bum shows up. I'm gonna sue every one of y'all for false arrest." The threat fell upon deaf ears as the guard stomped down the corridor and slammed the outer door.

Marnie sat silent and appalled. The city jail's clientele was even cruder than the accommodations. Selma Garrett looked as gaudy as she sounded.

"What're ya in for, honey?" the hardened lady asked, her wary eyes assessing Marnie from head to toe.

The trite line and absurd scene struck the widow as ludicrous, like something out of a 1930s gangster movie. A hysterical giggle swelled in her throat. She swallowed hard before answering. "I believe they call it murder one," she replied sarcastically, receiving the reaction she'd intended—a gasp.

"You're in some mighty heavy trouble, girl," Selma finally responded. "Who'd you waste?"

"Waste?" Marnie repeated, unfamiliar with street lingo.

"You know," Selma grunted. "Kill...blow away...do in," she tutored.

"Supposedly my husband." Marnie could fairly feel Selma's curiosity peaking. She stood and began to pace once more, wishing to be invisible, wanting to be far, far removed from the prying Selmas of this world.

"More than once I wanted to kill my old man." Selma flopped upon the cot with a nonchalant shrug. "He was a miserable low-life who got his kicks by whipping up on me for no good reason. I lucked out, though. One night he got into a brawl over some woman in a bar and ended up as dead as I'd wished him a hundred times. I didn't shed any tears, I can tell you for sure." Selma critically surveyed her chipped nail polish as she spoke. Marnie halted her pacing, thoughtfully surveying the flashily dressed and cheaply perfumed woman. It occurred to her to inform the callous Selma that Seth wasn't a low-life who deserved shooting, but then she just as quickly dismissed the notion. She didn't have to defend him or herself to anyone. This tragedy was a private affair. Let people wonder and speculate. Didn't they always assume the worst, anyway?

"You don't look the type," Selma said with a saucy cock of her head.

"Pardon?" Engrossed in her own thoughts, Marnie was caught by surprise.

"I said," Selma drawled in a miffed tone, "you don't much look like the violent sort. You kinda remind me of Grace Kelly. She was one of my favorites. A real class act. I'll never forget her in *Dial M for Murder*."

The comparison of her to the star who'd become a

princess had been made before. A faint smile tripped
across Marnie's lips at the recollection. Ironically it
had been a visiting French ambassador who'd first
commented on the likeness that Selma had just spoken
of. It was during a state dinner that had been held in
the dignitary's honor. Afterward Seth had teased her
unmercifully about the elderly gentleman's obvious infatuation. She could still hear his infectious laughter as
he pretended to be outraged over the flowery tributes
bestowed upon his wife. During those first and good
years in Washington, Seth had been so wonderfully
good-natured and attentive. So often of late, Marnie
found herself reminiscing and yearning for those
sweet, bygone days.

She snapped from her nostalgic state when Selma
harshly questioned her. "Hey, are you okay?" Nodding, Marnie began to retrace the length of her
cramped cell.

"Well, you don't look so good. Maybe you're getting light-headed from all that pacing?" A loud sigh
followed the deduction. "You might as well save your
energy. All the walking in the world won't bring ya
one step closer to getting out."

Her frazzled nerves made Marnie want to shout,
"Oh, will you please shut up!" but her perfect-lady
control prevailed. Silently she sought the cot, stretch-
ing out and staring blankly at the ceiling.

"You're not much of a talker, are you?" Selma said
between pops of her gum.

"I haven't had much sleep," was all Marnie responded, hoping she'd take the hint and desist.

"Me neither. I sure hope that worthless attorney of
mine gets here soon. I got what you might call a busi-

ness engagement later tonight and if I don't show, some conventioneers are gonna be really sore.''

This time Marnie could not help herself. A soft, rippling laugh spilled from her. She knew she was transcending rational response, but didn't care. Slowly, surely, she was going, as Selma would call it, stir crazy.

''What're you laughing at?'' Selma demanded, jumping to her feet and striking an angry pose—one hip jutted out, a hand perched haughtily upon it.

Marnie tried to compose herself, but an incautious giggle or two escaped her all the same. ''I was only thinking that since you're entitled to one call, perhaps you could phone the gentlemen and explain how you've been unavoidably detained. I see no reason why our keepers should object. In fact, I view it as poetic justice.''

A comprehending grin spread over Selma's worn face. Soon she was laughing robustly. ''You've got a warped sense of humor, honey, but you kinda break up the monotony.''

Marnie was about to reply when the recognizable sound of the lock springing on the outer door drew their attention. Keys jangled with each approaching step of the matron.

''Well, it's about time,'' Selma huffed, smoothing her dyed red coiffure in preparation to exit her cell. Her face sagged as the custodian turned in Marnie's direction and began to unlatch the door.

''Your bond's been made, Mrs. Hill. You can collect your personal property at the booking desk,'' the jailer instructed.

Marnie was too stunned to move at first. The unexpected sight of the cell door easing open caused her heart to race.

"Hey, what about me?" Selma whined. "I gotta get out of this crummy hole. I got a business engagement tonight," she pleaded.

"He'll keep, Selma," came the dry comeback from the savvy matron as she placed a leading hand on Marnie's shoulder, then shut the cell door behind her.

Selma became irate, beginning to expel a rapid succession of expletives again. "You're trying to sweat me," she yelled. "You think I'll say I was in on that liquor-store heist. But I won't, 'cause I wasn't," she bellowed after them. "I'm innocent. Dammit! I am!" she continued to wail even after the door thudded shut.

Marnie couldn't help but relate to Selma, not that they had much in common. Perhaps no more than a mutual plea of innocence. And she had her doubts about Selma's sincerity. In all probability, Selma was equally skeptical of hers. What did it matter, after all? In the end, it would be a jury who'd decide their innocence or guilt. Meandering in a depressed fog, she followed the matron to the booking desk to await the return of her personal articles. An envelope was passed to her, the faceless officer requesting that she be certain each item was accounted for before signing the standard release form. One by one, she retrieved then replaced the expensive pieces of jewelry until she came to the jade-and-gold wedding band. For a long, thoughtful moment, she could only stare at the sentimental object. Finally the impatient officer was forced to ask if something was amiss.

"No, nothing," she answered in an unsteady voice,

unable to bring herself to accept the ring back on her finger. Instead she dropped it into the beaded clutch bag, hastily scribbling her signature across the blurred document in front of her.

The officer gestured toward another set of doors, muttering, "Your sister's waiting in the lobby outside."

"Thank you," was all she answered, wondering if she had strength enough to leave the building. Head held high but her limbs feeling like jelly, she exited the jail area.

"Marnie," Grace hailed her the second she emerged into the dank lobby. Marnie nearly collapsed under the weight of her anxious hug. "Are you all right? You look so tired. I'm sorry it took so long, but finding an attorney wasn't easy. I've been frantic with worry. What an awful place! Did they treat you well? Gracious, Marnie, you look positively drained." Grace bombarded her with pats, questions and apologies.

"I'm a little tired, Grace, that's all," she answered numbly.

"Well, of course you are," the elder sister said in a maternal tone. "Oh, I nearly forgot." Abruptly she turned to a man standing with his shoulder braced against the wall, hands thrust into his pants pockets as he intently observed the reunion from a few feet away. At her signal, he slowly straightened, then strode purposefully in their direction. Instinctively Marnie became wary as she noted his disconcerting study of her. It was as if he were cataloging each and every detail of her appearance, every microscopic flaw in her character.

Though forewarned by Grace how stunning her sis-

:er was in the flesh, Ian was totally unprepared for the initial encounter. From the first moment he set eyes on his lovely client, he was struck by the genteel beauty he beheld. She was an angel—an earth angel—as fair and as fragile and seemingly untouchable as mankind's perception of the celestial myth. Only one element marked her as mortal—the very real sadness he perceived in her crystal-blue eyes.

"Marnie, this is Ian Dunn. He arranged for your bail and has graciously consented to represent you," Grace explained, touching her sister's arm as if to jog her from the lethargy that shrouded her.

Marnie reacted coolly, meeting her champion's assessing gaze with remoteness. "I wonder which you are, Mr. Dunn—ambitious or reckless?" she murmured in a defeated voice.

"Marnie, please," Grace scolded, squeezing her arm imploringly.

A wry smile broke on Ian's lips at Marnie's blunt remark. "Actually a bit of both, Mrs. Hill," he countered. "We can debate my character after we discuss yours. Shall we go?"

Her only acknowledgment was the adjusting of the lace wrap about her slim shoulders as she swept past him toward the exit staircase. In her wake lingered a fragrance, one Ian couldn't quite place at the time. Yet in the weeks to come the scent would haunt him—this rare essence of a wild rose.

CHAPTER FIVE

NADINE MIMMS PAUSED outside the library. For the first time during her many years of service, she cocked an ear to the door and intentionally eavesdropped. Not a sound could she distinguish. She pursed her lips, uncertain if she should intrude with a knock and solicitous inquiry. The old judge had been in his dead son's private office for hours, locked away with his grief and surrounded by painful reminders. Perhaps the strain was too much. After all, he was nearly seventy-two years old.

She rapped lightly, wincing at his admonishing, "I asked not to be disturbed."

"It's lunchtime, sir. I thought you might like me to bring you a tray. Something light, perhaps?" Nadine's voice penetrated the oak door, filtering into the gloom.

"I want nothing but privacy," came the terse reply.

"As you wish, sir." With a discouraged sigh, she proceeded down the hall.

Judge Aubrey Hill sat statue still within the darkened chamber. The draperies were drawn as tightly as his lips. He moved not a muscle; only his mind was active—erupting with memories and seething with bitterness. The thirty-six hours preceding his seclusion in the library were hazy. He hardly remembered the night-coach flight to Rosehill or his managing of the on-going crisis. By the time he arrived, Seth's body had already been claimed by the coroner's office and Marnie taken into custody for questioning. Only the physical evidence of the shooting remained—a chalked outline where his son's body had fallen, a crimson stain on the rug, a pair of homicide detectives still lingering on the scene. After receiving a secondhand account of the fatal incident and assurances that the entire matter was being thoroughly investigated, he was faced with the deplorable task of funeral arrangements. But now, after fulfilling his obligations, Aubrey Hill was left with empty time and a broken dream. For him, the instant of Seth's death marked the hour of his own private Armageddon.

Slowly he stood, then balanced himself on his ivory-knobbed walking stick and began to browse the eerie quiet room. Here and there he would stop to touch a memento of his son's impressive past—a college football trophy (Seth had been an All-American wide receiver at S.M.U.), a bronze star (Seth was a Vietnam hero, decorated twice for valor), a photo of him being sworn into office (Seth held the distinction of being the youngest senator ever to serve from the state of Kentucky). From one sentimental object to yet another honor, the judge drifted. There wasn't a corner of the room or his mind where memories didn't dwell.

He paused beside a heirloom family Bible resting on a pedestal table near the window. Aimlessly he ran a gnarled hand over the embossed leather. Without thinking, he pushed back the drapery a bit, allowing a stream of light to seep across the Bible's surface. Then, reaching into his pocket, he withdrew a pair of glasses, slipped them on and opened the "good book" to a place reserved for the recording of marriages, births and deaths. The records dated back to his grandfather—over a century of heritage. His eyes skimmed the page until he found the line that documented his own marriage to Rae Beth Anderson on Thanksgiving Day, 1941. It had been a triumphant day for him—marrying the only daughter of the prominent tobacco tycoon Mitchell Anderson. For though Aubrey Luther Hill was considered by many to be the sharpest legal mind in the state and possibly a man destined for greatness, he still needed the social credibility that such a merger with Kentucky hierarchy would reap. Mitchell Anderson was of the old guard, his name was synonymous with wealth and tradition. When he gave his daughter in marriage, he also virtually guaranteed Hill's political aspirations.

Now, looking back, A.L. (as he would later become known) wondered if he might not have been better off without the Anderson endorsement. Never before had it occurred to him to question the arrangement. At the time it seemed the surest course to an end he envisioned. Mitchell Anderson wished to realize the one obsession his vast wealth couldn't buy—a male heir to carry on the bloodline. It was agreed that the first male child born to A.L. and Rae would pass on the name of Anderson as well as the lands and heritage it entailed. In his impetuous youth, A.L. had thought the request a small concession. But now, when recalling the loveless years and strokes of fate that kept him from accomplishing his dream, the old man began to believe he'd struck an ill bargain.

Rae Beth was an attractive woman, but hardly passionate. Their years together were best described as excruciatingly dull. They were of different temperaments and completely opposite goals. She fancied herself a blue blood and hated the bawdy political rallies and the grueling pace of the campaign trail. Her aloof nature hindered his bid more than once. She remained an enigma and a sore spot with the common voters. Her unsupportive attitude coupled with a long-term illness and a few naive but crucial errors in judgment had cost Hill dearly. Much to his dismay, the judge finally had to accept the fact that his dream would have to be passed on, like the Anderson name, to his son. He never forgave Rae Beth for her part in his defeat. He blamed her for the fact that glory day by day eluded him. Right or wrong, she bore the burden of his eventual reconciliation to mediocrity. It didn't matter that he'd become the behind-the-scenes power, shaping and bending other ambitious men to his will, that he was now the old guard whose endorsement meant political life or death. He'd had to relinquish a dream, and the hunger became an even more compelling fixation than Mitchell Anderson's.

The old judge's arthritic finger eased down the page to the spot where his son's birth was recorded. There scrawled in Rae Beth's distinctive script was the name of Seth Anderson Hill—the heir to an obsession and a dream.

The reminder of his son's birth brought back long-forgotten memories. Seth was born in the midst of a snowstorm, icy roads and poor visibility making the trip to the hospital endless. Rae Beth wasn't a strong woman and had no tolerance for pain. The difficult birth left her fearful of another pregnancy. Her excuse of frail health to reject A.L. in bed became monotonous. Yet her abstinence was only exceeded by his lack of desire for her. As far as he was concerned, the original bargain had been kept. Mitchell Anderson and his beloved daughter could go straight to hell. Obliging women were always at his beck and call. And several disillusioning years later, he came to fully appreciate the blessing of his only son, a namesake through whom he could live out his dream.

Aubrey Luther Hill had almost succeeded in his endeavor. From early on, he'd groomed his son for the glory that only thirty-nine other select men had achieved—becoming president of the United States of America.

The old judge's hand quivered as he smoothed the page. At his age, reflecting on one's life could be depleting. Soul searching never came easily. Much had been sacrificed in the name of glory. He had been single-minded in his purpose and had committed many sins while fanatically pursuing his objective—a Hill occupying the Oval Office. Unforeseeable misfortunes had prevented his own grand march to the White House. Yet he had laid the foundation, the road to the presidency. It was his one and only desire that his son follow in his footsteps and acquire the fruits of his long quest.

Some had called his ambition crazy, but nobody said it to his face. Everyone knew him to be a formidable force who'd usurped almost dictatorial power within the state. Seth became an extension of that power. Moreover, he had the Anderson look—fairhaired and refined. The combination of genes and clout made him a charismatic candidate. Under the judge's shrewd guidance, Seth had skyrocketed to political prominence. That he might've wished to follow another road, lead another life wasn't even a consideration. His course had been set, his die cast; his ultimate triumph was a foregone conclusion.

Though the old judge had never had any regrets about rough-riding his son's career, at this morose moment he was sensitive to his own failure as a father. He'd not taken the time to really know his son—either as a boy or as a man. He'd been too busy building a political dynasty—trading favors for future support, making beneficial alliances and prudent choices, wooing the minorities and placating the affluent—in other words, cupping a landslide win in the palm of his hand. Seth's destiny was preordained. He was, A.L. thought, content with the grand scheme. That was until Marnie Hastings entered his life. At first A.L. had thought her a passing fancy—a summer fling that all young men find irresistible. But gradually he began to realize that she meant more to his son. Suddenly Seth wasn't as devoted to the commitment they shared. He started missing important social engagements and showing up late for crucial civic affairs, began balking at the public pressure and resenting the exposure, even daring to be photographed with his common and detrimental paramour. She was all wrong for him, a disastrous choice.

The old judge's cheek ticked with suppressed rage as he recalled the woman whom he'd always feared would be his son's Waterloo. For the first time ever, Seth had ignored his counsel and openly defied him. "All my life I've been what you wanted. Now I want something just as passionately as you do. Don't force me to make a choice, A.L. I'm going to marry her with or without your approval." As long as he lived,

Aubrey Hill would never forget the resolve in his son's voice. The fool was in love. Only a bigger fool would interfere and risk jeopardizing a lifelong dream. Even though he felt betrayed and intuition warned him that the union was as calamitous as his and Rae's, he acceded to Seth's wishes that one and only time. It was perhaps his gravest mistake. For in the end Seth sacrificed everything for the love of that woman—even his very life.

Sheer fury engulfed his withering body. A. L. Hill was a father who'd lost a son. But more than that, he was a power deprived of immortality. He looked at the opposite page of the old Bible—the chronicle of deaths.

He had always supposed that his name would be added to the family record by Seth—never the reverse. A tightness gripped his chest as he picked up a pen lying beside the Bible and began to write Seth's name and the date of his death. His hand shook. His dull eyes blurred. He snatched off his glasses and bent his gray head. This was the most difficult duty of his life—to consciously admit the loss of his only child, to give up the dream. He underscored the date—June 21, 1984— the darkest day in all of his seventy-one years.

Unimaginable bitterness consumed him as he flung aside the pen and raised his walking stick, then whacked it across the page. *She* caused this! *She*, this reason for Seth's disobedience, this nobody from nothing roots who'd bewitched his son. Again he raised his cane, lashing out at the injustice recorded on a page and in his heart. Marnie Hastings, an opportunist with a sultry smile, had dashed his most fervent hope, his life's purpose. He had but one reason left to live—to exact revenge.

He felt heady with hatred, his feeble body tingling with a rush of adrenaline. Slowly he lowered the walking stick, taking deep breaths while stepping cathartic circles around the room. One thought kept pounding in his head: *she* would pay for her sin against him. This vendetta, and this alone, would inspire his every breath. If it was Seth's destiny to be assassinated, then it should not have been in vain, without dignity or immortality. Oh, how he despised this malignancy called Marnie—this killer of dreams. If it was his last act on this earth, he vowed that she would know the same emptiness she had bequeathed to him. During his reign, a few other brash and unfortunate souls had provoked his revenge. They had been swiftly and utterly annihilated. So would *she* be!

A.L. collapsed into a nearby chair. Again he sat stock-still, staring into space and absorbing the silence. He had little else left to do in his life but to wait for retribution.

ALL GRACE'S IMPLORING hadn't changed Marnie's mind. She couldn't ignore the strong attachments pulling her back to Rosehill. She felt in her heart that Aubrey Hill deserved an explanation. She knew she couldn't divulge everything, knew he'd probably reject and expel her, yet she had to at least make the gesture. But she was emotionally unprepared for the somber expression of grief that hung on the stately double doors. A weakness gripped her. She clutched an adjacent wrought-iron railing to steady herself. The pain of seeing a pair of black-ribboned mourning wreaths was almost more than she could bear. Eyes lowered, she braced herself, then climbed the wide veranda steps and rapped the brass knocker.

Nadine herself answered the summons. Alarm registered in her ebony eyes as she entreated, "Please, Miss Marnie. You mustn't—"

"Allow her in, Nadine," came the icy command as Judge Hill's walking stick tapped his entrance on the marbled foyer. "Would you deny me a last word with this sore my son foolishly wed?"

Nadine cast her ex-mistress a sympathetic look before obediently opening wide the door. The widow fought for her composure as she stepped across the dreaded threshold. Graciously she spared the housekeeper from having to endure the impending confrontation, excusing her with, "Leave us, will you please, Nadine?"

"That is the *last* instruction you will ever issue at Rosehill, madam," came the venomous promise as the old gentleman turned his rigid back, then limped into the parlor.

Nadine's chin quivered at his scornful tone. Marnie was touched by her distress. With an encouraging pat of her shoulder, she dismissed the loyal servant, then strode into the parlor to face her hostile father-in-law.

"Is it forgiveness you seek, madam?" he said with dispassion, presenting his austere profile.

She advanced a step or two toward his formidable figure. "I wanted to try and explain as best I can this nightmare we're living, A.L.," she softly answered. "What happened was an accident, a terrible freak accident," she said apologetically.

"Do you expect me to believe that?" he growled, never blinking or turning in her direction.

"I'd hoped you might." Abruptly she drew up. "I know there's never been any love lost between us, but surely you can't believe that I'd intentionally harm Seth? My God, A.L., he was my husband.'' She begged his understanding, but only incurred his wrath.

His head snapped around, his lip curling with contempt as he rasped, ''That you were his lawfully wedded wife was a fact you conveniently discounted whenever it suited you. You made a mockery of your marriage vows. I find your claims of devotion almost as repugnant as I do you.''

Her chin lifted at the insult. ''If you're implying that I was unfaithful to Seth, you're wrong. I never—''

''You never loved him,'' he boomed, cutting her off effectively. ''Oh, you were clever, seducing him into marriage and then pretending to be the perfect and dutiful wife for several years. And you were patient, too, making sure you were indispensably entrenched into every aspect of his life. Only after you'd assured your position did you show your true colors—flaunting your indiscretions, publicly humiliating him. You knew he couldn't seek a divorce—not without forfeiting his chance at the presidency. But breaking his spirit wasn't enough for you, was it? You wanted to be rid of him and the future obligations but still enjoy the status and benefits being his widow would bring,'' came the knifing accusation.

Marnie flinched at the attack. ''You really are a vicious old man. From the very beginning you never gave me a chance—labeling me a fortune hunter and maliciously fueling Seth's jealousies. It wasn't enough that you deprived him of your love; you also begrudged him mine. I should have known better than to try and explain anything to you. You always drew your own conclusions and had all the answers, didn't you, A.L.?''

"I know that if Seth had listened to me when I warned him about you, he'd be alive today," he countered, his jaw setting like granite. He glared at the woman before him, hating her with all his heart, all his might. "Nothing you can say will convince me otherwise. You've taken my son's life and ruined mine. And I intend to see that justice is done."

"I'm supposed to be presumed innocent until proven guilty." She stood up to his threat.

"Maybe in the eyes of the law, but not in mine. I'm going to do everything in my power to assure your conviction."

"I'm sure you will, A.L.," was all she replied, turning toward the door to hide the sense of defeat she felt. She wasn't strong enough to engage in an emotional duel with her father-in-law—not on the heels of everything else she'd endured. Her coming here had been a disastrous mistake. She desperately wished to flee Rosehill and his spite.

"Just a minute, madam." He halted her retreating steps. Slowly she turned to face him. "There is something I feel obliged to discuss with you."

"That is?" she said warily.

"Sunny," came the answer in a word. "I think she should remain in Vicksburg with Connie and the children. As much as possible she should be sheltered from this tragic affair."

He referred to his niece, whom Sunny was visiting at the moment. Connie Hill was one of the more respectable relations—a strong-minded and energetic woman who relied on both qualities in order to keep up with four vivacious children. Sunny adored vacationing on the rambling cotton plantation and frolicking with her distant cousins. Marnie had agreed weeks earlier to the visit. Sunny had only just left the day before the fatal shooting. Though Marnie had phoned this morning to tell her daughter of Seth's death, she was still undecided whether or not to recall her home. Things were in such a turmoil. Of course, she wished to spare her daughter from the sordidness. Moreover, she was too distraught from the clash with A.L. to suspect his true intent. "Yes, I think it would be best if she remained in Vicksburg for the present," she agreed.

Shrewdly A.L. masked his relief. "Then for once we concur," he grunted. His shoulders stiffened as he readied himself to deliver the first of many premeditated blows. "I ask that you do me the courtesy of not attending Seth's funeral. It would be a sacrilege to his memory. You are never to set foot in Rosehill again. These disillusioned eyes of mine only want to see you once more—when judgment is pronounced and they may witness your Jezebel misery." He snorted his disgust as he limped past. "Now gather your belongings and get out of my house. I can't bear the sight of you."

Marnie couldn't have been more devastated if he had struck her across the face. She stood immobile, unable to tear her gaze from his departing figure. In her stricken state, she began to question her own character. For suddenly it dawned on her to wonder why she had tolerated the old judge's abuse all these years. Had she somehow felt unworthy, and unconsciously accepted his cruel remarks as her penance for daring to intrude upon hallowed ground and breathe Aubrey Hill's air?

"Miss Marnie?" came the soft entreaty.

Her eyes focused on Nadine in the doorway. "You mustn't linger long. He's near out of his mind with grief and bitterness," she warned.

"I shouldn't have come at all. I wonder if I will ever learn?" she asked more of herself than of Nadine, unable to disguise the utter despair in her voice.

"He's always been a hard man. Poor Mr. Seth seldom heard anything but criticism from his lips." Atypically, Nadine expressed a personal opinion, then immediately looked contrite.

Marnie sighed, remembering Seth's insatiable need for affection. Neither of his parents had filled the void in him. In fact, through his formative years, they contributed greatly to his hunger. The old judge was aloof and domineering and, by every account, Rae Beth had been incredibly shallow. It was no wonder that Seth was prone to be insecure at times. "I'd better do as the old judge wishes and remove myself from Rosehill." Marnie refused to meet Nadine's eyes as she crossed to the spiral staircase.

"Don't go up there, Miss Marnie," the old housekeeper blurted. "I can collect your belongings and have them sent on. I'm afraid if you go in that room...." She choked on the trepidation she would've expressed. Her shoulders heaved as she succumbed to the melancholy mood that clung as closely as the sweet smell of condolatory bouquets beginning to collect in the parlor.

Quickly Marnie went to her, enfolding the brokenhearted servant in her consoling arms. "There, there, Nadine. Please don't cry," she murmured, unshed tears shimmering in her own eyes.

"Why, oh, why did this have to happen?" Nadine

sobbed. "I can't believe Mr. Seth is gone. And I'll miss you Miss Marnie," she sniffed. "You were a breath of fresh air in this musty old place. I didn't want to say anything against you. But the policemen kept asking the same questions and telling me I had to be truthful. I told them over and over again that you were a good person—" she ran a trembling hand over her puffy cheeks "—and that you didn't mean to shoot Mr. Seth."

"You mustn't fault yourself, Nadine. You had no choice." With soothing pats, Marnie tried to reassure her.

"The hardest thing I'll ever have to do is testify against you. If only...."

" 'If onlys' won't change a thing, Nadine," the widow crooned in a fatalistic voice. How many times during the past days had she silently uttered the same lament, she thought. Favoring the devoted housekeeper with a forgiving smile, she then gently kissed her cheek and walked to the front door. "I'll let you know where to send my things. Be strong, Nadine," she softly encouraged before exiting from the Hill mansion. Rosehill was a closed chapter of her life. With a slam of a door, a sway of a mourning wreath, a storybook love affair was ended, a sensational murder trial about to begin. And the principal character in the ongoing saga would not be able to escape the memories as easily as she fled the neatly manicured grounds.

"Forever" the loving inscription inside the gold band had read. "Forever" could quite possibly haunt Marnie for the rest of her life.

CHAPTER SIX

THEY HAD GATHERED TO PAY their final respects to a dynamic man whose life and brilliant future had been snuffed out in his prime. The assembly of family, friends and dignitaries was solemn indeed as the minister quoted the Twenty-third Psalm. Heads bowed, they issued a concluding, "Amen," then slowly dispersed, each offering condolences when parading past the judge and filing out of the cemetery.

It was late afternoon: the amber sun set low in a drowsy Kentucky sky. Within minutes, all that remained were the tombstones of the forgotten, the rustle of the wind through the treetops, and the dainty flutter of flower petals atop the senator's casket.

A distant slam of a car door resounded in the somber stillness. Soon after, a slender figure dressed in a chic, two-piece black suit and trimmed in a white piqué collar appeared on the stone path leading to the family plot. The lady wore a matching wide-brimmed summer hat dipped low over a brow and carried a solitary crimson rose. She approached the casket cautiously, glancing back over her shoulder every now and then as she made the journey. Then, halting beneath a majestic elm that shaded the spot where the casket stood, she bowed her head to say goodbye in her own fashion and in her own time.

The widow had much to say to her deceased husband, and for once he had no choice but to listen. She
was experiencing so many feelings at this moment—
anguish, hurt, anger, confusion, pity, disgust. Lost in
an emotional collage, the lady was disoriented,
segregated and beyond any external displays of grief.
This was a meeting of spirits, a bridge between the past
and present, an instant when the reality, the truth, the
waste of a bronze casket gleaming in dusky sunlight
became a living hell.

The reality was that Seth was dead, Marnie alive.
The truth was that his premature death was precisely
as he'd wished, that perhaps the alternatives had been
nil. The waste was that it should have happened at all,
that two so deeply in love could not have altered the
outcome.

"They say there's a thin line between love and hate,
husband," she murmured aloud. "At this moment I'm
afraid to know what it is exactly I feel for you."
Resignedly, almost reluctantly, her eyes skimmed the
flower-bedecked casket. *Loyalty!* her subconscious
cried out. *Isn't it loyalty that bound you for the past
few years?* She reached up and jerked off her hat,
shaking loose her platinum hair as a surge of memories
overcame her.

She could speak frankly now, if only in her mind.
Was Seth's spirit attuned to her thoughts, she wondered. Did it really matter?

*Do you recall how sweet it was in the beginning,
Seth?* She sighed. *Oh, how well I remember you in
those days—so young, so dashing. You were magnificent. And I was in awe. You told me I was all that mattered, made me believe that we were invincible. I recall*

the day you read excerpts to me from Ralph G. Martin's tale of The Woman He Loved. *We were both swept away by the romanticism of the Duke and Duchess of Windsor's story... the king who'd abdicated for the love of a commoner. You said that unlike them, we'd prevail—attain our dreams and still not compromise our love. You promised that, Seth. I remember vividly.*

In slow, measured steps Marnie began to pace the length of her dead husband's casket.

And we almost succeeded, dear Seth. She sighed again. *We defied them all—mama, the old judge. I loved you so passionately; you craved me so desperately. We were magnetic—attracting everyone's attention, evoking their envy. Oh yes, we were "the chosen ones"—full of spirit and ideals and love. They made us their symbol—Sir Lancelot in shining armor, Guinevere in white satin—Camelot resurrected from the Kennedy days. I remember. But, oh God, how I wish I could forget!*

She glanced up at the cloudless sky, inhaling a deep breath.

We took them by storm, you and I, Seth. We were fantastic together—sweeter than the cherry-blossomed springtimes we shared in Washington and stronger than the harshest of Kentucky winters. Sometimes when I close my eyes and drift, I can still recall the splendor of our past. Funny, how certain moments stay special in one's mind, like the night we sneaked away from another of those tedious receptions to have a moonlight picnic. We drank champagne from a thermos and danced under the stars to a car radio on the banks of the Potomac. I remember thinking how handsome you

*looked in the dawn light as we waltzed. And what a
very fortunate woman was I.*

A sad smile touched the widow's lips at the recollection. She cleared her throat, then shifted her gaze to
the gently swaying branches of the elm tree.

*Something else I relive at the strangest times is the
night when Sunny was born—your squeezing my hand
and coaching me through the natural birth, saying,
"I'm here, sweetheart. I'm with you. Don't give up.
Together we can do this." And we did. She was exquisite and we were so smug, as if neither one of us
had the slightest doubt that anything we conceived
together could be anything less than perfect.*

A grim expression crept into Marnie's brimming
eyes as she looked back upon the casket, whispering
aloud, "But our world didn't remain perfect, did it,
Seth? Perhaps because we were too cocky, too convinced that we were immune to heartache. We believed
the chanting crowds, the flattering press releases. You
were meant to be president and I to always be your
First Lady."

She looked away from the casket, a rebel teardrop
escaping down her cheek as she brushed the velvet rose
across her trembling lips.

Damn you, Seth, for making me love you so much,
her heart screamed. *For relying on me, using me. . .for
day by day, month by month, these past two years disillusioning me! I don't want to remember the fanatical
and brooding man you became. I'd rather relive the
time when you were the prince in a fairy tale. The man
I once loved and thought I knew.*

As she allowed her memories to surface, her ache to
come forth, Marnie could not contain her sorrow any

longer. Flashes of Seth illuminated her grief-stricken mind—the spirited and handsome young man who'd won her heart; the mature husband who'd adored and depended upon her so greatly; the diseased and tortured Seth who cleaved to her so desperately. She was the guardian of the senator's secrets—one she bore alone; the other Dr. Merkland, the family physician, shared. He could be trusted, she knew. At her request, he'd promised to keep Seth's file confidential. As in so many times past, she'd had to intercede on Seth's behalf.

Throughout the years and different phases the senator had undergone, she'd given him her understanding, loyalty and love. For ten years she'd devoted herself to his happiness, at times at the expense of her own. She loved him both as a woman and as his best friend. Then, the one time she had demanded, not selfishly but because she sensed him retreating from her and feared his secret reasons, Seth denied her.

"How could you do this to me, Seth?" came the miserable sob. "Leave me to face this alone? I would have shielded you," she whispered. "I will always protect you," she vowed.

Only the rustle of the wind answered the widow. The silence was almost as intolerable as the accusations she must withstand alone. "Murderess!" was the public outcry. She was the convenient scapegoat on which the people could vent their frustration and anger. Didn't they understand? She'd loved him as they never would...knew him as they never could. It wasn't fair! Was it any less a crime to sacrifice a soul and spare a life?

Silhouetted against a copper sunset, Marnie buried

her face in her hands and, for the first time, wept bitterly. "Forever" the inscription had read. One incoherent question kept beating in her mind and heart. *If love wasn't meant to be everlasting, what's forever for?*

THE WIDOW THOUGHT SHE WAS ALONE with her grief, but someone watched from a distance—an intrigued voyeur hidden by dusk's shadows. It wasn't especially significant that Ian Dunn had attended the senator's funeral. After all, he was only one of many colleagues in attendance. What was strange is that he'd known the widow would put in an appearance. He'd waited and observed, not really understanding why.

Maybe to convince himself that Grace's assessment of her sister was correct—that Marnie was incapable of cold-blooded murder. Or perhaps because he merely wished to see her again—the earth angel.

Only one thing did he know for certain. After witnessing the lady's pain, encroaching on her privacy, he felt his client, not the deceased, was the real victim. The ostracized lady wasn't behaving like a woman without conscience or feeling. He yearned to hear her explanation of the incident. Yet he sensed the widow would not reveal all. Behind the angel veneer lurked secrets. But what were they? And how detrimental to her case could they be?

As he watched the widow in black kiss the velvet rose, then place it atop her husband's casket, a twinge of envy coursed through Ian. For he knew that if he died tomorrow no lady would grieve his passing. His partner, Rory, might hoist a few in memory of him, but that would be about the extent of the mourning. His eyes trailed Marnie's slim figure as she departed. He saw her pause and then turn to cast a final gaze at the casket; saw her stumble, upon which he almost forgot himself and dashed from the shadows to lend assistance. He was overcome with an urge to help this vulnerable widow. But she recovered from the stumble and he from the gallant impulse. The widow would've resented his intrusion. She was a proud woman who wished only to avail herself of his legal expertise, not his pity.

That she was lovely, prideful, brave and hurting was established in his mind. He wished he could be as convinced of her absolute innocence. He'd agreed to defend her because he believed her to be a victim of discrimination and the system. But he needed more than a hunch on which to base a defense. He needed her trust and cooperation. *"Marnie confides in no one."* Grace's statement whispered like the evening breeze through his mind. "This once you must, Mrs. Hill," he vowed beneath his breath, his eyes as intent as his commitment as he watched the stunning blonde get into the silver Mercedes and drive off. He remained rooted until the European auto disappeared from sight. Hardly was he aware of the burial crew's arrival. Easing his hands into his pants pockets, Ian began strolling in the direction of his Cadillac. Upon passing the gravediggers, he couldn't help a cynical thought— if, as he suspected, the illustrious senator was a sham, he'd move heaven and earth to see him in Hell. This he promised himself and the corpse about to be interred.

A CRACK OF LIGHT spilled through the slightly ajar door, an unintelligible mutter drifting out into the hall. Soundlessly Ian proceeded through the darkened reception area and down the hall to his office. He eased open the door, standing undetected for a moment and observing Rory Connery. The senior law partner sat conversing with thin air, his back to the door, a half-empty bottle of bourbon at his elbow. Ian knew from past experience that trouble loomed ahead. Whenever Rory drank alone and talked to himself, it meant his Irish dander was up.

"Sure 'n' I'll not be having it!" Rory grumbled. "I want no part of dead senators and scandal." His mutter was followed by a disgusted slap of a newspaper on the desk. Ian had already seen the headlining story that had provoked Rory's ire. The article mentioned that the firm of Connery and Dunn would be representing Marnie Hill—a small detail that Ian had neglected to tell Rory, especially since he'd known very well the effect it would have on the conservative partner. Long ago, the passion for burning causes had dwindled in Rory. About all that remained of his Irish heritage was a taste for fine whiskey, a quick temper and a hint of a brogue. So Ian was not at all surprised by the scene he encountered. Rory's reaction was precisely as he'd anticipated—one of irate opposition.

He squared his shoulders in preparation for the battle ahead. "It's a little late for you to still be here. Something on your mind, Rory?" he asked, purposely adopting an air of nonchalance.

The senior partner snapped around in the chair, barking, "Where've you been all afternoon?"

"Attending the burial services for Seth Hill," Ian answered, paying no heed to Rory's purple expletive.

"Were you suffering under some grand delusion that your presence there would be welcomed or appropriate?"

"I had my reasons for going," was all Rory received in answer, as Ian slipped from his suit coat and loosened his tie.

"Well, now, I'd love to be hearing them," came the condescending quip. "The same as I'm yearning to know why a bright, seasoned attorney like yourself would risk his future and the firm's reputation by associating himself with such a smut case." Rory snatched up the bottle and splashed a goodly amount into a water glass. He took a greedy swig, wiped the back of his hand across his lips, then lowered the glass to the desk with an irked *slam*. "Well?" he bellowed.

"Considering your foul mood, I'm not sure this is the proper time to discuss the Hill case," Ian said, easing into his desk chair, tilting it back and smiling cordially. "By the way, is that bottle from my private stock or yours?"

"Yours," Rory grunted. "'N' don't be trying to change the subject."

"Could I at least sample my generosity before we argue the point?" A hint of mirth crept into Ian's voice.

Grudgingly, the blustery senior partner complied, sloshing a stingy amount of liquor into yet another water glass, then sliding it over. "Now, do you suppose we could settle this matter of discord between us?" he huffed.

Ian sipped, exhaled an appreciative, "Ahh," then nodded.

"You did a foolish thing, Ian. The case is poison. You must withdraw," Rory said flatly.

"I can't do that," the younger partner replied without a second's hesitation.

"Oh, but you can, me boy. It's simply done. You return the retainer and render your regrets." Connery took another gulp, then slanted Ian a censuring look.

"Let me rephrase my answer. I won't withdraw," Ian said simply, at which Rory's fist rammed the desk.

"Can you not recognize an exercise in futility when you're in the midst of one? Are you pigheaded or blind? You're doomed before you begin. There's no future in crusading for lost causes. What is it you hope to prove?"

"Her innocence." Ian met his snarls with logic.

"Her innocence, he says!" Rory mocked. "Considering the circumstantial evidence alone, I'd say you've about as much chance of gaining an acquittal as I have of becoming pope."

"That's a ridiculous analogy, Rory. You haven't practiced the faith since you were a scrub-faced altar boy," Ian cast him an impatient look over the edge of his glass.

"My point exactly," Connery retorted, slugging down another gulp. "From all accounts, the lady's about as faithless as I."

"She's not being tried on a morals charge."

"The hell she's not! You know as well as I that her character will be a major factor. The D.A. and press will have no compunction about tearing her and anyone associated with her to shreds. That courtroom's going to become like an ancient Roman arena, the spectators screaming for blood, the lions hungry for prey. And in the end, it'll be A. L. Hill, not the jury, who'll enact a caesar's privilege, turning thumbs down. I don't know about you, me boy, but I've neither the temperament nor the inclination to be a martyr."

"Neither am I inclined to refuse my help because of incurring one sour old man's disfavor." Ian's voice grew stern with conviction.

"Are you daft? We're speaking of Aubrey Hill. The man buys and sells influential favors every day. Have you no conception of the extent of his power? Hell! He plays golf with Supreme Court justices and dines regularly at the White House. The governor doesn't make a move without first consulting him."

"I'm not intimidated by his contacts in high places," Ian scoffed.

"If you haven't a healthy respect for the man's clout, then you're a fool indeed." The senior partner shook his graying red head, then poured a hefty refill and drank again. "Listen to reason, Ian—" he wheezed, the stout liquor taking his breath "—you've heard the old phrase 'you're judged by the company you keep'?"

Ian nodded, a bit wary of Rory's mellow tone.

"Well, it's the same with a law firm. We're judged by the clients we represent. Are you following me so far, me boy?" he asked, his entire manner becoming suspiciously patronizing.

Ian was thoroughly schooled in the clever tactics of Rory Connery. Since his ranting and raving had thus far proven ineffective, he was now resorting to subtle persuasion. He was a crafty old fox. Next he would be coercing Ian's cooperation by feigning an impending stroke from the stress of it all and declaring to his dead wife, "He'll be the death of me yet, Megan. I'll be joining you soon, me darlin'." Rory was also a consummate actor. His theatrics were impressive in a courtroom but hardly convincing in private. Ian managed to retain a placid expression when nodding.

"The road to success hasn't been an easy one for either of us. Like me, you scrapped your way to the top and asked no favors as you went. So naturally you feel you've earned the right to pick and choose your own cases. Now I realize that we're both shanty Irishmen at heart, loving a good fight and fine whiskey." He leaned over the desk, generously refilling Ian's glass, then his own, then dropping the empty fifth into the trash. "But there comes a time when you must consider a debt you owe yourself. We've struggled too long, worked too hard to jeopardize everything now. And believe me, Ian, allying yourself with Marnie Hill could cost you dearly. She's a very unpopular woman. The very same community that has been financially beneficial to you will just as quickly turn on you. Seth Hill was a hero to these people—one of their own. They'll consider your defense of his killer a betrayal. Step aside, Ian. For your own good, decline the case."

"And what about Marnie Hill? Who'll serve her good? The law says she's entitled to a defense. But how's she going to avail herself of that right if every attorney in Lexington refuses to become involved because they fear the probable consequences? To decline in the name of self-interest sounds dangerously close to a breach of ethics."

Ian's argument stung Rory. "Judas!" he boomed. "I'm talking professional suicide, and you're theorizing about ethics! Well, me boy, let me be more blunt. If you insist on taking this case, you could very well find yourself a grossly underpaid and highly over-worked public defender back in New York City again," he blurted without thinking, his Irish temper getting the best of him.

Ian's face went rigid with shock. The desk chair creaked as he righted himself. "Are you telling me that if I insist on taking the Hill case our partnership is severed?" The question he posed to Rory hurt—hurt deeply.

The partner who'd been like a father to him for many years shifted uneasily under his gaze. Turning his glass bottoms up, he nervously cleared his throat. "I've a flip tongue and nasty temper. You know that, Ian," he mumbled ashamedly. "If ever the partnership dissolves, it won't be my doing. I only meant to say, in my crass way, that we, the firm, may not survive the bad press and animosity." He sighed, then met Ian's forgiving eyes. "I can retire early—not gracefully, mind you, but early. But A. L. Hill will hound you. He'll make certain that you are penalized for your insolence. They'll not be space enough in Kentucky for both you and him."

Ian exhaled a held breath. "I could win, you know, Rory," he said, casting his old comrade a cocky smirk and lifting his glass. "Even with all the cushy cases we've handled lately, I believe a little of the brash Irish kid who fought his way up from the streets of Brooklyn still exists inside me. I can be a tough adversary."

"Sure 'n' no one knows that better than I." Rory flashed him a cocky grin. How well he remembered Ian in the early days—a maverick with a chip the size of Texas on his shoulder. It had taken Rory Connery considerable time and effort to win the young man's trust. Immediately Rory had recognized the aggressive quality about Ian that made him such a sterling lawyer. He never took the defensive in a courtroom battle; he always attacked. In the beginning his tactics were almost crude, but after a few years under Rory's capable tutorship, Ian became a very polished and competent counselor. The lad of humble beginnings and deep emotional scars became a "blooming success."

Yet to this day Ian fought himself almost as fiercely as he challenged the system. He was devoted to the idealism of the law and disillusioned with the realities. He envied power, but had no patience with those who misused it. He was an earthy man who constantly tried to channel his lusty nature constructively. Nine times out of ten he was successful. Yet once in a great while old wounds made him lash out against injustice—injustice as he perceived it—and he would become impassioned and entirely too reckless.

"You're determined to do this," Rory sighed defeatedly, slumping back in the chair and leveling a capitulating look at Ian.

"I am," he answered in a subdued voice.

"Is it the challenge or compassion that rules you?" Rory demanded.

"Need you ask?" The question was its own answer.

"No, I suppose not," the Irishman replied in a somber voice. "Ian, you must not confuse her with a past that haunts you. It would be disastrous and could be fatal for you both. I understand how you might misconstrue her plight. You see her as abandoned and unloved and—"

Ian's facial muscles tensed. "I appreciate your concern but you're worrying needlessly, Rory," he cut in.

"Am I now," the perceptive elder gentleman persisted. "Aren't you both, in entirely different ways, society's outcasts—you the unfortunate and unwanted child, condemned to a dreary orphanage till the age of eighteen; she, the misunderstood and unjustly maligned widow, who might possibly be institutionalized for the rest of her natural days? Isn't it possible that you may have transferred the unforgettable ache of being scorned, Ian? Might that not be your main motivation?" Rory verbally pummeled Ian with conjecture.

"That's nonsense," Ian protested.

"Then answer me one question," Rory hounded.

"If I can," came the wary response.

"In the cold light of fact—powder residue on her hands, the point-blank projection of the bullet—do you believe she didn't pull the trigger?"

"There could be an explanation for that," the junior partner argued.

"Are you convinced that she didn't knowingly and willfully take her husband's life?" Rory relentlessly pursued an answer.

Ian rose from the chair, diplomatically turning his back on the grim-faced Rory in the pretense of staring out the window. He was tired and plainly disturbed. "I don't know," he answered in a drawn voice. "I honestly don't know."

"And if you discover she's as guilty as sin, then what, Ian? Will you *knowingly* defend her?"

There was a poignant pause. Ian rubbed the back of his stiff neck as he contemplated Rory's words. At last he spoke. "We've defended our share of the guilty, Rory. Hell! It goes with the territory."

"We've not ventured into territory as hostile as this before," the old gentleman was quick to clarify.

Ian sighed, then turned to face his peer. "No, we've never had our necks stuck out this far," the young attorney conceded. "But I'll not compromise my values for anyone. And I won't be bullied by Judge Hill." His steadfast hazel eyes affirmed his pledge.

Rory gave a comprehending nod of his head, then hoisted his bloated figure from the chair. "Then I'll say no more on the subject except to ask that I be kept apprised. I've had my fill of smooth whiskey and hard talk for one night. So, good night to you, Ian," came the husky mumble as he lumbered toward the door.

"Rory," Ian called after him. Connery abruptly pulled up, then glanced back over his shoulder. "Your shoes," Ian reminded with a smug grin.

The senior partner looked dumbfoundedly at his stocking feet. "Sure 'n' there was a time when I held my liquor better," he grunted, marching back and retrieving his shoes from under the desk.

"I wouldn't get alarmed, were I you, Rory. Your absentmindedness might be nothing more than a symptom of senility." Ian couldn't resist taunting him a bit.

"Ahh, 'n' here's me thinking my condition might be serious." The elder gent shot Ian a parting wink, then swaggered out the door.

Consumed by silence and doubts, Ian strolled to the bookcase, slid back a paneled door and secured another bottle from his private stock. He returned to the desk, slumped to his chair, unscrewed the cap and poured himself a stiff one. Snapping off the desk lamp and leaning back, he propped his feet on the desk, took a long, savoring gulp, then breathed a deep, deep sigh. Tomorrow his schedule included a late-afternoon appointment with Marnie Hill. Tomorrow he would hear her version of the shooting. And tomorrow he must fully commit or regretfully decline. He pictured her as she'd been today—so lovely, so troubled, so damned compelling. He rubbed his forehead as if trying to erase the image from his mind. Tomorrow he'd have to be totally objective. But could he?

He gulped another swallow of mellow bourbon, wondering if it were possible both to anxiously anticipate and dread an encounter. One thing became clear in the dark—tomorrow and Marnie Hill would come, and he mustn't let a sensitivity from the past play a part in the future.

CHAPTER SEVEN

As was inevitable, tomorrow and Marnie Hill came to Ian Dunn. He waited for her in his office, wishing he'd had more sleep and less to drink. The dull headache swelling in his head wasn't enhancing his mood or appearance. A scowl resided on his face and the fact that Mrs. Hill was inexcusably late for her appointment only added to the indigestion that had plagued him since lunch.

The intercom buzzed, the receptionist announcing, "Mrs. Hill has arrived, sir."

"Show her in, please," came the brusque reply as he began to adjust his shirt collar and fumble with his tie. "Hell with it," he grumbled, yanking free the silk tie and hurriedly stuffing it into a desk drawer.

There came an announcing knock, then the door eased open. And for a moment in time Ian found himself struck mute as a vision in gauzy violet entered his office and heart.

"I apologize for being late, Mr. Dunn," came a lilting voice that drifted into his consciousness.

He collected himself, mechanically answering, "That's quite all right, Mrs. Hill," as he gestured toward a chair in front of his desk.

Was it his imagination or did she actually glide across the room, he wondered. Objectivity was fast escaping him. He sank into his chair, pretending to clear his desk of paperwork while mentally shaking himself. She did as he bade, gracefully alighting inches away and crossing one long, slender leg over the other. He tried not to notice but, much to his chagrin, soon discovered that he had little immunity and great admiration for a fine pair of legs. Again he silently berated himself.

"May I smoke?" she asked, drawing his attention to her fantastic face.

"Of course," he answered appropriately, searching for the buried ashtray on his desk. Where was the blasted thing, was all he could think as he lifted first one folder, then another. At last his hand zeroed in on the elusive object, and he placed it before the widow. She smiled her gratitude before lighting up and exhaling a hazy stream of smoke.

"Thank you." She cast an appraising glance about the room.

"You're welcome." He appreciated her classic profile while her attention was otherwise distracted.

"You're fond of plants," she said by way of idle conversation, obviously ill at ease at the prospect of what lay ahead. Her gaze shifted to him, the faintest apprehension glimmering in her expressive eyes. Suddenly he noted more than her apparent beauty: he saw the toll of little sleep and private grief etched upon her lovely face.

"Yes," was all he replied, unable to detach himself from her aura. "I spend a lot of time surrounded by these four walls. So I try to make my surroundings as pleasant as possible."

She acknowledged his response with a polite nod. The lady was extremely disciplined. That was, except for the brief look of tension he detected in her eyes.

"Are you staying with your sister?" he asked, beginning to relax a bit and settling back in his chair.

She inhaled deeply before responding. "No. I thought it better for Grace and her family if I made other arrangements."

"I see." Again he uttered a standard reply, though in fact he truly did perceive and commiserate with her exile. "Where are you staying, then?" He studied her as she extinguished the cigarette.

"Different places," she answered with a shrug. "Since my release I've checked in and out of a series of anonymous motels. It usually takes the press about a day to catch up with me. They're very resourceful and persistent."

He could only imagine—imagine the harassment she endured and admire her courage. The ordeal of 'The Damned' had to be a living hell. No longer was Marnie Hill the Kentucky darling that everyone who was anyone wished to be near. No! In the circles she traveled, scandal was akin to leprosy. She was an outcast left to suffer her fate in solitary. Ian had great empathy and hated to add to her misery, but the D.A. was pushing for, and more than likely would be granted, an early trial date (owing mainly to the Hill influence, no doubt). So he had precious little time in which to prepare her defense. As yet, the only details he'd learned of the shooting came from a sterile police report and biased newspaper accounts. Ian was banking on discovering the human element—the emotional factors behind the brutal facts. Unfortunately, in order to do so, he hadn't time to tiptoe around a still-fresh ache. For the sake of expediency, he had to pressure his client into revealing all, no matter how painful it might prove to be.

"I'm sure the past days haven't been easy," he murmured, meeting her eyes and prefacing his next words with an implied apology. "Try to keep in mind that though their methods may be a bit extreme, they're only doing their job."

Noting the subtle change in his attitude, she sensed that the small talk had ended and he wished to proceed. She disengaged herself from his intent gaze. "As you must do," she said softly, mentally preparing herself for the impending interrogation.

He clicked the ball-point pen and positioned it over a legal pad. "Yes, I'm afraid so. Shall we begin?"

"Have we a choice?"

He chose to interpret her reply as more resigned than flippant. "I'd like you to tell me as simply and honestly as you can what precipitated the shooting." He masked his personal susceptibility by accentuating the client-lawyer association.

"We'd retired after a late dinner party," she said with a sigh. "We were both exhausted and somehow a trivial discussion developed into an argument between us." Her tone was exact and expressionless.

He continued. "About what were you arguing?" came the same dreaded question for what seemed like the hundredth time.

"Nothing in particular and everything in general," she hedged, shifting in her chair and recrossing her legs. "As I told the authorities, our argument wasn't especially vicious and had nothing to do with what occurred later."

He glanced up, a brow arched skeptically. "I'd prefer to judge that for myself, Mrs. Hill. Please tell me about the disagreement."

"I really can't specifically recall, except to remember that it wasn't significant." She stubbornly refused to discuss it.

Ian had the answer he sought. It was important—important enough for her to either deliberately lie or subconsciously block it from her mind. Sometimes the shock from such a traumatic experience could cause partial amnesia; other times, blind rage could obscure one's memory as well as confiscate reason. He decided to pass on the sensitive issue for the moment.

"All right, let's go on. How did the gun come into play? In whose name was it registered—yours or your husband's? Who first introduced it that night?"

"I can only answer one question at a time, Mr. Dunn," she complained.

"Of course. I'm sorry. We'll take it step by step and question by question," he relented.

And so it went, back and forth, for hours—he grilling her with pointed questions, she responding in various ways—detached, resentful, resigned. Her version of the shooting was sketchy and pat—a bit too pat. Ian pressed her for details, emphasizing the discrepancies in her account. She professed ignorance to the questions she couldn't explain, never deviating from her original statement.

"We were arguing," she explained once more.

"Violently?" He tried to trap her.

"Loudly," she rebutted, refusing to meet his eyes. "Seth wasn't himself . . . was extremely agitated."

"About what?" he pursued.

"I don't know," came the pat response. "A gun was in the nightstand drawer. Seth took it out, a strange expression on his face. Impulsively I reached for it. I was afraid. I wanted to remove it from his sight."

"Why were you afraid?" he probed.

Again, "I don't know." She bowed her head, brushing a speck of imaginary lint from her skirt. "The gun was in my hand. Seth made a lunge for me, grabbing the barrel in a wrenching motion. And—" she raised her gaze to his, a flash of something inexplicable in her eyes "—and then the gun discharged."

"Wounding your husband?"

"Yes," came the barely audible reply. "Seth slumped to the floor. It was then I fully realized what had happened."

"So it was your husband who initially produced the Smith & Wesson?"

She nodded.

"Why did he do that?"

"I don't know," she sighed. "Perhaps, as I told the district attorney, he only meant to check that it was loaded." She lit another cigarette. The ashtray was quickly accumulating the evidence of her stress.

"The senator must've said something at the time. Did he normally flaunt a gun during a marital spat?"

Her electric blue eyes snapped. "Of course not. He wasn't in the habit of slinging a Smith & Wesson at any excuse."

"Then something must've provoked him. What, Mrs. Hill? What was it you said or did that incited your husband to react so irrationally?"

"It all happened so fast. You're asking me for answers I can't give. Why don't you believe me? The shooting was accidental. Dammit! I wish someone would accept my explanation!"

The violet sundress flounced about her shapely legs as she abruptly stood and paced a few steps. She presented her back to him, her eyes fixed dead ahead, her arms wrapped about her midsection. She hadn't meant to lose control. But he kept asking, insisting on clear-cut answers, of which there were none. And she was tired of evading and masquerading. She needed space, some respite from the ceaseless pressure.

"I don't mean to sound unsympathetic, Marnie." His use of her first name was unintentional but effective. Ever so slowly the rigidity receded from her body. "Like the reporters, I'm just trying to earn my pay," he explained in a calming voice. "If I do my job well, you'll be spared a prison sentence."

He noted the sigh that shook her slim figure. "I understand," she finally answered, turning in his direction. "It's my turn to apologize. Ask me whatever's necessary."

He couldn't help thinking that though she reluctantly gave her permission, she did not as willingly offer her cooperation. "Let's discuss your marriage on the whole, shall we?"

"I thought it was a matter of public record," she replied as she sat down again, with a toss of her silver-blond hair.

He ignored the sarcasm, entreating her compliance with an easy smile. "You and your husband spent much of the time separated during the past few years." Though the fact was expressed in the form of a statement, it came across as another privacy-invading query.

"Yes," was her only reply.

"Why?"

She braced her temple against her fingertips, wishing he'd quit dissecting every facet of her life. "Contrary to the gossip sheets, it's not indicative of anything more than my fulfilling the obligations that are expected of a politician's wife. It's quite natural for a senator's spouse to stand in for him. Seth was in great demand. I simply went where he could not.''

"Didn't the extended separations put a strain on the marriage?''

"Not to my knowledge," came the terse response.

"You traveled far, Marnie, and kept company with some very—" he paused, choosing carefully and kindly the phrasing of his words "—highly visible men.''

A caustic smile stole across her full lips. "You're being diplomatic, counselor. You mean infamous gentlemen.''

"Yes, even borderline notorious," he admitted.

"All of whom were either politically influential in this country or deeply involved in foreign policy abroad. Surely you see the connection?''

"Perhaps you could enlighten me," he prompted.

"Seth had aspirations of becoming president. These men were crucial to his bid. On occasion I was his emissary.''

"That wasn't how your extensive trips and whirlwind socializing were viewed," he put forth, striking the pen on the pad, the incessant *tap*, *tap*, *tap* grating on her nerves.

"As always, my associations were misconstrued.'' She looked him directly in the eye, unintimidated by his innuendo. She was quite accustomed to the liberal interpretations people made about her private life— accustomed but hardly flattered.

"Your name was linked with a movie star in Beverly Hills, a Canadian financier and a Greek shipping tycoon, to name but a few. All wealthy and powerful men of dubious reputations.'' His tone was insinuating in itself.

Her delicate face paled, betraying a sensitivity. ''My name was also associated with numerous charities and many prominent women throughout the world but not nearly so often is that fact mentioned.''

''I'm only presenting the character-damaging picture that will be painted by the D.A. He will try to intimate—''

''It's been intimated many times and in ingenious ways, Mr. Dunn,'' she interrupted. Her frayed nerves could withstand little more of this derogatory conversation.

''I want to know if—''

''If I'm as scandalous as has been insinuated,'' she said curtly.

''You're putting words in my mouth,'' he protested.

''I'm sorry, counselor. I thought fidelity was the topic under discussion,'' she challenged.

Suddenly they were sparing with each other. Marnie had no more strength to draw on. She was drained and discouraged, wanting to lash out at whoever was symbolic. Ian was perplexed and impatient, wishing to goodness he could make up his mind about her. Was she cool and cunning or vulnerable and afraid?

He tossed aside the pen and leaned forward in the chair, his face and entire manner somber. ''You seem to be forgetting that we're on the same side,'' he reminded her.

''Are we, Mr. Dunn?'' she scoffed. ''Then why are you badgering me so?''

Ian's frustration got the better of him. His temper flared at the accusation. ''I'm trying to prepare a case in your behalf, Mrs. Hill, and you're behaving like a hostile witness. It's almost as if you're deliberately trying to sabotage any chance you might have.''

"How many more times and different ways can I say it?" she exploded. "I told you that the shooting was accidental and that I'm innocent. Yet you've all but called me a liar!"

"I don't think you're lying. I think you're being evasive. There's a difference. I can't defend you based on the bits and pieces you wish to reveal."

"I've told you the truth," she declared, a hysterical note creeping into her voice.

"Probably," he conceded. "But only the truth you wish me to know."

His uncompromising expression and tone cut to the quick. Marnie was seized by a suffocating panic. "Do you want to withdraw from the case?" The rash question tumbled from her lips before she realized.

Prideful blue eyes clashed with passionate golden ones. The moment was at hand to commit or retreat. Ian glanced at the legal pad before him on the desk, considering the meager facts and slim chances she'd given him. Raking his fingers through the sides of his light brown hair, he at last addressed himself to the crucial question.

"I want to win an acquittal. Don't you?" He deferred the decision.

His bluntness stunned her. She hadn't expected him to react so swiftly or positively. She lowered her gaze and swallowed her pride. "Very much," she finally admitted. "I'm sorry if I appear unappreciative. It's late and I'm tired. Maybe we could continue this tomorrow?"

The suggestion had merit. The stressful interview had certainly taken its toll on them both. She looked as drained as he felt. "When's the last time you ate, Marnie?" His voice grew mellow, his hazel eyes kind.

"This morning," she lied.

"Does a steak and salad sound good to you?" He rose from his chair while issuing the invitation.

The dinner suggestion was tempting. It was the first act of kindness anyone other than Grace had offered in days. "No more questions over dessert?" She asked for reassurances.

"No more tonight, Marnie," he acceded, realizing she could handle little more. "Tomorrow is soon enough."

"Then, yes, Mr. Dunn. I would very much like to join you for dinner."

They agreed to disagree tomorrow. For a few short hours they would pretend the serious circumstance that bound them did not exist. It wasn't an act of negation, merely a postponement of the inevitable.

"WE'LL HAVE COURVOISIER and coffee now," Ian requested, leaning back against the cushioned booth in a subtle indication for the tuxedo-clad waiter to clear his plate.

Marnie studied her escort's profile across the candle-lit table, suddenly aware of him as a person or, more precisely, as a man. Until now, she hadn't considered Ian Dunn much more than another faceless interrogator in a nightmare inquisition. But he most definitely had a face—a strong, striking one with remarkable eyes. It was as if they had the power to penetrate to one's soul—read your thoughts and learn your secrets. God! She hoped not!

He looked back at her and instantly she blanked her face and mind. "I thought an afterdinner drink might make us both sleep better tonight," he said.

"Do you suffer from insomnia?" she asked.

"Not normally," he said, grinning.

She elected to ignore the deeper implication of his remark. "Tell me why you chose to go into criminal law?"

"I'm not sure there was any cut-and-dry reason. I guess mostly because I hadn't the temperament for civil or the patience for corporate practice."

"Have you ever had any regrets?" She leaned her chin on a palm, looking pensively sultry and ever so appealing in the flickering candlelight.

He rested his forearms upon the table, a smile tripping over his handsome face. "That's a very complex question, Marnie. It depends on which aspect of my life we're discussing. Professionally speaking, no, I haven't had any regrets. Oh, once in my idealistic youth I considered the priesthood, but not seriously or for very long."

"Really," she said, amazement animating her voice and pretty face. "Somehow I can't imagine you as Father Dunn."

He grinned broadly at her candor. "That was about the same comment I received from the monsignor at my declaration of a true calling. Though he admired my intellect and tenacity, he doubted my devotion and discouraged my application to the seminary. He thought my volatile nature was better suited to a secular rather than a spiritual vocation."

Marnie could neither conceal nor contain her curiosity. Ian Dunn was a disarming individual who constantly surprised one with the unexpected. "I suspect that he was right, but I wonder what inspired you originally."

He withheld his answer until the waiter had served the Courvoisier and coffee. After swirling then savoring the liquor, he finally responded. "I was influenced a great deal by a man who literally molded my life. You see, at the age of seven I became a ward of the state of New York—another illegitimate child abandoned to the streets by a mother who had no options or conscience."

"I'm sorry," came the sympathetic murmur.

"Don't be," he replied a bit defensively. "I was a tough little punk—street-wise and obnoxious as hell. At the time the only thing I had going for me was being Catholic. I could've just as easily ended up in one of those sterile state institutions, but since I was 'of the faith' I became a ward of St. Timothy's Home for Boys—a Catholic charity for wayward kids like myself."

Marnie did not interrupt. She merely sipped her smooth liquor and listened with an open mind and heart.

"It was perhaps the worst and best time of my entire life. Like all such places, the home was overcrowded, underfunded and minimally staffed. The dormitory leaked with icy rain in the winter, then reeked with musty stagnation in the summer. Potato soup was our mainstay, religion our escape. My comrades were of every ethnic group and as rebellious and resentful as I. We were unkempt, underprivileged and defiant. But there was something that united us—one man—a simple but devout priest. His name was Father Pat."

He gazed into his snifter, as if the past he spoke of were contained therein. "With infinite patience, a sense of humor and a strong hand, he reached out to us. To him we weren't just a collection of misfits without advantage or value. He saw us as individuals with specialized needs and diverse potential. We each had a gift to share with society, and he was determined to make us recognize, develop and contribute the talent we had to give. He taught us that it didn't matter if the world didn't perceive our gift as a major contribution; it only mattered that we realize our self-worth and exercise our God-given potential." He paused, raising his reminiscing eyes from the snifter and the past.

"I can certainly understand your admiration. He sounds very special indeed," she commented.

"I have a purpose in telling you of him. You see, Marnie, Father Pat impressed on us the need to trust—that there are crucial times in our lives when you *must* rely on a reaching hand—a gesture of faith. Had Julio Ortega, the Hall of Famer, rejected his saving hand, he would've been just another delinquent who pitched bottle caps in a ghetto lot instead of Yankee Stadium. Had I refused his assistance and mocked his undaunted belief in my ability, I would not have graduated summa cum laude from law school. There comes a moment when the strongest of survivors can be swept under by life's swift and fickle undertow. You have only a split second in which to make a decision whether to react on instinct and grasp the hand extended to you or chance the struggle alone. My hand is out to you, Marnie...."

His bronzed and muscled arm stretched across the table, his steady hand encouraging her trust. She sat stunned and immobile, deeply touched by his plea but terribly afraid of the symbolism. Once before she had put herself in another's hands, only to be betrayed. Seth had let go—had left her to drown in a sea of disillusionment.

"I can't," came the desperate whisper. "Not again," she choked.

"Yes, you can, Marnie. Trust me," he entreated, inching his hand closer. "I've a firm grip and I'll hold on tight. I promise," he pledged.

"The water's deeper than you think, counselor. With all your good intentions, you may not be strong enough. I could just as easily pull you under with me," she warned.

"I'm willing to risk it," he assured her.

Slowly, reluctantly her hand left the snifter, timidly melding with his. With a firm clasp, his vow became a tangible sensation. She lifted her tear-filled eyes to his steadfast gaze, the wordless strength he lent dispelling her doubts as keenly as his magnetic touch warmed her cold flesh.

"Father Pat would be proud of you," he murmured in a soothing voice, squeezing her fingertips tighter when they trembled.

"In light of the situation, I'd prefer Father Pat's prayers to his esteem," she said in a vanquished tone, withdrawing her hand, clutching the snifter and needfully gulping the potent liquor. The fumes stung her eyes. Ian's naiveté pierced her heart. For she knew she could only trust him so much, no matter how desperately she wished to do otherwise.

Intuitively Ian sensed her resistance—sensed and was willing to gamble on it. For the memory of his own wariness clung to him. Trust was a slow process; deep wounds heal slowly.

He signaled the waiter, ordering two more Cour-
voisiers and a refill of the coffee. "I prefer the company to being alone tonight. Let me impose on you for
a little longer," he implored with a boyish smile.

His easy style was much more difficult for her to
resist. The dynamic counselor was a breed of man she
had never before encountered: tough yet sensitive;
polished but sincere. During the past few years she'd
dealt one on one with lustful men who personified
power. Ian Dunn was refreshingly different. He was
simply, unequivocally, a powerful man—not a fac-
simile but the force itself.

"I have the feeling that we could drink Courvoisier
and chat till dawn and still not know each other, Ian."
For the first time that evening, she actually smiled.

"I'm not looking to define you, Marnie," he answered honestly. "I'm merely trying to understand
and befriend you."

"Am I so complicated?" she said, baiting him, leaning back with a challenging look. The fact that she
chose to retreat rather than move closer was significant
in itself.

"I believe you are," he answered, never taking his
eyes from her lovely face as the waiter approached.

"And what if I'm no more than I've been depicted,
Ian? Would you still defend my honor?"

They both fell silent as the waiter served their
drinks. It was a tense intermission, and the mood that
remained in its wake was heart-pounding.

"You're testing me, Marnie," Ian at last replied.

"No, I'm merely making a distinction between defend and befriend." Her eyes involuntarily fell upon
her barren ring finger. "You ask for trust; I want reas-

surances. Are we speaking two different languages? And aren't we both seeking definition?''

"You're more than a glamorous woman exploited by the media, Marnie. Infinitely deeper than a headline and far more explosive than a blast from a Smith & Wesson. And I intend to discover the 'why' and 'what's really real' of you.'' He cocked a brow and lifted his glass.

"Are the words, 'mistaken' and 'regret' in your vocabulary, counselor?'' For some unfathomable reason, she measured him more. She wondered if he could ever truly understand the entanglements that bound her and might he ultimately regret his involvement.

"I can only reiterate what I stated earlier—not in any professional sense, Marnie.'' He clinked his glass against hers, playing her word game and fervently hoping the lady was worth the risk.

AND AS THEY CHALLENGED each other, life was also challenging them. Like the sheerest of mist, fate engulfed them. An Indian legend mingled with Courvoisier and, with the cleaving of two hands, the "faith of the abandoned" would not be denied.

CHAPTER EIGHT

FORTUNATELY ONE POSITIVE DECISION was reached during the table debate that occurred between the persuasive counselor and his reluctant client. Ian had wisely suggested that she take up temporary residence in his summer cottage a safe distance outside Lexington. It proved to be a very prudent and timely offer. For in the weeks that followed, the media had a heyday with the sensationalism surrounding the upcoming trial. The scandalous overtones increased circulation and they milked it for all it was worth.

Years' worth of negative publicity was rehashed: character-assassinating newspaper articles appeared, depicting Marnie Hastings Hill as a budding prima donna, a jet-setting socialite and neglectful wife. Always printed alongside was a recent interview with Judge Hill, eulogizing his son's outstanding accomplishments and moral fiber. Daily the old man emphasized the same question—what more might his son have contributed if his life had not been terminated at the zenith of his career?

The tide of public opinion was running strongly against Marnie. Television and radio stations nationwide were repeating old clips of Seth at different stages of his public-service career. Senate peers, both liberal and conservative, Republican and Democrat, were invited to comment on the personal and national tragedy of his premature death.

Since Marnie was unavailable for comment, Ian took the "heat." Constantly he was harassed for a statement. The offices of Connery and Dunn became a haunt for reporters and scandalmongers. The partners were besieged upon their entrance and exit, and the simple task of conducting routine business became an impossible ordeal.

Rory was tested beyond endurance. Rather than risk being mobbed by the swarming vultures who hovered ever near, he took to spending most of his day in the quiet bar across the street, being certain to park in a private lot around back, then sneak through the rear door.

On this particular afternoon, he was in an especially foul humor: for today, he couldn't go into his office or home, either. He blamed his exile to the gloomy bar on Ian. Ordering another mug of beer, he listlessly dropped a quarter into the jukebox, then flopped his flabby body back on the bar stool.

"Look at 'em," he complained to the bartender as the sallow-complected fellow set a frosted mug before him. With a flamboyant gesture, the tipsy Irishman directed the disinterested barkeep's attention to the law offices across the street and the praying-mantis reporters collected outside. "It's a flippin' zoo. Do you suppose we should charge admission?"

"Dunno, Rory," the bartender said, shrugging. "I got my own problems. That night barmaid I hired a week ago quit yesterday. So guess who's got to double up?"

"Precisely my point, Artie." Rory swigged the brew,

then licked the foam from his lips. "Seems as if not a soul has the least consideration anymore. It's every man for himself, 'n' tough luck if you happen to be standing in the way."

"Yup," the bartender agreed, exhaling his stale breath on a glass and polishing with a vigorous rub. "It's a cruel, hard world."

Rory grimaced at the cliché. "I'll tell you what's hard," he groaned. "Hard is a sister-in-law's spite when your eligible bachelor partner has stood up her moony daughter for the second time. Cruel is having to bear a testy mother's screeching tantrums and mollycoddle a simpering niece. Sure 'n' he promised me he wouldn't forget this time," Rory griped. "Didn't I tend to all the arrangements? 'Twas a small favor I asked."

The bartender nodded dumbly. He hadn't the vaguest notion what Rory was muttering about.

" 'Insensitive and rude,' my sister-in-law yells in my ear before she bangs down the phone. 'You did me no favors matchmaking my sweet Eileen with the likes of him!' she spits in my eye when barging into my home like a raving lunatic this morning. I tell you, Artie, Maggie O'Shay is a vindictive woman. She'll not be satisfied until I make amends. 'N' do you suppose my partner cares that I'm suffering the effects of his thoughtless neglect?"

The barkeep yawned as Rory slurped an angry sip.

"Hell, no! He's too preoccupied with that notorious widow to even take the time to make some flimsy excuse. 'I forgot,' he says. Sure 'n' that's supposed to pacify Maggie O'Shay and her darling daughter. The spiteful witch is refusing to do my shirts until Ian apologizes properly. 'N' does he care if I'm doomed to a Chinese laundress who binds me in starch?''

"Life can be a bitch," Artie commiserated.

"So can Maggie O'Shay," Rory groaned, draining his glass. "'Tis a sad day when you've no idea where your next laundered shirt is coming from, Artie. I'll have another," he said dejectedly.

"You want a chaser with this one?" Artie inclined his head toward the back door, tactfully warning Rory of Ian's approach.

The elder gent grunted affirmatively, then shoved a handful of goldfish-shaped pretzels into his mouth.

"What'll you have, Ian?" Artie asked, mopping up the varnished bar.

"Tonic water with a twist of lime," came the weary reply.

"Hard day?" The bartender chatted as the miffed Rory ignored Ian's presence on the bar stool beside him.

"I've had better." Ian forced a phony smile before taking a long, reviving drink.

Rory slugged down the schnapps and said nothing until the bartender moved off. "Judging from your glum mood, I take it that your request for a change of venue was denied," he grudgingly mumbled.

"Emphatically denied," Ian answered. "It looks like we'll have to do battle on Judge Hill's territory."

"'N' the jury selection? Are we winning any ground there?"

Ian's jaw flexed as he stared into his glass. "All I know for sure is that it's slow and tedious. With all the publicity, I'm having a hell of a time trying to find twelve unbiased jurors."

Wordlessly Rory picked up the bowl of munchies and gestured for Ian to follow. "Bring another round to the booth," he hollered to Artie, cramming his large figure into the cubicle.

Ian lingered to bring the drinks himself. Rory's retreat to the secluded booth meant one thing—he wanted to parley. In his fatigued state, Ian preferred to postpone the confrontation as long as possible. He chanced a glance over his shoulder. Rory was shedding the wrapper from a plump cigar—a sure sign of an impending harangue. Ian all but cringed.

"I'm putting everything on one tab," Artie announced, interrupting Ian's thoughts.

"How long has he been here?" Ian inquired.

"Since before noon. Don't worry. We take credit cards." Artie cast him an amused smirk.

"Somehow that doesn't ease my mind, Artie," Ian quipped, taking the drinks in hand and strolling to the booth.

A repugnant blast of smelly cigar smoke and a curt, "Sit down, Ian. I'm believing it's time for us to have a candid talk," introduced the verbal Irish brawl that Ian feared Rory was hell-bent on having.

"Are we going to argue the case or your niece again?" Warily, the young counselor slid the drinks across the table, then slung his body into the booth.

"You're a cocky cuss," Rory snarled, his teeth gnashing the cigar. "Sure 'n' it's not *your* shirts that'll bear the brunt of Maggie O'Shay's wrath."

Ian buried his forehead in his hands and rubbed his palms over his burning eyes. "For pete's sake, Rory. Drop it, will you?" came the exasperated request.

"It's not my jilted niece and crazy sister-in-law I was wanting to discuss," Rory huffed and puffed.

"Then, it's got to be the Hill case. Lately those seem to be the only two topics on your mind." Slinking his fingers through his hair, Ian raised his head.

"I glanced over the Hill brief yesterday. And frankly I don't think you've a snowball's chance in hell of winning," Rory blurted. "The old man doesn't just want her convicted, he wants her crucified! You can't get a change of venue, the judge won't grant you another delay, and so far your basis for a defense isn't only weak—" he plucked the cigar from his mouth and expelled a discouraged sigh "—it's bloody pathetic!"

As if he hadn't the strength to deny any of Rory's assumptions, Ian slouched back against the vinyl cushions, stretched out his cramped legs and slowly rolled the glass of tonic water between his palms.

"What may I ask do you plan to go into court with? Bejeesus! She shot a man whom the press and public want canonized. And why? Because she was afraid? The D.A.'s going to depict him as damn near a second Messiah, and you're supposed to convince a jury that Mary Magdalene put a .38-caliber slug into his heart because she was afraid of him? Bull!"

"You're right," Ian snapped. "It is bull. It's too contrived—his image and her explanation of the shooting. Nobody's as pure as he's being presented—a bronze-star hero, American as apple pie and truer than true blue. And Marnie's not as conniving or callous as she's being portrayed. It's all hype and makes for good copy. Dammit, Rory, there's a cover-up here. I can smell it. I believe she was a loyal wife. For some reason, I don't know why, she's protecting him."

"And maybe she's just what she seems and you're blind to it—a cold-blooded bitch who did away with her husband when he was about to rain on her parade," the seasoned partner argued.

"Shut up, Rory. You're playing the devil's advocate and I'm not in the mood." Ian jerked his drink to his lips, swallowed a gulp, then slammed down the glass on the table. Rory was purposely riling him, but it was nearly impossible to take issue with his logic. Ian had no defense and he knew it. Worse yet, he didn't have a prayer of getting one if Marnie didn't see the light and cooperate soon. She was concealing something. He was sure of it. He'd tried to gain her trust, to find the key and unlock her secret. But she was always leery. Suspicion held her at bay and every now and then a fleeting glimmer of dread shimmered in her eyes.

"He's not in the mood, he says!" Rory cynically mimicked. "Well, I'll tell you now, me boy. You'd better dig up some proof of your neat little theory or you might as well be convincing the jury they should also believe in the wee people 'n' legends of gold."

Ian checked his temper and fought back the biting comeback itching his tongue. "She's a very complicated woman. I've got to gain her trust before pressing her. She's got one vulnerable point. It could break her, but I don't want to have to use it unless I've no other alternative."

"If you've an edge, then for God's sake use it, man. You're out of time. Get hard on her if you think she's holding back. Make the woman help you defend her. If you don't, we're all going to go down the sewer." Rory had no compunction about pressuring their client.

"That's all you care about, isn't it? Your lousy

reputation! A woman's whole future is at stake here, and you're worried about some adverse publicity.''

An odd expression stole over the ornery Irishman's face as he fiddled with his cigar. "No, Ian. You're wrong. I'm concerned over more than my reputation and her acquittal.''

"Yeah? And what might that be?" Ian growled.

The blustery old gent hesitated, considered, then munched the pretzels instead of explaining. "Not now," he muttered. "Maybe when you're ready to hear. But not now. So be about gaining her trust. You got two days to do it in. Go on," he urged. "I got some thinking and drinking t'do and you're disturbing me."

Ian instantly regretted his rashness. "I shouldn't have come down on you so hard, Rory. It's not that I don't respect your opinion.''

"Don't be apologizing for speaking your mind. It's unhealthy to repress your feelings. You were bound to flare up, anyway.'' Rory's atypical contriteness alerted Ian.

"Why's that?" he quizzed.

"Maybe it'd be better if I told you tomorrow," the cagey old fox hedged.

"Tell me now, Rory," Ian demanded.

"First you give me your word that you'll not be flying off the handle.'' Rory squirmed and puffed in double time.

A sneaking suspicion began to gnaw at Ian. "First you assure me that this has nothing to do with your niece," he insisted.

"Dammit, Ian! You broke the girl's heart. A dozen roses is poor compensation for the grief you've caused.''

"You talk as if I were committed to more than a play and dinner. I broke a date, not a betrothal."

" 'Tis no difference in Maggie O'Shay's books," Rory grunted. " 'Twas a public humiliation."

"What dozen roses are you referring to?" Ian backtracked.

Rory buried his mouth in the foamy beer, his muttering barely intelligible. "The bouquet I sent in your name along with a note of apology," he confessed.

"I don't believe it!" Ian exclaimed, his head collapsing against the cushioned back of the booth. "You're purposely compromising me."

"I'm vindicating myself is what! You broke a promise I made to my niece not once, mind you, but twice. Eileen is a sensitive bit o' fluff."

"She's ugly as sin and has the disposition of a dead fish!" Ian quoted Rory's own articulate description of his kin. "I only agreed to take her out because you insisted."

"Sure 'n' I had your best interests at heart when I did," the Irishman snapped. "Do you think people don't wonder about your celibate ways? When a man shuns women as consistently as you, it stirs suspicion and sets tongues to waggin'."

Ian choked on his drink. "Are you suggesting that...."

"I'm merely apprising you of the gossip that has periodically surfaced in regard to your reclusive ways." Rory signaled Artie for refills. He strongly suspected he needed fortification against the counterassault ahead.

"I live my life the way I choose. It's no one's business if I refrain from casual and meaningless rolls between some empty-headed, glitter-girl's satin sheets."

"When a fine-looking lad like yourself displays no interest in the lovely and willing prospects you've encountered, it tends to create doubt about his virility."

"How about you, Rory? Are you among the skeptics?" A muscle ticked in Ian's cheek as he stared unwaveringly across the table at his partner.

The elder gent held his tongue until Artie had served the drinks, then wisely retreated. He took a long draw on his beer, a thoughtful puff of his cigar, then answered. "No, I understand your strong aversion to commitment of any kind. Rejection is a bitter experience. You've your reasons for being wary. Tender scars become tough adhesions through the years. Your stay at St. Timothy's and the countless disappointments you suffered at being passed over for adoption turned a supple twig into hard hickory. You'll not be swayed by a pretty smile or a promise of fleeting pleasure. You're wanting something of a deeper substance."

Ian hid the ache that clutched him. Instead he salved the old adhesions with tonic. "I'm curious. How much did this flowery apology to your niece cost me?"

"A mere seventy dollars," Rory said and beamed. "'Tis a bargain when you include my properly laundered shirts."

In spite of himself, Ian grinned. "You're a conniving old reprobate," he said with grudging respect.

"Ahh, but Maggie O'Shay will be appeased 'n' I'll come out smelling like a sweet Irish Rose." Rory chuckled, first chugging down his mug of beer, then sweetening his breath with a shot of schnapps. "I've had my limit. I'll be scooting myself home now. Consider strongly my advice about the case. Sometimes a good lawyer must make necessary but distasteful

choices. Press her,'' were his final words as he left the
booth and bar with a jaunty wave to Artie and a cheery
whistle on his lips.

Ian sat motionless, lost in a pondering fog. Rory's
disturbing revelations left him shaken in more ways
than one. The man who had been a loner most of his
life, whose fear of rejection ruled his desire, found
himself after all the many long, lonely years questioning the price he had paid. At the age of thirty-seven, he
had only known two special women. His sex life was
hardly what one would call active. Yet it was secure—
no risk, no complications, no regret, no chance of
pain. His two lovers had been older, more worldly,
more prone to be slow and sensual than fevered and
emotional. They'd tutored him in the art of lovemak-
ing and excused him from the hard lessons of love.

"Can I get you another?" Artie intruded upon his
reminiscing.

Steeped in nostalgia, Ian merely nodded, swigged
what was left in his glass, then handed Artie the
empty.

His mind returned to the ladies of his past. Marisa
had been the first—a fellow law student who now was
a corporate barracuda in a prestigious law firm in New
York. She specialized in 101 tax loopholes and 1001
ways to pleasure a man. Prim and proper on campus,
wild and inventive between the sheets, Marisa was a
study in contradictions. She had a quick mind and fantastic body and had no compunctions about exposing
either attribute.

"How about a refill on the pretzels?" Artie claimed
his attention when setting the sparkling tonic water
before him.

"No, thanks. This will be just fine." Ian glanced up, acknowledging but not really seeing the barkeep.

His mind returned to Marisa and the nights they'd crammed for upcoming exams till midnight, then relieved each other's tension till dawn. Marisa was a divorcée with years' worth of experience to share. He was a quick study with an abundance of suppressed passion to give. It was a mutually beneficial arrangement. He remembered the wink she'd cast him when he'd marched up the aisle to the podium to receive the coveted diploma. Her message was loud and clear. He'd graduated in more ways than one. They'd made the rounds of festive graduation parties together, then held a private celebration of their own. He would never forget her last words as she smoothed his tousled hair and softened the touchy moment that descended upon them as inevitably as the breaking dawn. "You're a hell of a fella, Ian Dunn. Too bad we won't keep in touch. No pun intended," she'd said, laughing.

"I hope life's good to you, Marisa," he'd answered. "Whenever I recall these hectic days and lazy nights, I'll remember you and smile," he vowed.

And he did, even at this moment when experiencing a pang of regret. Not that Marisa had been his ideal, only a vivid memory of a good, good season.

He sipped the lime-flavored tonic, vaguely aware of the tune someone had selected on the jukebox. Strands of a torchy blues song and visions of another extraordinary woman crystallized in his mind.

Simone was her name—and she was as sexy and French as any man could ever imagine. Sometimes soft and purring as a kitten, other times primitive like a sleek cheetah was Simone. He had been touring Europe,

sight-seeing, as it were. And Simone was a sight to behold—Parisian through and through—naturally beautiful and more provocative than a pure dram of
outrageous perfume. The lady had done well, marrying
into the family that owned one of the wealthiest and
most renowned vineyards in all of France. Yet sadly her
husband was a withered old man twice her age and a
paralytic. The marriage was open, and Simone had no
qualms when it came to exercising her option. They met
on the steps of the Louvre, ended up in a lavender loft
she rented under an anonymous name on the outskirts
of Paris. It was a steamy summer that European holiday. Simone had an insatiable need; he had a thirst for
fine French wine and a hunger for a spicy woman with
the pouty look of Brigitte Bardot and a throaty laugh
that bubbled like champagne. Her touch was memorable, her lust remarkable. In the immortal words of
Chevalier, Ahh, yes! He'd remember it well!

He raised the glass in silent salute to the two women
he'd known. Maybe his experiences were slim in comparison to other men, but they were unforgettably gratifying. So, maybe the Irish punk from Brooklyn wasn't
what one might call sophisticated in the realm of
women; he was nonetheless content with his indoctrina-
tion into the wonders of the opposite sex. Simone and
Marisa were vital, wonderful teachers. They made no
demands and were wise in the ways of a fickle, no-
guarantee world. They'd understood that part of
himself he could not relinquish; understood he'd paid
too dearly in his youth. The two women of his past had
loved him and left him a better man for the enriching experience.

The blues melody had ended, but not Ian's sentimental mood. There still lurked a haunting question in his mind. Why couldn't he resist Marnie Hastings Hill? Something about her intrigued him more than any other woman he'd ever met. He found himself wanting to draw her into his arms, hold her, console her. She was the dark corner of his own self that he both feared and longed to explore. Unlike Marisa and Simone, he was the one with a need, not the needed. And it frightened the hell out of him to have to admit, if only privately, his infatuation with the notorious widow.

He gulped down the last of the tonic. Instinct warned him that it wasn't smart to linger or ponder the inexplicable attraction he harbored for the aloof beauty. For he might not be able to abide the answer he sought. Perhaps she was as deadly as a black widow, and he was flirting with danger. Determinedly he shoved back his glass and maneuvered his large frame out of the booth.

"How much do I owe you, Artie?" he asked, reaching into his pocket for his wallet.

"The damages come to thirty-one dollars even," the bartender said in a chipper voice. "I can show you the tab if you like."

"I trust you, Artie," Ian replied, slapping down two twenties on the varnished bar, then strolling toward the door.

"Hey, ain't ya gonna wait for your change?" Artie hollered.

Ian flung him a negative wave, then vanished into the misty rain outside. The dewy moisture on his face felt refreshing after the smoky bar. He struck out walking, going no particular place in no particular hurry.

"Press her! Make her help you defend you!" Rory's

words clung to him like the misty rain. There was a way—her name was Sunny. He hated the thought of using a mother's protective love for her daughter as a tactic, but the child seemed to be Marnie's only vulnerable spot. She was devoted to her daughter, as he suspected she'd been to her husband. On several occasions when they had conferred at the cottage, he couldn't help but notice the change in her at the mention of Sunny's name. Marnie Hill may have insulated herself against the flak the press was flinging at her and reconciled herself to the grueling judicial process that lay ahead, but she had not prepared herself for the unthinkable prospect that she might be legally and irrevocably separated from Sunny.

The rain grew steadier, his thoughts even gloomier. *How he hated to use the child to get through to her!* It was such a drastic thing to do. But she left him no choice. The trial was two days away, and he'd yet to gain her confidence. Dammit, he silently cursed. What was she concealing?

He paused beneath a street lamp, its dim light emphasizing the stress that scored his face. Who was this enigma named Marnie, he wondered. Was she a charming opportunist capable of elaborate deception? He thought back to the widow at the cemetery and doubted the conclusion very much. Then why was she avoiding explanation? Refusing to give him a chance to exonerate her? The lady was playing with dynamite—with her very life. And *he*, with his doubt and infatuation, trifled with fire.

He sighed and rubbed the glistening moisture from his face with a forearm. As he turned to retrace his steps to the Cadillac, one truth pelted him as relentlessly as

the heightening rain. The lady had an effect on him—
an intense effect! Their association was much like
engaging in Russian roulette—except he had a gut feeling that the odds were even more perilous.

CHAPTER NINE

THE WHISPERED *ping* of raindrops hitting against the cottage window barely registered in Marnie's mind as she stared into the misty purple night beyond the glass. They had much in common, she and the crying night. They were each stricken with gloom.

Listlessly she shed her rain-soaked scarf and combed her fingers through her damp hair. She was chilled through and through, both in body and spirit. Thinking that perhaps some brandy might warm her, she forced one foot in front of the other and walked to the bar. In the vague recesses of her mind, Marnie recognized that she had all the classic symptoms of being on the verge of a physical and mental collapse. The frenetic trip she'd undertaken to Vicksburg to see Sunny had nearly pushed her over the brink. Her hands shook as she splashed the stout brandy into a snifter and then guided it to her lips. But then gradually the liquor's benevolent glow ignited a flicker of life within her and she breathed a deep, languid sigh.

The visit with Sunny had been depleting. Her daughter was full of childish tension and wounding curiosity as only a seven-year-old could be. It was only natural, Marnie knew, but the confrontation was also very distressing.

"I think daddy's sad in heaven," Sunny had said.

"Why would you think so, darling?" Marnie had asked.

"Because he never got to be president before he died. Do you think he minds very much?" came the profound question from such a sensitive little girl.

"I believe not," she'd comforted her daughter. "In heaven, you're at peace," she explained.

"Are you lonesome without daddy?"

"Very."

"Would you rather be with him?"

"Oh, Sunny. Are you afraid I'll be taken from you, too?" She'd clutched her daughter close, hugging her tight, then tighter still. "I won't leave you, sweetheart. Not for a very long time. I promise."

The pledge seemed to release Sunny from the apprehension and sorrow that claimed her. She wrapped her arms tight around Marnie's neck and pressed her cherub cheek close, whispering, "I miss him, mama. I love him so much."

"I know, baby. I know," she'd crooned. "Time is a mender, Sunny. You'll always love and remember him, but the ache fades. It's the same as when you fall down and skin your knees. It's terribly painful at first, but then the hurt heals."

Marnie blinked back the tears and gulped again from the snifter. If only she could be as easily consoled as her daughter. She had serious reservations that the wounds inflicted by Seth's sudden death would ever mend. They were so deep and raw. She found herself resenting the past and dreading the future—one had been a charade; the other was murky at best. Past, present and future began to run together in her mind. Lately she couldn't seem to distinguish or make sense of anything. The cool, collected widow was falling apart.

She returned to the window and sipped from the snifter, succumbing to a tidal wave of memories, visualizing scenes from the past. On Sunny's fourth birthday, Seth had lavished gifts and affection on her and laughed so gaily at her mischievous antics. In the purple beyond the window she pictured Seth lying beside her in bed, stroking her tenderly and whispering his gratitude for her and Sunny; then Seth a few years later, cradled in her arms and crying brokenly, begging her to leave him some dignity and the comfort of their daughter.

Marnie shuddered at the recollection. Suddenly she felt cold again. Would this shiver ever leave her? Was there enough brandy in the world to warm her again? She took another sip, seeking oblivion but finding instead even clearer pictures of the past: the tinsel recollection of Washington; she and Seth, a striking couple, cast against political splendor. In her mind she relived unforgettable moments: the homespun girl from Kentucky meeting the prime minister of Great Britain and being smiled upon by an Arab king; waltzing with the president and sharing a chat with the First Lady; graciously accepting the admiring glances bestowed on her but none more appreciative than her dashing husband's. Those had been sweet and incredible days of glory—moments she'd shared with her invincible Seth.

But the fragile and fleeting times were gone now. And she was suffocating in "used to be's." One would have thought she'd have adjusted better. After all, hadn't she mourned the loss of her husband nearly two years before his actual death?

Marnie deserted her post at the window and sought the brandy bottle once more. She didn't want to think on the past. It hurt too deeply. Yet she was afraid to consider the future. It disturbed her too greatly. For so long now she had been denying and suppressing her feelings. She was a woman who'd become quite accustomed to squelching her desire and sleeping alone. If only her accusers knew the restraint she'd exercised over the past few years, the tempting offers she'd resisted. It could've been incredibly easy to succumb to the flattery, to fall into a pair of comforting arms and then tumble into an anxious admirer's bed. But she'd remained loyal to the last, disregarding her own needs in deferment to Seth's.

During the past few weeks she'd become acutely cognizant of her smoldering passion. The sexual abstinence she'd endured mocked her constantly. If she were honest she knew she felt desire every time Ian Dunn came near. All her senses were heightened in his presence. Should his knee accidentally brush hers under the table, she was aware. Should his breath caress her neck as he bent over her shoulder to discuss something, she was aware. Should he happen to flash her a disarming smile quite unexpectedly, she was aware.

Damn! Why was she so alert to him as a man? It was irrational and totally inexcusable. Perhaps she was going mad. How could she even consider.... Her trembling hands lifted the snifter and she drank to steady herself. She closed her eyes as if the act would block the absurd and unthinkable prospect of a torrid interlude from her mind. She mustn't allow her rampant desire any expression. It was only the loneliness that caused her to attach such significance to a natural regard. Didn't it happen all the time between patient and doctor, student and teacher? Ian Dunn was her only hope. Of course she transferred her need to him. It wasn't uncommon, especially taking into account the desperate circumstances that bound them.

The rationale comforted Marnie—not much, but enough to deceive herself into a dangerously lax mood. It was either that or the brandy at work. She couldn't distinguish which. For finally her heart didn't palpitate like a captive bird's and the self-recrimination dulled.

Though she thought her physical attraction for Ian was accounted for, there were stronger, even more compelling ties drawing her to him—emotional ones. Never in her life had she known a man quite like him—a man who gave new meaning to words such as decency, solidity and devotion. He accepted so much on faith and risked such a great deal in the process. Within him was harbored a virtual wellspring of strength and integrity, intelligence and sensitivity—enough for ten men. Yet he wasn't cocky, merely confident.

During the past few weeks as she sat in his pleasing company, absorbing his quick wit and slow, easy style, she'd find herself alternately wondering about his unselfishness, then marveling at his competence, confused by his restraint, then grateful for his amazing patience. He was an extraordinary man—successful but humble, full of conviction but still compassionate. His emotional barometer fluctuated only on occasion, and then only when provoked. Unlike Seth, he was steady and firm, consistent and reliable. Oh yes, Mr. Dunn had much to recommend him. Marnie might possibly resist his physical magnetism but his charismatic personality was much more difficult to deny. She had to be constantly on her guard lest his good qualities override her good sense.

She blinked, refocusing her thoughts. As always,

she'd master her circumstances. Ten years of marriage to Seth Hill had taught her to adjust and adapt to life's variables.

Should you fail, there were no excuses acceptable, no second chances allowed. At this crucial stage of her life, she mustn't let loose the tight rein she'd kept on herself, mustn't let panic run away with her. This time the race wasn't for a senate seat or the presidency; it was for her very life. This time it wasn't Seth's political future at stake; it was her freedom. Yet she was handicapped by secrets. She'd promised Sunny to win—to be a firm influence in her impressionable life. But how could she do both? Supply the explanation that would gain her an acquittal and still protect her daughter? There had to be a way! Silky blond hair spilled over her face as she buried her head in her hands. God help her! There just had to be a way!

At the unexpected knock on the front door, her head snapped up. She glanced to the clock atop the mantle. It was nearly midnight. The rapping summons echoed again.

Warily Marnie crossed to the door, opening it the length of the chain latch. "Ian," came the baffled response. "It's rather late for a social call, don't you think?"

"It's pretty nasty out here, Marnie. Ask me in and I'll explain," he answered.

The door shut for a second, the scrape of chain latch slipping from its slot resounding before she beckoned him inside.

"You're drenched. I've been sampling some excellent brandy that the previous tenant kindly left behind. Would you care to join me?" The offer was spoken in a much more casual manner than her constricted stomach muscles would have indicated was possible.

Once more she was caught off guard by the infectious grin he cast her. "That's gracious of you," he replied, slipping out of his wet sport coat and running a hand over his rain-slicked hair.

She retreated to the bar, refilling her glass and pouring another for him. "Since it's nearly midnight and foul weather, I take it that something urgent is on your mind." She approached him cautiously, passing him the brandy but mindful to remain at arm's length.

"We're two days away from going to trial, Marnie." He wasted no time getting to the point as he took a hefty swig of brandy.

"I'm aware of that, Ian." She studied his solemn profile. He kept his eyes averted, contemplating the shimmering liquor.

"During the past few weeks, I'd hoped to gain your trust and perhaps learn the complete truth of the shooting." He looked up, his expressive eyes pinning her. "But you persist in being evasive and we're running out of time."

She turned from him, unable to contend with the determination on his face.

"The possibility of losing is very real, Marnie. The D.A.'s got a strong circumstantial case and juries are fickle. Help me defend you. Tell me what it is you're withholding from me."

She eased the glass to her lips, remaining silent. Only a dramatic pause answered his plea.

"Dammit, Marnie! Your loyalty is commendable but masochistic. What about your daughter? Do you care what will become of her when you're found guilty?

You'll lose her forever!'' His words struck her with brutal reality.

"Don't say that!'' She spun on him, her blue eyes wild, the glass trembling in her hand. "Don't... don't,'' she repeated, her voice fading to a groan as she shook her flaxen head in dazed agony.

His advance was slow, purposeful. "I have to make you face the possibility of a guilty verdict. You have to understand the consequences of your silence.''

"No! Stop hounding me, please.'' She denied him, retreating until there was no room left to run. "I can't betray....'' She caught herself. "Don't ask. Please don't ask,'' she pleaded. The glass dropped with a dull thud to the floor, spilling amber liquid onto the carpet in the same way as the glazed grief trickled from her eyes.

He reached for her, his powerful hands clamping her shoulders and shaking her hard. "You have to tell me why you spent the last few years on the jet-set run. Give me something, a reason, to counter the elite whore image you created. You've got to, Marnie! Tell me your secret!'' he demanded.

The tight rein snapped. No longer was she mistress of her emotions. "Seth asked me to,'' she blurted hysterically. "He begged me to stay as far from him for as long as I could.''

"Why?'' he badgered. "Why would he make such a request?'' His grip intensified and he nudged her again, prying the truth from her lips.

"Because he was impotent the last two years of our marriage. My nearness was torturing him!'' She choked on the admission a second before she swayed.

Ian caught her in his arms, pulling her tight against his stunned heart. The sounds of her broken sobs filled the cottage. He felt her tremble beneath the strain and found himself overwhelmed with sympathy.

"Don't cry, Marnie. Please don't cry," he soothed against her temple, at which she raised her misery-laden eyes to his, making him ache as never before in his life. "I don't want to hurt you. I never want you to grieve again," he pledged through lips that kissed her salty cheeks, her whimpering mouth.

He didn't know why he was saying these things, why he was kissing her. She was clinging to him, soft and yielding beneath his touch, moaning under his consoling mouth. And he was absorbing her, not just her despair, but *her*, this angel in his arms.

"Believe in me," she sobbed. "Oh, God, please don't desert me. I need you, Ian."

He winced at her words, gently lifting her in his arms and walking into the bedroom. He placed her on the quilted coverlet, his sincere hazel eyes holding hers as he eased down beside her. Reassuringly he captured her fragile face between his steady hands, promising in a husky whisper, "I believe in angels, Marnie, even tarnished ones. I won't forsake you." She stared up at him, confused and vulnerable. He kissed her deeply and with commitment.

His kiss was warmer, smoother, more stimulating than the life-sustaining brandy. She was so in need, so terribly susceptible. His gentle hands soothed her, stroked her in easy, mesmerizing glides—through her silky hair, through her sheer blouse, through her inhibitions. Her arms entwined around his neck, drawing him closer, borrowing his strength. She felt heady from brandy and desire, her body responding with ardor, her conscience wrestling with denial.

"Ian," came the hoarse and breathless whisper as she placed her palms on his shoulders, recoiling from the magnetic pull of his lips. "It makes no sense. We mustn't do this." Her plea was shallow and futile.

The word "sense" had no meaning to an impassioned man. His eyes were glazed, the touch of his fingers raking, then tangling in her hair was tenderly possessive. He needed, too, even more strongly than she did.

"Don't deny the moment, Marnie," he implored. "There are no right or wrong reasons for the chemistry between us. There's only you and me and the rain. I care," he whispered, molding his muscled body closer, stringing beads of kisses along her sleek neck like the crystal droplets of rain that shimmied down the windowpane. "I want you, Marnie," he confessed, "as I have never wanted any other woman before."

His trembling hand relinquished her hair to seek the buttons of her blouse. One by one, he unfastened the dainty catches, the eager lips following the trail his fingertips made from the hollow of her throat to her satin midriff.

She trembled at his desire. Never before in her life had she felt so cherished and at the same time so utterly inept. His brawny arm slipped under her blouse, holding her slim back and lifting her from the coverlet. In one swift motion he peeled the garment from her body and gently lowered her upon the bed. She closed her eyes, her tapered nails weaving through his soft, damp hair as he grazed a cheek across her swelling breasts. The contact of his flesh on hers was like eighteen-karat-gold gilding, luscious honey coating—precious and sweet beyond compare.

Take our fashion tote plus two exciting romance novels...

free

YOURS FREE

Two best-selling Superromance novels and a fashion tote to carry them in.

The editors of Harlequin would like to share two of their best-loved books with you, and at the same time, send you a fashion tote bag—FREE!

You'll find plenty of compelling reading in your *free* HARLEQUIN SUPERROMANCES. And you'll find plenty of uses for your *free* Harlequin tote. Take it on shopping sprees or out-of-town trips...to the beach or to the gym...on picnics or overnighters. It's perfect for carrying everything from parcels to your Harlequin novels.

The two Harlequin novels and the fashion tote are yours to keep—**FREE**—just for sending us the postpaid card at right.

More good news! You can also look forward to a long love affair with Harlequin *at a terrific savings.* As a subscriber, you'll receive four newly published HARLEQUIN SUPERROMANCES every month, delivered right to your home up to 4 weeks before they're available in stores. Each novel, over 300 pages of exciting reading, is yours for only $2.50. You save over $1.00 per shipment off the retail price.

Begin your rendezvous with romance right now by accepting our two free novels and tote bag. Rush the attached card to us today!

HSUA

Your rendezvous with romance

Watch as TV talk show Host Russ Marshall betrays author Sara Daniel's trust and love right on television.

Never Strangers by Lynda Ward

Follow through Dr. Robin Mitchell's struggles to convince Dr. Paul Wilcox that marriage is the ultimate expression of love.

Reach the Splendor by Judith Duncan

Free Gifts/Savings Card

Yes, please send me my *free* tote bag and my two *free* HARLEQUIN SUPERROMANCE novels, *Never Strangers* and *Reach the Splendor*. Then send me 4 new HARLEQUIN SUPERROMANCE books every month as soon as they come off the press. I understand I will be billed only $2.50 per book (for a total of $10.00—a saving of $1.00 off the retail price). There are no shipping, handling or other hidden charges. There is no minimum number of books I must purchase. In fact, I may cancel this arrangement at any time. The tote bag and novels, *Never Strangers* and *Reach the Splendor*, are mine to keep even if I do not buy any additional books.   134 CIS KAVG

Name_____

Address_____ **Apt. No.**_____

City_____

State_____ **Zip**_____

Offer limited to one per household and not valid for present subscribers. Prices subject to change.

Mail to:
HARLEQUIN SUPERROMANCE
2504 W. Southern Avenue,
Tempe, Arizona 85282

LIMITED TIME ONLY
Mail today and get a
MYSTERY BONUS
GIFT

Take it, tote it, swing it, sling it —

You'll just love this stylish tote. Perfect for shopping, traveling and your Harlequin novels. Made of durable cotton canvas with two sturdy straps and snap closure. Topstitched. Bottom-gusseted. Natural color attractively highlighted with Harlequin diamonds in lovely shades. A $6.99 value — it's yours *free* along with two *free* HARLEQUIN SUPERROMANCES.

His expert fingers moved to the front clasp of her scanty lace bra. She stiffened with a desperate clutch of his hand, the sound of her voice competing to be heard over the frantic beat of her heart. "I haven't the strength to resist again, counselor," she warned. He captured her petal-soft lips, trying to thwart her reluctance. Desperately she fought him and her own outrageous response. "Please listen," came the urgent murmur. "It isn't fair, not to you or to Seth."

The clasp of her bra surrendered to his will. Her breath exhaled in a gasp as he touched first one sensitive breast, then the other.

"To hell with what's fair, angel. I want to linger in paradise," he rasped, groping for the side sash and zip of her skirt, finding it and adeptly undoing and discarding what remained of her encumbering clothing. He was knocking on heaven's door and nothing would stand in his way. He didn't care if the moment was perishable. He'd gladly suffer eternal damnation for an instant of bliss.

Marnie was incoherent with longing, her willowy body cleaving to his manly contours, her mind intoxicated with his musky scent. Dreamily but, oh, so intensely greedily she undressed him and explored him and devoured him. The months of unfulfillment seemed to vanish as thunder rumbled and flashes of lightning streaked across the Kentucky sky beyond the window. He was magnificently passionate, absorbing her sensuality like the dry earth receiving the revitalizing rain.

Two silhouettes raged like the storm—rolling, twining, undulating in a tempestuous fever. In the glare of intermittent lightning, he could distinguish her cameo face—alternately taut with desire, mellow with euphoria. Then, the same as the distant thunder, her features would fade with his own yearning and ecstasy. The sounds of her purrs and gasps, the smell of her perfume, the sweet taste of her lips and velvet texture of her tongue engulfed him. She was as natural and exciting as the swirling storm winds that mingled with their moans.

"Say you're not sorry, Marnie." The darkness swallowed his whisper as he blanketed her body with his, melding his need with her own. He was beside himself with wanting, dazedly kissing her throbbing temples and stroking her lithe hips.

"I'm not sorry," came the breathless reassurance. "I'm only impatient," she moaned. "Love me, Ian. Love me senseless."

He wouldn't have denied her if he could. And regardless of the outcome, he hadn't the luxury of choice. Fate had chosen for him. With compassion, without a second's reservation, he cast reason aside and entered paradise. And in the wondrous moments that followed they both experienced indescribable rapture and more; they found the bliss that poets had immortalized and myths had promised—boundless love.

The storm and passion receded; the patter of two hearts and dwindling raindrops remained. Ian refused to let go of Marnie or the moment, wrapping his arms and affection about her and rolling over with a satisfied sigh onto his back.

"No regrets?" he asked in a hushed and concerned voice.

She snuggled against his solid length, cradling her head against his shoulder. "Only one," she murmured, tingling his bare chest with a lazy, contented weave of her fingertips. "That time can't stand still."

He pulled the coverlet over their linked bodies, hugging her close, then smoothing her tumbled hair. "Unfortunately that's a wish I can't grant, angel."

"I know," she replied forlornly. "You need answers to your questions."

He brushed her forehead with an apologetic kiss. "I hate this, Marnie. But it's necessary."

"Can't we postpone a little longer? I'd like to freshen up." She raised her hand and cast him an entreating smile.

"Of course," he relented. "But only if you promise to come back to bed and my arms again."

She lowered her eyes. "Usually I'd enjoy pillow talk," she murmured.

He tilted her chin with a fingertip, then leaned and touched her lips with a tender kiss. "The afterglow may not be as it should, but I haven't a complaint about the magic we just shared. Did I fail to tell you that you're heavenly, angel?"

"No, counselor." Her lashes fluttered, her soft blue gaze beguiling him. "You're a very skillful and vocal lover."

"Your choice of words makes you sound very worldly. But after being with you, I know better. You were starved for expression, Marnie. I'm glad you chose me as the means to convey it."

Wordlessly she withdrew from his arms and slipped from the bed. Instinctively he let her go, though his eyes stalked her moonlit figure and his heart pounded with regret. He began to wonder if she really was but a fleeting vision. If perhaps he would never truly hold her to him for long. He swung himself from the bed, absently straightening the covers and fluffing the pillows. His chore complete, he lay back down, folding his arms behind his head and staring up at the ceiling. If Marnie was a beautiful apparition who only materialized on occasion, he prayed he was fortunate enough to be present at every appearance. For he was absolutely enchanted by her.

As if she'd read his mind, Marnie emerged from the adjoining bathroom wearing a gown of abalone satin, her sleek-brushed platinum hair cascading over her shoulders and tumbling down her bare back. She was beyond a shadow of a doubt the loveliest vision he'd ever beheld.

He turned back the quilt, then patted the burgundy sheets in a gesture for her to come lie down beside him, thinking her poetry in motion as she glided to his side.

"I can't decide which I prefer," he said, "an angel in white satin or a sorceress in the buff?" Adoringly he pulled her near.

"Are you still having difficulty making up your mind about me?" She cast him a faint grin and stretched languidly.

"You are an enigma, Marnie," he answered honestly. "What I haven't decided is whether it's intentional or not."

"I'm just plain me, counselor, and all that that encompasses—good and bad, hard and pliable, evident and vague." She reverted to word games once more.

He fell back on the pillow, still embracing her in the bend of his arm, his hand slowly stroking her creamy shoulder.

"You are intriguing," he murmured more to himself

than to her. "Perhaps the answers you promised to give will shed some light."

He felt the slight stiffening of her supple body, but he made no remark. "What do you want to know, Ian?" she said with a sigh.

"Everything that is pertinent to the case. Most especially I want you to tell me about the senator's problem and the effect it had on your marriage."

She, too, rolled onto her back, pinning his arm beneath her. And by the time she was finished confiding the private details of Seth Hill's impotency and the ensuing problems it posed, both Ian's mind and arm tingled—his arm from the lack of circulation, his mind from the significant information she'd imparted.

It seemed that several years ago Seth Hill was diagnosed as having diabetes mellitus. He had ignored the symptoms too long and by the time he sought help the disease was advanced and severe. Within six short months he experienced impotency—one of the stages of the disease. Unfortunately, in his case, the incapacity wasn't psychological but physical, and the only treatment was experimental. Seth's depression was extreme and two-fold, according to Marnie. Primarily he had always been a very passionate man who unashamedly lusted for his wife; secondly he realized he was vulnerable to even worse disabilities—blindness or the amputation of a limb. He became obsessed with keeping his illness private. He wished no one to pity him and wanted to make his bid for the presidency while he was still capable. The thought of Marnie near and untouchable drove him to distraction; the fear of forfeiting his political future made him fanatical.

She told Ian that the senator begged her to make both

easier for him—to take away the temptation he could never again know and use her charm to woo influential support wherever she traveled. Reluctantly she'd agreed. In her words, ''because he seemed so desperate...because it seemed to be the only thing that brought him any peace...because he merely had to ask and I couldn't refuse.''

But Seth Hill was tortured by contradictory demons— his goals and his jealousy. In time he became a dual person—the public image and private martyr. He would coerce Marnie into extended trips and social maneuvers, then become irrationally jealous of her efforts on his behalf. She recounted the numerous times she'd endured ugly scenes and untrue accusations following an absence or political affair. Again, in her words, ''it became a vicious cycle—him wanting me and knowing physical expression of his love was impossible and also desiring the presidency of the United States at any cost; me wanting to ease his manly anguish and help him realize his fervent dream before a debilitating illness claimed his only chance for immortality.'' She recalled the incidents when she would remind her husband of his request for assistance and distance, then his subsequent begging for her forgiveness and understanding.

Ian was encouraged by the revelation. At last he had some basis for a defense. If he could defend Marnie's character, persuade the jury that she was not all black or the senator all white, then he could establish doubt as to her deliberate intent. He could also hint at the unstable state of Hill's mind at the time of the incident. Marnie could very well have had cause to be afraid. The momentum of public opinion could swing in their direction, the scales of justice tip in their favor.

He was immensely relieved. She was strangely passive. He attributed her lack of enthusiasm to strained nerves and sudden weariness. She turned onto her side, facing away from him. He draped an arm around her waist and gathered her spoon fashion next to his hard body. The lady had had a very tense night. He understood her need for rest.

As he embraced this misunderstood and brave woman in his arms, he did not realize the mysteries that worked against him—what Marnie had chosen not to reveal; what his heart had unconsciously admitted. He, the man who swore never to expose a need so great it could consume him, had done so without realizing. He was falling in love with an enigma named Marnie, without knowledge or consent.

Marnie lay still and silent, guilt and remorse gnawing at her. How she wanted to tell Ian everything. But her vow was sacred. Seth might be beyond the heartache of his mistakes, but Sunny wasn't.

AGAIN, FATE TWISTED THEIR LIVES and the bittersweet legacy of the wild rose enveloped the pair. One of them was falling in love, the other hovering in a dangerous limbo. After their intimacy, Marnie knew she cared for Ian deeply, but she was still bound by a covenant that not even death could dissolve. Her conflicting allegiances tore her apart. If anything, accepting Ian's blind devotion only added to her burden. Again she was trapped in a vicious circle. Ironically Ian Dunn was losing his heart to a woman whose false pride might cost them both a price too dear to pay.

CHAPTER TEN

THE COMMENCEMENT OF THE HILL TRIAL was exactly as Rory had prophesied, only worse. Press and spectators swarmed the courthouse steps for a glimpse of the alleged murderess in a crime of passion. The excited mood outside the legal amphitheater was much like the frenzy associated with the annual arrival of a traveling circus—even to the street vendors who peddled cold drinks and snacks on the corner.

As Ian turned the corner, he realized their predicament, but it was too late to avoid the fiasco. He was grateful for the human barricade of uniformed officers who fought to maintain order.

"Best go round the back, me boy. Try the rear entrance." Rory straightened his bulky figure in the back seat, trying to shield Marnie from the celebrity hunters.

"I won't begin this trial by sneaking in the back door. We're going in with our heads high," Ian decided, braking and gearing into park.

Immediately a grim-faced officer approached, touching the brim of his cap in respect as Ian rolled down the window.

"Leave it running, sir. We'll take care of your car. I suggest that y'all not pause between here and the doors. It's a mite sensitive out here, sir."

"I understand, Sergeant, and we appreciate the assistance."

"It's our job, sir. Good luck," was the fellow's spare reply.

Ian and Rory gathered their briefcases, then exchanged concerned glances. "Okay, Marnie," Ian said, turning to her with an encouraging smile. "Stay between us and don't answer any of their questions. I'll run interference for you."

She did not respond at first, her eyes and attention focused on the heckling crowd. Some even carried signs—No More Excuses; This Time Marnie Loses! She Killed Our Beloved Senator; Now Execute Her!

The viciousness momentarily paralyzed Marnie. Though she knew Seth had been popular with the people, she failed to realize the near-fanatical devotion he'd inspired. As much as the masses loved and excused him, they hated and accused her. Like Marie-Antoinette or the czarina, Alexandra, she was a tangible symbol of all that was wrong in the land.

"Marnie. . ." Ian said, claiming her attention. "It's a long walk to the doors. Are you up to it?"

Her blue eyes shifted to, then quickly dismissed, him. She tugged her floppy hat lower over her pale face. "I'm trained at maintaining my composure, Ian. Once the limo Seth and I rode in was stormed by radicals in South America. I was up to it then and I won't panic now."

Ian drew a deep breath. "Ready, Rory?" he asked, sliding over and gripping the car door handle.

Rory blessed himself, then swung open the door, protectively reaching back for Marnie's elbow and pulling her to his side. Ian took the left flank, Rory the right as the crowd converged, straining against the police line.

Flashbulbs exploded everywhere at once, partially blinding the threesome as they edged forward.

"Have you any statement for the press, Mrs. Hill?" an aggressive reporter yelled.

"None," Ian boomed, squeezing Marnie's arm and propelling her onward.

"How will you plead?" Another voice called from the multitudes.

"Not guilty to any and all charges!" Ian answered with amazing confidence.

"A zoo...a blasted zoo!" Rory muttered under his breath, then cursed in pain as an officer was shoved backward onto his tender instep.

Marnie was trying to shield her face from the barrage of photographers, saying nothing and moving fast. To most in the crowd she was only a blur in a plum-colored hat and summer suit.

Then a voice screamed out, "I hope you get life for what you've done. You're a murdering whore!"

Marnie went rigid at the vile accusation. Suddenly the crowd's jeers sounded remote and the mass of angry faces became a haze. Ian's arm clamped around her waist, literally holding her up as they took the final steps to the courthouse door.

"They're a bloodthirsty lot," Rory grumbled, yanking open the door and covering Marnie and Ian's retreat within the hallowed halls.

Ian didn't bother to answer as he surveyed his client. She was plainly shaken, yet bravely trying to collect herself. "I won't put you through that again, Marnie," he promised. "I'll make other arrangements for our arrival for the duration of the trial."

Her mouth quivered as she attempted a weak smile.

"Please do. I'd rather face another run-in with South American radicals than a repeat performance of this sort." She removed her disguising hat and shook free her lustrous hair.

"We've only a few minutes before court convenes," Rory reminded, glancing from his worried partner to their wilted client, then checking his watch again. The expression on their faces told the savvy Irishman more than they'd intended him to know. The widow looked to Ian for strength; he lent it with a serene smile.

"Go ahead, Rory. We'll be along shortly," Ian said to excuse him.

The senior partner considered insisting, then thought better of it. He knew Ian well enough to realize the futility of arguing. "I'll save you a seat," he grunted, swiveling on his heel and disappearing down the corridor.

Ian and Marnie stood silent for a second, her polished fingertips methodically turning the brim of her hat, Ian examining his recently shined shoes.

"Would you like a smoke before we go in?" he finally suggested. "It's not allowed inside, you know."

She nodded and he gently took her elbow, escorting her to a designated smoking area. She handed him her hat, then fumbled in her purse for her cigarettes and lighter.

"Here, let's trade," he said softly, exchanging the hat for her purse, locating the elusive articles and lighting one for her.

"Thank you," she sighed, inhaling deeply.

He tucked the purse under his arm and leaned against a marble column. "I forgot to instruct you what to wear today, but you're dressed perfectly for the court appearance.''

A wry smile flitted across her lips. "Conservative with a hint of bereavement.'' She stared beyond him, her fine features taut with tension. "Long ago I learned the importance of making the right impression. Funny,'' she went on, her voice subdued and distant, "how if you dress to fit a role hardly anyone sees beyond the superficial.''

"And what do you think passersby surmise about me?'' he countered in an amused tone. "They're probably appalled at my sporting a black clutch bag with a brown silk suit. Terribly gauche, don't you think?'' His teasing grin was charming.

"Terribly,'' she mimicked. "I should spare you the humiliation.'' She reached a hand out to relieve him of the attention-getting accessory, but found it trapped in his own.

"If only I could spare you as easily,'' he murmured with a gentle press of her hand. "I'll do my best to make this ordeal as bearable as possible,'' he pledged.

She looked up and crystal-blue disillusionment clashed with emerald-and-amber sincerity. "I know you will, Ian.'' She eased his anxiety with a shy smile. "Please don't take my foul mood personally. You're not responsible for the situation.''

"I do take you personally, Marnie,'' he vowed. "Someday, when all of this is far behind us, I'll tell you how much.''

She lowered her eyes, then withdrew her hand. His declaration meant so much to her, and still she couldn't bring herself to reciprocate the trust he so freely gave.

"My somedays are uncertain, Ian,'' came the dif-

ficult but accurate assessment as she took a last puff,
then extinguished the cigarette. Ian was oblivious to the
tap, *tap*, *tap* of a walking stick on the terrazzo floor, but
Marnie immediately recognized the sound. Slowly she
turned and faced the glare of Aubrey Hill.

He stood a few feet away, his searing eyes riveted on
her regal figure. Noting the ever-so-slight tensing and
lifting of her proud chin, Ian followed the path of her
gaze to the old judge. Instinctively Ian knew him.

"Smoking again, Marnie?" the old man mocked.
"Strange how quickly one reverts to former trashy
habits, given the opportunity. I shall send you a carton
in prison."

"Don't concern yourself, Aubrey. I want no more
favors from the Hills," came the sharp retort.

Ian was trapped in the cross fire. Since Marnie
seemed to be holding her own, he did not intervene.

"I decided to come and observe the proceedings. I do
hope you won't detain me longer than necessary," he
needled her.

"You came to gloat," she answered with a defiant
toss of her head. "Has the possibility occurred to you
that this once the final outcome may not be as *you*
decree?"

He smirked and did not bother to respond. His expression said everything. No, the possibility of the jury
finding on Marnie's behalf was totally abhorrent and
completely irrational. And not only was he smug in his
belief, but dedicated to his crusade. He dismissed her
with a scoffing grunt, then limped away.

Marnie's whole body wilted at his departure. Wordlessly, Ian embraced her slim shoulder. "Would you care
for an injection of antivenom serum before we go in?"

She shook her head, smiling in spite of herself. "No, but if you happen to have a silver bullet I could bite, I wouldn't object," came the unsteady reply.

He led her down the corridor, opening the massive door on what would become a pivotal chapter in their lives. A murmur rippled over the gallery of spectators at their entrance. Ian's steadying hand remained at her back until they'd marched through the swinging gate and seated themselves next to Rory at the defense table.

District Attorney Sutter Cane acknowledged Ian with a curt nod as he took his seat. Both he and his assistant were dressed for a kill—impeccably tailored yet duly modest. His paperwork was arranged methodically before him. He was ready to seek the maximum sentence for the state—ambitiously primed.

"Cane's bursting to begin. He's smelling the capital and the attorney general's post," Rory muttered across Marnie.

"Well, if he doesn't believe I'm going to do everything in my power to deprive him of it, he's underestimated me." Ian cast Rory a covert wink while sorting through his own paperwork.

"All rise!" The bailiff summoned the court's attention.

The participants came to their feet as Judge Simon Greer took the bench.

"The Ninth Criminal District Court is now in session, His Honor Judge Simon Greer presiding. The defendant is charged with a violation of Article 144 of the penal statutes," the bailiff recited.

"How does the defendant plead?" Judge Greer asked.

"Not guilty, Your Honor," Ian responded.

"Be seated," came the magnanimous command from the bench. Judge Greer glanced to the prosecution's table. "Are you ready to proceed for the State?"

"We are," Sutter Cane answered in a positive voice.

"Is the defense also prepared?" Judge Greer's benign gaze shifted to Ian.

Ian rose slightly, answering, "We are, Your Honor."

"Then present your opening statement, Mr. Cane," came the reply.

As the D.A. rose from his chair, Marnie studied for the first time the faces of those who would decide her fate. The jury consisted of five men and seven women, each looking discreetly blank. What might they be thinking, she wondered. Did they wish, like her, to be anywhere else but in this courtroom? To be John or Jane Doe and far, far removed from the responsibility they must fulfill? Perhaps. But their faces revealed nothing as they fixed their eyes on the energetic figure of Sutter Cane and absorbed his opening remarks.

"Ladies and· gentlemen of the jury," he began, strolling toward the jurors' box, a brief in hand. "You are charged with the grave duty of measuring the invisible line between guilt and innocence in a murder that is perhaps the most lurid crime of this decade. It is a difficult task." He paused for effect, his head bowed. "It is the State's contention that the defendant, Marnie Hastings Hill, did willfully and intentionally take the life of her husband, better known to all as Senator Seth Anderson Hill. It is our obligation to prove to you beyond a reasonable doubt that *she*—'' he pointed an accusing finger at Marnie; the widow remained poised ''—while in the midst of an argument and completely lucid, did cold-bloodedly and for self-serving reasons shoot at point-blank range her spouse of ten years.''

His eyes drifted over the captivated jurors, seeking to make allies of them from the first. ''I intend to make your duty clear by presenting such solid and overwhelmingly conclusive evidence that you will have no other choice but to serve the principles of justice and find the defendant guilty of first-degree murder.

''There is no crime more barbarous than the calculated murder of one who was devoted and unsuspecting. Seth Hill was both. *He* had no inkling of his wife's intent. *He* had no reason to fear her. *He* trusted her and she betrayed him—betrayal delivered via a lethal bullet from a Smith & Wesson,'' he dramatically inserted.

''The State doesn't ask that you surmise or conjecture about the tragic incident that occurred on the night in question. We only ask that you listen to the irrefutable facts in this case and do not be swayed by hypotheses or theatrics. Unfortunately Seth Hill cannot testify or accuse his murderer. He depends on each and every one of you to see that justice is done.''

Ian was impressed with Cane's ability to subtly burden the jurors with accountability. Their expressions were solemn indeed. Sutter Cane was going to be an able adversary. He hit 'em where it mattered—and quite slickly, too.

''Seth Hill spent nearly all his adult life trying to preserve the ideals that made this country, this very exercise in equity we are participating in today, possible.

He was struck down in his prime, a victim of the violence he sought to abolish by his avid support of stricter gun-control legislation. You, ladies and gentlemen of the jury, have the opportunity to make an example of his tragedy...to take a stand against the crimes of passion that are affecting our society at an alarming rate. To allow such blatant disregard for human life to go unpunished is criminal in itself.''

He strolled the length of the jurors' box, his footsteps echoing throughout the still courtroom. "The State depends on your wisdom. We seek the maximum sentence for this defendant, not with the unconscionable malice that Marnie Hastings Hill aimed at her husband, but with impartiality. It is imperative that you not be influenced by the exalted status of the principals in this case. Seth Hill was mortal and died violently. His alleged murderess should so be judged. Be sure and swift in your judgment, ladies and gentlemen of the jury. Any verdict other than a guilty one, any less a sentence than life in prison, would be a license for others to also kill.''

With a solicitous last glance at the jury, Sutter Cane resumed his seat.

"The defense may present their opening remarks," Judge Greer decreed.

Ian sat motionless, his gaze panning the jury and smug D.A. Alarm registered within Marnie. Why was he hesitating, she wondered. Her thoughts were precisely the same as Rory's. He cleared his throat.

"Mr. Dunn?" Impatience sharpened the judge's voice.

Ian snapped to attention. "I'm sorry," he apologized. "I thought the court might need a second to catch its breath from my esteemed colleague's impassioned, though a bit windy, speech.''

A twitter of snickers filtered through the gallery. Judge Greer was not amused.

''I suggest that counselor not concern himself with the court's disposition. Make your opening statement, Mr. Dunn.''

Ian rose to his feet, unbuttoning his jacket, sliding his hands into his pants pockets and approaching the jurors' box. His diversionary tactic worked. He had their undivided attention. He stood relaxed and confident before them, his quiet energy engulfing each man and woman of the jury.

''I agree with my colleague's appraisal. This is undoubtedly one of the most sensational cases of the decade. I also concur with his assessment of the ever-increasing statistics that document family violence in America. But the collective ills of our society are not on trial here today. I remind you, ladies and gentlemen of the jury, that you sit in judgment of *one* woman, a solitary set of circumstances. I suggest to you that it would be an injustice to make my client accountable for each and every Saturday Night Special tragedy in this country.''

Ian singled out faces, addressing his remarks personally. ''I regret, as do my client and every one of you, the victims of such needless slaughter. Yet I put to you that Marnie Hill is not responsible for the moral decay that has swept our land.

''No!'' The jurors flinched involuntarily at his startling expletive. ''The defendant is only accountable for one regrettable instance of chaos—one split second of misunderstanding to which I, Marnie Hill and even you are humanly susceptible.''

He paused, removing his hands from his pockets and bracing them on the jury box. "Reasonable doubt," he said in a contemplative tone. "What does that mean, ladies and gentlemen?" he put forth. "To me, it means that you must be thoroughly convinced that my client did in fact knowingly and with premeditated intent shoot her husband. There can be no question, not the slightest doubt in your mind. You have been given the power to incarcerate her for the rest of her natural days. It is an awesome power that must be tempered with common sense and compassion. That's what makes our judicial system work. If it weren't for your innate sensitivity, a computer could just as well judge Marnie Hill's fate—feed in the law, supply the facts and obtain the clinical result."

His gaze swept the jury. "My colleague asks that you disregard the incontrovertible fact that the Hills are public figures. I contend that you, in all fairness, cannot. You *must* take into account the pressures of their lives—the human factors that contributed to the tragedy. For if you isolate the act and fail to consider the chain reaction that ignited the explosion of a Smith & Wesson, then, *that* is an injustice!"

He withdrew a step, once more slipping his hands into his pockets and spreading wide his brown silk suit coat. "Mr. Cane suggests to you that you have an opportunity to make an example of this highly publicized case, then in the next breath claims to be impartial in his pursuit of a guilty verdict. I only ask that you be open-minded, that you listen with your heart as well as your intellect. For the ultimate decision is yours— reprieve or punishment is in your hands. I need not remind you, as did the district attorney, that the Hills were and are mortal—both subject to the human frail-

ties that plague the species. So are you mortal—
capable of grievous error and immense compassion.
Our judicial system relies on your sensitivity. It is not
infallible and neither are you.''

Slowly he straightened, then let his gaze assimilate
the chosen twelve. ''I believe my client is innocent of
malice. I believe she is as much a victim as her slain
husband. And I ask that you be objective to extend to
her the inalienable right of a fair trial. Do not be influenced by politics or public opinion; merely judge
her no more harshly or leniently than you would the
man or woman seated beside you. Mr. Cane said that
you must measure the invisible line between guilt and
innocence. In closing, I'd like to leave you with a
thought that I hope you will mull over in the days
ahead, not mine but a quote from Leigh Hunt. 'There
are two worlds: the world that we can measure with
line and rule, and the world that we feel with our
hearts and imagination.' In the interest of justice, I
hope that you make every effort to feel and imagine
the extenuating circumstances that ended in the accidental death of Seth Hill. Because, ideally, a blend of
both worlds is necessary in order to arrive at a truly
just decision.''

Marnie was as stunned as everyone else in the courtroom. Ian had been magnificent—his carriage, his
delivery, each expressive word and flawless motion.
Sutter Cane looked deflated. Marnie couldn't help but
be heartened by his sullen expression as he analyzed
Ian's effect on the jury.

''You were wonderful,'' she murmured under her
breath as Ian seated himself.

''That was only the warm-up. It'll be tough going

from here on in," he muttered, impersonating a ventriloquist, his lips barely moving. "What do you think, Rory?" He ignored Marnie's praise, directing his concern to his partner. "I can't get a feel for the jury."

The Irishman leaned over Marnie, unintentionally forcing her to withdraw from the conversation. "You got a slight edge. 'Twas probably the ending quote that impressed 'em. Who the devil is Leigh Hunt?" came the bewildered query.

"An old flame of mine," Ian lied with a mischievous grin. Rory grunted his disbelief, then sat erect in his chair.

Marnie glanced from one to the other, completely addled by their behavior. Their detachment bothered her. Actually, and more precisely, it galled her. They were behaving more like tennis partners participating in a casual game—discussing strategy, then indulging in good-buddy banter. Their attitudes were much too blasé to suit her.

Her tapered nails drummed the table irritatedly. She stared ahead at the judge, refusing to look at either lawyer again.

"I prefer to wait until the afternoon session to begin hearing testimony. Court will reconvene at 1:00 P.M. You will call your first witness at that time, Mr. Cane." Judge Greer pounded the gavel with a flat, "Court's adjourned till then."

"All rise!" the bailiff boomed.

Judge Greer's black robe rustled as he retired to his chambers. Sutter Cane shot Ian a sizing look before breezing through the gate and down the aisle.

"Why don't you go get us a burger, Rory? Marnie

and I will be in one of the vacant anterooms down the hall." Ian stood and stretched his cramped muscles.

"Sure 'n' do I look like some errand boy?" Rory protested.

"I'm not hungry," Marnie stated flatly.

"Sure you are," Ian insisted.

"No, I'm not," she resisted in a haughty tone.

"Is it to be burgers or dueling pistols?" Rory chimed in.

Ian quirked a brow. Suddenly Marnie was acting as hostile as during their first interview. He hadn't the vaguest notion what was wrong with her, but her stubbornness was only fueling his determination. The burgers were now insignificant; it was the principle of the matter.

"Get some fries, too." He snapped shut the latches of his briefcase.

"Three orders?" Rory was purposely pursuing the sensitive issue. He received a negative and affirmative answer at once. Hardly could he smother the smirk tickling his lips. "Well, now, I'm glad we're all agreed," he said cheerfully before beating a hasty retreat.

Skeptical of the press and curiosity seekers who hovered outside the main door, Ian chose not to risk an aisle exit. "Let's use the side door and work our way around." Grasping his briefcase in one hand, he gently clasped her elbow with his other.

"Not in the mood to live dangerously, counselor?" she challenged.

His fingertips tensed a bit more authoritatively, maneuvering her toward the side exit. "What the Sam Hill is the matter with you?" he muttered under his breath. "One moment you're complimentary and the next instant you're sarcastic."

"If you don't mind, I'd prefer to discuss it in private," she snapped, her expression cool as ice as she brushed past him through the door he'd gallantly opened.

"Whatever you prefer, Mrs. Hill," he retorted, becoming more and more agitated by her rebuffing manner. She walked ahead of him, her slim body rigid. He checked out anterooms as they proceeded down the hall until finally locating one that was unlocked and vacant. "I think this should be private enough," he called after her, slinging wide yet another door. This time he forsook all gentlemanly gestures, leaving her stranded in the hall.

He discarded his briefcase on a table and sauntered to the window, loosening his tie and rolling his stiff neck. She marched into the small quarters, throwing her hat atop his briefcase, then perched at another window at an opposite end of the room. Blankly she surveyed the bustling noon activity on the street below.

"Well, are you going to tell me what's bothering you?" Ian finally forced the issue.

"You and Rory make me feel like an outsider. You discuss my case as if it's some sort of private game you two play and I'm not allowed to participate. Damn! It's my life on trial here and you both act as though I'm not involved." She slipped off her jacket and threw it across a chair, then stared sulkily out the window once more.

"What did you expect? For us to have a cordial huddle and slap each other on the back? I consult with Rory because he's a pro and I need his experienced feedback.

You're a novice in courtroom strategy, Marnie. There's maneuvering going on in there that you can't begin to comprehend," he patiently explained.

"I'm shrewder than you think, counselor. I absorb more than you realize, too. You're different in that courtroom. It's almost as if you get a natural high from the uncertainty of it all. You perform in there. Suddenly I don't know what's genuine about you. Do you really believe in my innocence or are you merely seizing an opportunity to be the dynamic attorney who can mesmerize a courtroom with a brilliant performance? Because if you are and if that's what it takes to win an acquittal, I think our legal system stinks!" Her chin quivered. Rarely in the past few years had she been so outspoken.

Ian was momentarily stunned speechless. He'd always thought of Marnie as more sophisticated. For a woman who'd been privy to the behind-the-scenes power struggles of the mighty, she was reacting quite uncharacteristically.

Sensing that she was ready to explode at the slightest provocation, he approached her with caution. The strained silence expanded to every nook and cranny of the room as he rested a shoulder against the window jamb and studied her tense features. "What's really wrong, Marnie?" he asked softly. "I know it's more than disillusionment with the system. You're too bright not to recognize the importance of playing the game."

She did not answer. She was lost in the maze of traffic beyond the window and a flash of picket signs outside the courthouse.

"Don't retreat from me, Marnie," he urged, reaching out and grazing the back of his hand along her sculpted cheek. "Instead, share with me," he earnestly beseeched.

"I'm frightened, Ian," she whispered. "You saw...you heard them this morning. They despise me." She gazed deep into his eyes. "The strangest thoughts went through my mind as we fought our way through that mob—they giveth and they taketh away. I never desired the acclaim. I merely fell in love with a man in the limelight. Why am I being persecuted for that?" she choked. "Why are they obsessed with my life?"

He enfolded her in his arms, rocking her like a babe. "I don't know, angel. They create their idols and then reject them. I haven't all the answers, Marnie," he admitted, tilting her chin and tenderly brushing his lips over hers. "I only know that I'm going to dish the dirt with the best of them if it's the only way I can protect you."

"Hold me, Ian," she implored. "If only for a moment, make this craziness disappear."

He pulled her tight against him, absorbing her disillusionment and fear. She sighed as he buried his head in her fragrant hair. "This Brooklyn punk adores you, Marnie Hill," came the aching declaration in the form of a muffled murmur. "He's not about to let you go."

CHAPTER ELEVEN

As THE DAYS PROGRESSED in the courtroom, love blossomed during private and wondrous weekends in the country. Because of, or in spite of, the difficult circumstances that bound them, Marnie and Ian cleaved to each other out of a basic and mutual need—two displaced souls looking for a haven somewhere with someone who made no demands or judgments. Amid the trial and tribulations, they found peace in each other, found what each had been searching for most of his or her life—unqualified love.

Ian accepted Marnie as she was naturally. He grew to know the woman of simple roots and deep sensitivity, began to penetrate the sophisticated veneer that years of incessant scrutiny had made necessary. Slowly but surely, clue by clue, he discovered the secrets of Marnie. And in the end, he absolutely adored her.

Ian wasn't alone in discovery. For Marnie was ascertaining much about him, too. The contrast between him and Seth was both striking and fascinating. She was in awe of Ian's earthy charisma. His trusting acceptance of her, without censure or expectation, was a gift she cherished. Never had she known a more robust and uncomplex man—one who was so easy to decipher, so easy to love.

It seemed sublime that they should find joy in a time

of stress and haunting sorrow. Yet they did. Perhaps because the moments were so precious; perhaps because it was destined to be.

The trial had been going as well as could be expected. Sutter Cane was doing his best to convict her, eloquently depicting Marnie as an unscrupulous opportunist. Through the testimony of a constant stream of witnesses, he branded her as a morally loose and exceptionally shrewd individual. But Ian was pacing his defense brilliantly, deftly countering every strike on Marnie's character with logical and sometimes witty cross-examination. The score was even so far, the jury uncommitted.

Ian anticipated Judge Aubrey Hill's taking of the stand for the prosecution on Monday morning. Cane was saving the most damaging testimony for last. It was then that Ian planned to play his ace in the hole—to confront the old man with his son's illness and subsequent impotency, then imply that Seth Hill was indeed a troubled and desperate man. Ian was confident that the introduction of the startling facts would instill that all-important shred of "a reasonable doubt" in the juror's minds.

But the confrontation with Aubrey Hill was two days away and he had another, almost as important, surprise up his sleeve. He had accidentally discovered that this August Saturday was also Marnie's birthday. Quite unintentionally he'd overheard a phone conversation between her and her sister, Grace, the preceding night. From snatches of the conversation he had surmised that Grace wanted Marnie to come to spend the day with her and her family. Marnie thanked her for the invitation but declined, saying she wasn't acknowledging the fact that she was thirty and preferred to disregard the auspicious occasion. Grace kept insisting; Marnie kept refusing, but then finally agreed to commemorate the event by sharing a private lunch on some unspecified date in the future when the trial and smutty publicity were over.

It was a typical Marnie response—always trying to spare others by sacrificing herself. Ian knew she longed for Grace's company just as she'd yearned for her support during the trial. Yet she'd forbade Grace to attend the sessions from the first. Her argument had been convincing. She didn't wish the press to use her sister's presence as an angle or pressure her for statements that might be misconstrued in print. Grace had been extremely upset but eventually cooperative. And, as usual, Marnie suffered through the ordeal alone.

Ian had not interfered with her wishes then, but he fully intended to now. Ever since he was a kid, birthdays had been important to him. Probably because Father Pat always made a point to remember and make a "big deal" about it. "Everyone should be special one day of the year," Father Pat had said. Then he would cart the boys who had a birthday that particular month to Coney Island and finance all the rides and junk food they could eat. Later, when they thought themselves too mature for such nonsense, he'd take them to Hoolihan's Pub and treat them to authentic New York cheesecake and "a sip of suds." Those were grand times that Ian never forgot. Father Pat's sentimentality about birthdays had just naturally rubbed off, and Ian could not let Marnie's pass without a very special celebration. He'd arranged everything. It took some doing, but all was in readiness except for persuading Marnie.

Getting up at the crack of dawn, he drove out to the cottage. Luck was with him. Marnie never roused at his tiptoe entrance or hushed preparation of breakfast.

The bedroom was filled with early-morning sunlight and the soft sounds of her slumber as he eased open the door and came to the edge of the brass bed. Soundlessly he set the breakfast tray on a nearby nightstand, then stood for a suspended moment gazing down at his fragile client. Silver wisps of tumbled hair fell across her face. He couldn't resist brushing them aside with a whisper touch. She sighed but did not awaken, rolling onto her back with a languid snuggle. Her face was serene and lovely minus makeup and stress. He couldn't help thinking how angelic she looked. What's more, he had no willpower against the magnetic attraction she inspired in him; asleep or awake, she drew him to her as the moon tows the tide. With a feather-light stroke, his fingertips caressed her sleek shoulder, then trailed along her arm. The satin texture of her skin never ceased to amaze him.

Her lashes fluttered, her eyes blinked open, but then her initial alarm was replaced by a lazy smile. "Do you make a habit of sneaking into ladies' bedrooms, counselor?" she murmured groggily.

"Happy birthday, angel." He grinned and leaned down to glide an airy kiss across her lips.

Her blue eyes opened wider. "Grace told you," she pouted sleepily.

"Not exactly," he hedged, grabbing her hands and pulling her into a sitting position, then stacking the pillows behind her back. "I overheard your conversation last night," he explained, guiding her back against the fluff. "I made the birthday lady breakfast. Nothing too heavy, mind you. I wanted to make sure that you saved room for some authentic New York cheesecake.'' Looking very smug, he placed the tray over her lap, then lifted the lid on a dish of fresh sliced cantaloupe and a flaky croissant.

"This was sweet of you, Ian, but you shouldn't have gone to so much trouble," came the expected reply.

He poured two cups of coffee, handing one to her, then seating himself on the edge of the bed and sampling his efforts. "Cantaloupe and croissants are not trouble," he said lightly. "The cheesecake was another matter."

She nibbled the cantaloupe, glancing at her tray, then eyeing him suspiciously. "I didn't know you were so domestic—all this and cheesecake, too."

"I'm afraid I can't take credit for the cheesecake. We're going to New York for that course."

"We're what?" she gasped, tilting the tray precariously as she lurched to attention.

The amber in his eyes glinted mischievously as he straightened the tippy tray, then edged from the bed and sauntered toward the adjoining bath. "We're flying to New York, the borough of Brooklyn to be exact, where you will partake of the most delicious cheesecake in this hemisphere," he replied in an even tone before disappearing from sight.

"We can't just leave town on the spur of the moment," she spluttered, freeing herself from under the imprisoning breakfast tray and cloying covers, then scampering from the bed. A blast of shower water was the only response. "It's a sweet thought but out of the question, Ian," she said, pattering to the doorway and peeking warily around the corner.

"Why's that?" he asked politely, stacking fresh towels and a washcloth outside the shower stall.

"Well, for one thing," she began, her skeptical gaze following his every movement as he removed a fresh bar of soap from its wrapper, opened the shower-stall door and placed the soap inside, then checked the water temperature. "I'm under bond for murder, in case you've forgotten. I'd be a fugitive from justice," she argued. Her sleepy mind was having great difficulty keeping up with him. "Will you stop flitting around and talk to me!" she insisted, placing her hands on the hips of her two-piece shorty pajama ensemble and striking a stubborn stance.

"You've been watching too many late-night movies, angel. You can only be a fugitive if you fail to return. I doubt that police will resort to a dragnet in the next twenty-four hours. I think the water's just about right." Clamping his firm hands upon her upper arms and mesmerizing her with an enticing smile, he managed to move her to a spot outside the shower stall. "Don't dillydally. We've got a plane to catch shortly." Playfully he popped a kiss on her nose before withdrawing to a discreet distance inside the bedroom.

"This is crazy, Ian. I can't just forget everything and fly to Brooklyn for cheesecake. Be sensible." The weak protest trailed after his retreating figure.

"You have precisely five seconds to get into that shower voluntarily, Marnie Hill," he declared. "Or else I shall come and bodily assist you," came the convincing threat. "Which is it to be?"

He smiled to himself at the slam of the bathroom door. Lately she was beginning to display more and more spunk. Though her feisty spells were exclusively directed at him, he still found it encouraging that she was starting to assert herself rather than coolly accept and adjust. For too long Marnie had allowed life to dictate to her. The same as Thomas Jefferson, Ian believed that a little rebellion was good for the soul. He figured she'd probably be a bit testy for the next hour or so, but then he'd charm her into a good mood for the remainder of the trip. Marnie was incredibly versatile and so easy to forgive. With a last sip of his coffee, he cleared the tray and his presence from the bedroom. He'd call a final time to be certain his pilot friend was standing by with the private Lear jet fueled and ready for takeoff. Every minute counted when there was so little time to spare.

Ian's meticulous planning proceeded without a hitch. He and Marnie would arrive in New York on time and, after being wooed with spicy Clamato juice and iced oysters on the half shell, Marnie was in a magnanimously festive mood.

"This is a frivolous waste of time and fuel, but I have to admit that I'm flattered." She fed him an oyster from a tiny three-pronged fork. "I feel deliciously wicked and carefree."

"A thirtieth birthday can be traumatic," he teased. "I wanted to reassure you that this is prime time."

"Actually, counselor, I strongly suspect that this is an elaborate seduction, but I'm also impressed by the lavish attention. You're a difficult man to refuse. Is it just me or do all women find you irresistible?"

"I haven't pursued any other women quite so earnestly," he confessed. "I just wanted your birthday to be special, Marnie," came the sincere and emotional reply.

"It is," she murmured demurely, reaching out and tracing the sharp angle of his cheekbone with a fingertip. "You are a remarkable man, Ian Dunn."

He caught her hand, blazing her palm with kisses. "The birthday celebration has only just begun. My friend Mike won't be taking off for Lexington until midnight, and I intend to spend the remaining hours indulging you."

"You're spoiling me, Ian," she warned.

"You were meant to be cherished," he replied, relinquishing her hand as the pilot poked his head through the cockpit door.

"Thanks for the lift, Mike," Ian said, grinning. "You haven't lost your touch for an easy landing."

"Glad to be of service, buddy. Remember the coach turns into a pumpkin at the witching hour," came the friendly rejoinder.

Marnie smiled her thanks as she disembarked from the elegant jet. "Where do you know him from?" she whispered as they briskly descended the steps to the field.

"We flew together in Nam."

"I didn't know you were in Vietnam. Seth was, too, you know."

"It seems we've more than one thing in common," he said wryly, whisking her through the terminal doors and toward the exit marked Limo and Taxi Pickup.

A shiny black limousine was parked a short distance away. The driver snapped to attention at their approach.

"Mr. Dunn?" he asked smartly.

"Yes," Ian confirmed. "You must be Robert."

"Yes, sir. At your service." The chauffeur opened the door with a practiced flair.

Marnie waited until they were seated inside the luxurious interior and under way before commenting. "This is costing you a fortune, Ian. I wish—"

"I wish you'd direct your attention outside the window, madam, and enjoy the sights. Robert has my itinerary and we've a lot of ground to cover before dinner." He cast her a persuasive smile.

"All right, Mr. Dunn—" she laughed gaily "—show me your town."

And for the next few hours, they cruised the boulevards of the Big Apple, Ian acting as Marnie's personal tour guide and taking her on a whirlwind excursion through the multifaceted city. From Wall Street to the Broadway theater district, Greenwich Village to Times Square, East side, West side, all around the town, Ian and Marnie traveled in style. Ian's witty anecdotes and native knowledge about the local color thoroughly fascinated her. And every so often, Robert would make a pit stop at a quaint or famous eatery and they'd sample whatever happened to be the specialty as they rode. It was an afternoon to remember forever.

Ian's home ground in the heart of Brooklyn was where they finally wound down the tour. At his instructions, Robert made a detour and cruised along the familiar street where St. Timothy's stood. There wasn't much to distinguish the brownstone except a weathered cornerstone and a collection of disgruntled youths moping on the wide porch steps.

Sensing Ian's nostalgic mood, Marnie suggested that they stretch their legs and stroll along the block.

Robert voiced a reservation. "This is a pretty rough neighborhood, folks. Are you sure?"

Ian smiled to himself at his concern. "We'll be all

right, Robert. I think I can still hold my own on these streets. Pick us up on the next block.''

"Yes, sir," the obedient chauffeur replied as he parked the limo and jumped out to open the door.

The commotion drew the attention of the bored teenage boys huddled on the steps. And as Ian and Marnie began a slow stroll in their direction, the teenagers roused from their moody slouches and donned smirking expressions.

"They must be slumming," one kid hooted as they drew alongside.

"Hey, my man?" another jeered. "You checking out the wild side of town?"

Marnie felt Ian's arm slip protectively around her waist.

Several wolf whistles broke from the youth's lips. "Hey, foxy lady!" a kid wearing a dingy muscle shirt called out. "You a social worker or something? You wanna come rehabilitate me?" The kid was incredibly obnoxious.

Ian halted and Marnie tensed.

"Don't bother, Ian," she urged in a whisper. "Please, let's keep walking."

He paid no heed, instead turning to the group of brazen boys and challenging them. "Listen, punk. You got a foul mouth and I don't like it."

The blue-jean set grew instantly hostile. "Are you catching this dude?" the loudmouth in the muscle shirt asked his comrades. "He don't like our manners, guys. Suppose you teach me some, high roller," he foolishly taunted. The others contented themselves with nasty chuckles.

A muscle twitched in Ian's cheek as he narrowed the

gap between him and the bold punk. "I ought to," he growled. "When I sat on these steps, I minded my own business and I expect the same courtesy from you."

"Were you waiting for a bus to take you outta the slums and back uptown?" the cocky teenager gibed.

"Hardly, punk. I was like you—this street was my territory," Ian snarled between gritted teeth. "And I didn't hassle anyone who strolled through unless they gave me a reason. Have we given you a reason, boy?" came the low and ominous grumble.

The tough kids exchanged glances, reconsidering their earlier threats.

"No, I guess not," the youth who'd been the most vocal relented. "Hey, answer me a question, will ya, mister?"

Ian gave a curt nod.

"How'd you get out of this crummy place? How'd you make it all the way to limos and classy chicks?"

"I applied myself, kid. I hit the books as hard as I intended on hitting you." He answered in terms they could understand. "There aren't any free rides in this world. You think you're pretty tough, I'll bet."

"Nobody messes with Howie Jackson," the kid replied with a proud toss of his head.

"Well, Mr. Jackson, I'll give you a little advice. Tough isn't just how many heads you can break, and smart isn't getting away with ripping off hubcaps. Tough is getting your act together and channeling that aggression constructively. Smart is getting an education and the hell out of here. You can do it if you're as gutsy as you say."

Marnie was as entranced as the youths. It seemed that

though he spoke a different language, Ian was as charismatic and persuasive as in a courtroom.

"I might just do that, mister." Howie cast him a respectful grin. "Would you like to come up and take a look around for old times' sake?"

"Not this time, son," Ian declined, turning to Marnie and starting to walk away.

"Wouldn't you like to go in and see Father Pat?" she asked in a stunned voice.

"He died five years ago, Marnie. It's a shame those boys won't have the advantage of his guidance." He glanced back as they walked along.

"I think they were lucky to have the run-in with you. Your example ought to inspire them." She slipped an affectionate arm around his waist, saying, "You know, Ian, until just now I really didn't fully appreciate the struggle you waged to fight your way out of the ghetto. You're a strong breed, counselor."

His arm around her shoulders tightened. "Hungry?" he asked, kissing her temple.

"Famished," she sighed, resting her head on his shoulder.

He flagged Robert, who promptly backed the limo down the street.

"Next stop, Houlihan's Pub." He waved Robert off and opened the rear door himself.

"Now are we having the cheesecake?" She laughed, sliding in and snuggling near as they headed toward what she thought would be their final destination.

"Patience, angel. You'll have dessert. I promise." He tweaked her dainty nose good-naturedly.

Marnie leaned back against his muscular shoulder, absorbing the assured quality of this amazingly gentle yet incredibly strong man. Not once this entire day had she thought about the uncertain future. He had the ability to make her forget everything but him and the joy he brought into her life. In his presence, she was the wanted child she'd never been, the complete woman she longed to be. Through his eyes, the world was fresh and new, full of hope and promise. In his arms was shelter from the cold and escape from the bitterness that stalked her. It was all wrong, she knew. She shouldn't have fallen in love with him—not so soon after Seth's death. Society would condemn her once more. There were the constant rules and standards to which one was supposed to adhere. And yet . . . there were the constant hungers that had to be contended with alone—dark caverns in one's life that must be stumbled through blindly. He was the light in her dark—a life-giving spark she couldn't deny.

Abruptly and inexplicably Marnie turned to him, weaving her arms about his neck and bestowing upon him a deep, unexpected and passionate kiss. "I do love you, Ian," she murmured against his lips before releasing her desperate clutch of his neck. "I've probably cursed you by admitting it, but I had to tell you, if only just once," she whispered against his cheek.

"Oh, Marnie," he groaned, embracing her fast against his hammering heart. "You could never tell me enough. I swear I don't think I will ever get my fill of you." His broad hand cradled the back of her head, drawing her to his love-thirsty mouth again. This moment was a dream come true for him, the alpha and omega of one man's lonely quest for love. So long he had yearned, so long he had searched, secretly hoping yet cynically discounting the possibility of finding a woman who'd fulfill him. The ideal of Marnie seemed so remote. And yet here she was—in his arms and feeling so heavenly. An illusion didn't writhe and purr or smell of perfume, he reasoned. Marnie was as real and committed as he'd never dared to dream she could be.

The limo had been parked outside the pub for a minute or two before Robert had the heart to inform them. He kept his eyes averted when giving a discreet tap upon the tinted window.

Reluctantly Ian and Marnie broke apart, he exiting first, then assisting her.

"We shouldn't be any longer than an hour, Robert. You do remember the itinerary?" He winked as he placed a fifty-dollar bill in the chauffeur's hand.

"Yes, sir," came the perky reply. "I'll take care of everything."

Marnie looked to Ian for an explanation, but he merely took her arm and escorted her into the boisterous pub.

The interior was filled with the din of jovial patrons, clattering dishes and the happy sound of Gaelic music. Ian went first, shouldering a path through the crowd to a hostess dressed in shamrock green up front.

"I have a reservation for two at nine," he hollered over the noise. "Dunn . . . Ian Dunn," he shouted.

"Ahh, yes, Mr. Dunn. Mrs. Houlihan said to expect you. Follow me, please."

Marnie held tight to Ian's hand as they weaved through the throng of merry makers. "Is it always this busy?"

He nodded and smiled, continuing to follow the hostess to a booth in the rear.

"Saturday nights are a bit rowdy," she apologized in

a thick brogue. "Mrs. Houlihan says for you not to be rushing off before she has a chance to chat."

"Tell her my eyes ache for the sight of her." Ian poured on the blarney.

"She's prepared her specialty for you. Irish whiskey is on the way and the waitress will be serving you promptly."

Marnie sat agape. Ian certainly had an "in" at Houlihan's. "Should I be jealous?" she teased, once the hostess had departed.

"You could humor me and pretend to be," he replied with a grin.

"How is it that you still receive preferential treatment after so long an absence?" she quizzed, smiling cordially at the barmaid who dropped off two Irish whiskeys for their pleasure.

"The Houlihans are old friends of Father Pat's. He used to bring us here on our birthdays," he explained, sipping his drink, then exhaling an appreciative "Ahh."

"Don't tell me. Let me guess. For cheesecake," she said with a mirthful expression.

"The best in this hemisphere," he elaborated.

She raised her glass. "Well, I feel very honored to be extended the privilege of sampling this gourmet delight." She took a sip of the whiskey, wheezing with its stoutness. "Good Lord, Ian. This is positively lethal!" she exclaimed, setting aside her glass.

"It takes a bit of practice," he admitted.

"Well, as I live and breathe!" came a gravelly shout a second before a plump, elderly woman stormed up to them. "If it isn't the glib-tongued attorney hisself!" Ian was instantly smothered in smacking kisses. "And aren't you ashamed of yourself? Neglecting your old friends so long!" The owner straightened herself with a prissy pat of her gray-streaked hair.

"I am indeed, Maureen," he said with mock contriteness.

"And could it be because you've found new and younger acquaintances to occupy your time?" Her dancing emerald eyes zeroed in on Marnie. "And a lovely thing she is."

"I'd like you to meet Marnie Hill."

Maureen Houlihan stuck out a welcoming hand. "It's pleased I am to be meeting you."

Marnie vibrated all over from the exuberant greeting. "It's nice to meet you, too," she managed.

"Ian is a rascal, you know? But I'd be telling you a lie if I said he wasn't a grand man," the owner of the establishment prattled on. "Father Pat had faith in him," she said, beaming.

"So do I," Marnie heard herself say. She glanced at Ian, feeling foolish at the admission. But he took her hand and smiled so warmly that she nearly forgot Maureen entirely.

"Well, I'll not be intruding upon your dinner party any longer." Maureen smiled her approval. "I hope you enjoy your meal. And come again soon," she said, addressing Marnie.

"I hope to," was all she answered.

" 'N' they'll be no forgiveness for you, Ian Dunn, should you stay away as long again." Another smacking kiss, a loving pat of his shoulder and Maureen bustled away.

"She's a character," Ian said, looking affectionately after her.

"She's adorable." Marnie gave his hand an understanding squeeze.

He took another drink of the Irish whiskey. "She and her husband and Father Pat were the closest thing to family I had."

"I know," came the sympathetic response.

"She likes to make a fuss." Uncharacteristically he was making excuses.

"I'm glad to meet her. I'm glad we came here. I'm glad to be sharing my birthday with you." She repeated herself, trying to reassure him.

"I could have taken you someplace more elegant."

"I prefer to be here."

"I could have gotten you something more appropriate than this," he mumbled, reaching into his shirt pocket and dropping a sterling chain and medal into her hand.

"Oh, Ian, it's lovely. It's Catholic, isn't it?" She draped it over her fingers and inspected the delicate craftsmanship.

"Yes. It's St. Jude—the patron saint of the hopeless. Father Pat blessed it and gave it to me years ago."

"I can't take this, Ian," she murmured. "It's...."

"It's yours," he insisted, his hand folding over hers and locking the chain in her palm. "That medal saw me through some hard times. Wear it for me."

"I don't know what to say." She raised her misty eyes to his.

"Say you love me again," was all he asked.

"I do, Ian, but you must understand that I'm also bound by obligations from the past."

He misinterpreted what she was trying to say. He thought she referred to her daughter. "I know that, Marnie," he responded.

"Do you really, Ian?"

"Yes, of course. Put the medal on, Marnie."

She did as he'd requested. Tonight she couldn't refuse him.

His eyes never left her as the waitress served the feast of spicy corned beef, carrots and fresh-baked brown bread.

"Save room for the cheesecake." His reminder brought a smile to her lips.

"I'll have to diet for a week after today," she complained while sampling the entrée. "This is fantastic, Ian," came her first of many praises.

It pleased him that she was deriving pleasure from the meal. This was the first time in weeks he'd seen her eat with any visible enthusiasm. And he could hardly contain himself when thirty minutes later and after becoming an honorary member of "the clean plate society," she was inquiring about the cheesecake.

"I'm afraid we haven't time," he apologized with believable sincerity.

"Oh," was all she responded, trying to hide her disappointment.

They left Houlihans dessertless, Marnie bravely masking the silly pang his broken promise had spawned. She'd taken his word that time was running short and they needed to hurry back to the airport. Just as she failed to realize where Robert was headed until the stately magnificence of the Brooklyn Bridge loomed into view.

"Want to go for another stroll?" Ian asked.

She cocked her head dubiously. "I thought we were running short on time."

"Come on, a quick one," he insisted. "You haven't

lived until seeing the lights of Manhattan from the Brooklyn Bridge.''

Robert parked the limo without being told. Ian stepped out and then opened the front door to retrieve a box and satchel from the front seat. By this time, Marnie was absolutely tingling with curiosity.

"What's in the box?" she quizzed.

"Be patient, angel," he said, grinning. "I'll show you on the bridge."

They walked hand and hand, he behaving strangely subdued, she fairly bursting with anticipation.

"It's the cheesecake, isn't it, Ian?" she bubbled.

"Don't be silly, Marnie," he admonished. "What kind of fool would want to eat cheesecake on the Brooklyn Bridge?"

Now she was certain of it. She pranced ahead, walking backward and badgering him with exuberance.

"You, that's who!" she chanted smugly. "I love it!" She twirled around, free as she'd never been in her life.

"Stay to the side, Marnie," he instructed in a worried tone. "There's traffic on the bridge."

She ran and threw her arms around his neck, kissing his forehead, his nose, his lips, his chin. "It is special, Ian—" she giggled "—I don't think I've ever felt so special in all my life."

"You've danced with kings and been wined and dined all over the world, Marnie. How can this compare?" he said with genuine humility.

"Because that was all so superficial, Ian. But this—" she hugged an iron span, leaning out over the bay and drinking in the sultry August night "—this is natural and sweeter than that honey-glazed moon."

Midway between Brooklyn and Manhattan on a rustic bridge, Ian served Marnie cheesecake from a box and champagne from a satchel. Halfway between New York and heaven, he embraced an angel and smelled wild roses on a summer's breeze. "Make a wish," he had told her after lighting a single candle upon the cake. She closed her eyes and prayed her silent request would come true. And in the hours between midnight Saturday and Monday's dawn, her wish was semigranted many times. They shared exquisite and precious moments making wild, passionate love. But her wish was only partially realized because trust is a perishable thing, and without it love doesn't last *forever*.

CHAPTER TWELVE

HANDS CLASPED, MARNIE AND IAN explored a woodsy trail behind the cottage, then strolled along a rippling brook's shale bank. Every now and then, they'd observe a lazy tortoise basking in the rays of the late-afternoon sun or rainbow trout shimmying through the pristine water.

Ian stopped to skip a pebble across the water's surface. Marnie perched on a nearby flat rock, enjoying his boyish play. She slipped off her Italian sandals and rolled her gauzy slacks to her knees, then dipped her toes into the cool brook.

"I wish you didn't have to go back tonight." The secret regret passed her lips before she could stop herself.

"Tomorrow's going to be pretty grueling, Marnie. Cane's going to put your father-in-law on the stand, and I've got to be prepared."

"I know," she murmured, watching her feet as he studied her. "A.L. will finally get the chance to publicly slander me. He's yearned to do that for years."

Ian was listening but also admiring how the sunlight threaded like gold through her hair. Gathered at her nape and tied with a black satin ribbon, then falling in loose curls down her back, her casual hairdo made her look especially soft and amazingly young. "Why is he so hostile toward you?" he asked.

She shrugged and for a moment he thought she might not answer. "I really don't know for certain. He just never approved of me. As far as he was concerned, Seth would've been better off taking poison than marrying me. I was, and will always be, trash in his opinion. Hardly what he considered First Lady material."

"But over the years you proved him wrong. From what I understand you adapted quite well to the social graces and pressures of Washington." He skipped another pebble across the brook, creating tiny ripples upon the water.

"I thought so, too. But A.L. never concurred. He capitalized on every opportunity to remind me of just who and what I actually was—a nobody, born of welfare-subsidized parents, a refugee from the wrong side of the tracks who merely pretended to be a lady. He's a malignant, intolerant old man. Seth defied him once and I was the cause. He needed no more reason than that solitary instance of mutiny to hate me."

"My God, Marnie. Didn't your husband stand up for you? What sort of man would let the woman he supposedly loved suffer such mental abuse?"

His expressing of the truth stung. Involuntarily Marnie flinched. "Like you and I and everyone else, Seth was a product of his formative youth. Those who come from deprived and difficult backgrounds are motivated to change their circumstances, to make something better of their lives. Seth lacked no advantage except one—love. It was harder for him to recognize the sole imperfection in an otherwise perfect existence."

She gazed off, lost in reverie. Ian patiently waited. He knew she had more to say.

"I came to understand that Seth always believed the

fault was his, that in some obscure and inexcusable way he was responsible for the emotional rejection his parents inflicted on him. That's why he was constantly pursuing recognition—in school, in war, in the public's eye. He craved the attention and approval that his father doled out like tidbit rewards to a love-starved puppy.''

She swirled the water with her polished toes. "A.L. is a shrewd manipulator. Oh, yes, he's a master at pulling strings and making others perform like puppets for him. He realized Seth's almost desperate need for his approval. And, oh, how he used it, convincing Seth that he would at last be worthy if he'd attain the glory that A.L. had been denied. He dangled his unfulfilled dream in front of his son's eyes like a hypnotist inducing a trance.''

Ian was fascinated. He was learning much about the legend he must face tomorrow. He came to join her on the rock, dropping a few pebbles into her hand. She cast him a faint smile, then aimlessly tossed a pebble into the brook.

"It must have been a terrible strain for you, knowing your father-in-law's fanaticism and contending with his hostility at the same time," he said with genuine respect.

"To know Aubrey Hill is to be wary," she said with a shrug. "He never relents. I used to dread the time Seth and I spent at Rosehill, especially toward the end. For then we were on A.L.'s turf and his influence over Seth was even stronger. He'd be patronizingly cordial to me in Seth's presence and then deliberately antagonistic in his absence. I was ensnared in his trap—if I retaliated it gave him an excuse to criticize me even more; if I retreated any ground he usurped more and more of my husband. He was sly, never really out-and-out attacking me so that Seth would be forced to choose sides, but bit by bit undermining me so that my hold on Seth would weaken.''

She slung another pebble out onto the water, her features taut, her frustration evident. ''Yet away from Rosehill and A.L.'s obsessions, Seth was an inspiring and confident man. We had genuinely good, good moments together. Funny,'' she sighed. ''I don't think Seth ever realized his own potential because of his father's gigantic shadow. He had amazing insight into the social problems confronting our society and the energy, not to mention the ability, to make some positive changes. He was a born statesman with great popular appeal. But he felt that he was not respected as a capable politician in his own right—a man of vision and sensitivity. References to his politically powerful father were made so often that he grew discouraged and eventually accepted everyone else's perception of himself.''

''I can almost have empathy for him in that situation,'' Ian interjected. ''It sounds like he was cast in a mold made of granite.''

She nodded. ''It was a bitter concession for him to admit that no matter how hard he tried, he could not dissociate himself from his father without forfeiting his own aspirations. Because you see, Ian, he did want to be president. Believe it or not, I think he desired it even more fervently than the old man. I, like no one else, knew the times when he was bone weary from the pressure, so terribly depressed over his illness, but he wouldn't withdraw from the race for the White House.''

Ian stroked her back as she talked. "He was so tormented the last few years. I ached for him. Sunny and I were all that gave him any solace. During the last couple of years, A.L. became, if anything, even more aggressive in his quest for vicarious glory."

"Was he aware of his son's illness?" Ian asked, a sudden surge of suspicion gripping him.

"No. That was Seth's and my secret. I'm certain he would've told me if he had discussed it with his father. I wondered once, though," she murmured in a sad voice. "After Seth was first diagnosed we considered an experimental surgery for impotency that was being conducted at the Medical Center in Houston. Seth had been semiagreeable originally. But then after a visit to Rosehill one weekend he became avidly opposed to the idea. I worried that he may have sought A.L.'s advice and that it was *his* objections that Seth was voicing. But he assured me he had not confided in his father and fiercely resented my lack of faith. Seth wouldn't have lied about such a thing, wouldn't have rejected the surgery just to appease his father. And even as obsessed as A.L. was with Seth's becoming president, he wouldn't have interfered or insisted that his son not risk the publicity if there was the slightest chance that his manhood might be artificially restored. No, I'm sure it was Seth's decision. I didn't agree with it, but I respected his wishes."

She fingered the St. Jude medal that lay nestled at the divide of her breasts. "Secrets," she murmured. "Why must there always be secrets?"

He pulled her fast against him, answering her ache with a question of his own. "Do you still keep secrets, Marnie?"

She refused to answer, instead capturing his lips and kissing him with wild abandon.

He clutched her closer, responding with equal ardor. In the back of his mind he suspected that her silence was an answer in itself, but his passion was a greater hunger than his need to know. His hand slipped inside the loose-fitting gauzy blouse she wore, his palm roaming her flesh as a nomad seeks an oasis.

"Can I ever resist you?" came the husky groan against her powdered skin as he buried his head in the enticing softness of her bosom.

Her fingertips webbed through his tawny hair. "Maybe you should, counselor," she murmured breathlessly as he singed her flesh with impassioned kisses.

Feverishly he unbuttoned and stripped off her blouse, then clasped her hands and pulled her with him onto their feet. His hard arms wrapped around her in a fierce embrace. "Undress," he commanded.

"Not out here, Ian. I...." Modesty jolted her to her senses.

"Oh yes, angel," he insisted, unsnapping and unzipping her pants, then letting them fall over her hips and slink to her feet. "We're going to make love in the daylight, in the sunshine...." He jerked off his shirt and jeans before she could recover from his Bohemian advances. "No inhibitions, no secrets are going to stand in our way."

He untied the ribbon from her hair, combing the silver strands with his fingers, then drawing her to him and making her tremble with sweet surrender as he confiscated her will with a deep and long and irresistibly tender kiss.

"Like you, I'm innocent, Marnie," he professed in a breathless voice, removing and discarding her frilly undergarments. Slowly, sensually, his hands stroked her slender sun-bathed body. "I didn't break your heart—" he murmured, shedding his briefs, casting them aside, then lifting her protectively into his strong arms "—but, by God, I'm going to do my best to mend it," he vowed, stepping out into the cool, cool water and submerging them both in recklessness.

Baptized with water and drenched in love, she gasped as they immersed, her arms draping about his neck as he turned loose her legs and clamped her tightly against his swollen manhood.

"Marnie. . ." he choked. "You feel so damned right. How can this be wrong?"

She pressed her fingertips to his lips, stilling his doubt and accelerating his heart. Then, gliding her glistening lips over his, whetting his desire with her tongue, she became the metaphoric pebble with the force to riffle him with passion.

He took her in the water, in the late-afternoon sunlight, in a fever. It was perhaps the most torrid experience of his life. Marnie revealed one of her secrets to him—that she could be hotter than a fiery August sunset, once freed of her inhibitions. He doubted another Sunday or burnished sundown would pass again that he wouldn't be reminded of the sweet-savage splendor they'd shared.

CHAPTER THIRTEEN

TENSION RAN HIGH in the courtroom as Judge Greer instructed the district attorney to summon his next witness.

"The State calls Judge Aubrey Hill to the stand," Sutter Cane announced.

Even above the speculative murmurs rising from the gallery, Marnie could distinguish the tap of the old man's walking stick. Her delicate features set like granite, and she stiffened in the chair.

Ian leaned toward her, whispering, "Try to relax. Your body language is practically screaming 'uptight.'"

She drew a composing breath, willing the visible signs of tension to subside. Ian shot her an encouraging wink, then nonchalantly settled back in his chair.

"Do you swear to tell the truth, the whole truth and nothing but the truth, so help you God?" the bailiff chanted.

"I do," the old man swore.

"Be seated," came the bland instruction.

As A.L. took the witness chair, Marnie and he locked gazes. The animosity between them was almost tangible. Nearly everyone in the room felt it.

Sutter Cane stepped forward, capturing Aubrey Hill's attention with a subtle clearing of his throat.

' Will you state for the record your full name and relationship to the deceased?''

"Aubrey Luther Hill. I was the victim's father.''

For the benefit of the jury and his own ambition, Sutter Cane cast him a compassionate look. "The court realizes this is very difficult for you, Judge Hill. I will try to be brief.''

"I want to see justice done, Mr. Cane. Ask all the questions you like,'' the old man offered, slanting a recriminating glance in Marnie's direction.

The jury did not miss the expressive look or for whom it was intended. Sutter Cane allowed a dramatic pause before resuming his examination.

"Much has been said about your son's character during the trial, Judge Hill. And yet probably no other witness, except perhaps the defendant, knew him better than you.''

"*She* never bothered to know him,'' came the venomous rejoinder.

"Objection, Your Honor,'' Ian interjected. "Please ask the witness to answer only questions asked of him. He is casting aspersions, not rendering fact.''

"Sustained,'' Judge Greer concurred. "Please confine your remarks to only that which is prudent and pertinent, Mr. Hill.''

Visibly offended, Aubrey Hill consented with a stiff nod of his gray head.

"Continue, prosecutor,'' the presiding judge commanded.

"My point is, Judge Hill, that you spent a great deal of time in your son's company through the years and are more than qualified to speak about him. I would like you to enlighten the court about his character and disposition.''

"Seth was a good boy and fine man. He was a prin-
cipled person, as devoted to his country as he was to
his family," A.L. answered proudly. "He graduated
at the top of his class from law school, was decorated
twice for valor in Vietnam and served as a United
States senator for almost twelve productive years."

"How would you describe his disposition? By that I
mean would you say that he was an even-tempered individual or prone to be volatile?"

"He was definitely not inclined to be brash. Seth
had immense patience and amazing self-control. Seldom did he succumb to pressure. At least that was true
of him until recently. But any man who'd endured the
abuse he suffered would've reacted the same." The old
man's knuckles grew white as he gripped his walking
stick tighter.

"By 'abuse' you are referring to his deteriorating
marriage, I assume?" Cane followed up.

"I am," A.L. responded emphatically.

"Your son and his wife resided at your home when
they were away from Washington, did they not?"

"That's correct. Off and on throughout the years
they shared my quarters at Rosehill. The family estate
was to be Seth's upon my passing."

"So you were quite often in their joint company and
in a position to observe the friction that, according to
previous testimony, was escalating between them?"

"I was, by the simple fact of living in the same
house, in their company a considerable amount of
time. And I most certainly witnessed numerous instances of discord."

"Did your son also confide in you? Perhaps tell you
of other disagreements between him and his wife when
you were not in attendance?"

"He did. He was greatly distressed over Marnie's risqué behavior and the detrimental effect it had not only on his life, but on their daughter's, as well." The old judge's parched lips curled in disgust.

"I object again, Your Honor." Ian rose to his feet, shaking his head. "The term 'risqué' is conjecture on the part of the witness and unfair to my client. I must insist that he restrict his prejudiced remarks and divulge only the facts."

"The deceased confided in the witness, Your Honor. I therefore submit that this testimony is relevant and should be allowed," Cane argued.

Judge Greer pondered the request for a moment, then ruled in favor of the prosecution, stating that he agreed it was relevant testimony if it pertained to the deceased's frame of mind and the mood of the marriage at the time of the shooting. He'd allow the questioning as long as it lent itself to this issue.

Ian sat down in time to hear Marnie's barely audible sigh. Now would come the slander she'd dreaded.

"Would you enlighten the court as to the exact conversation?" Sutter Cane asked smugly.

A.L. turned his attention to the jury, addressing his remarks to them personally. He'd been practicing courtroom theatrics long before Sutter Cane and Ian Dunn had even begun to learn their ABCs. Oh yes, he knew how to play to a jury and had every intention of doing so now.

Marnie's heart turned to stone as she also scanned the jurors. Their wooden expressions did indeed make them look like marionettes. And the puppet master was about to pull the strings once more. She could sense it, and the thought of being publicly maligned by that vicious old man made her seethe with indignation. She had no doubt that he would embellish the truth. An oath meant nothing to him if he desired something. And only she knew how much he desired revenge.

"Three months ago my son had an occasion to visit me at Rosehill. He was at his wits' end trying to cope with a bitter marriage." He paused, turning and quirking a brow at Ian. "His words, not mine," he pointed out, then faced the jury box once more and resumed. "Marnie had been enjoying yet another extended holiday in Europe, supposedly staying with mutual friends in England. She traveled a great deal the last few years of their marriage. She seemed to prefer it to spending time with her husband and child."

Marnie was breathing laboriously. Ian and Rory could hear her exasperation. They both secretly worried she might explode at any moment.

"Sunny, my granddaughter, missed her terribly and my son needed her desperately. As you know, he was preparing to run for president. He had tremendous responsibilities and pressures and no one but me with whom to share them. Marnie took very little interest in his plans. Oh, she attended the parties and would consent to appear at an occasional luncheon, but that was about the extent of her support. Seth was embarrassed by her absences and humiliated by the gossip her activities incited—"

Marnie's nails began to drum on the table. Ian scribbled a note on the pad before him, then shoved it under her fingertips. "Easy does it," it read. The nervous motion stilled.

"Did he complain specifically about his wife's jet-

setting habits during that visit to Rosehill?" Sutter
Cane interrupted.

"Yes; he said he couldn't ignore or abide Marnie's
constant flirtations any longer. It was degrading to
him. He told me he knew she'd been unfaithful in the
past but more and more she grew less and less discreet.
In his words, 'she was flaunting her indiscretions.' "

"That's not true!" Marnie denied the accusation,
lurching from her chair. "Seth wouldn't have said
such things," she kept insisting as they maneuvered
her back into her seat.

"Order, order!" Judge Greer banged his gavel, attempting to still the chaos her outburst had caused.
"Mr. Dunn, you must caution your client not to interrupt this court again. I will tolerate no further out-
bursts of this nature."

"It won't happen again, Your Honor," Ian promised before reseating himself and huddling with Marnie and Rory.

"Maybe you should ask for a recess?" Rory suggested, squeezing Marnie's hand.

"I know this is hard for you, Marnie, but it won't
get any easier thirty minutes from now." Though Ian
commiserated with her ordeal, he wanted to proceed.
The sooner he got a crack at Aubrey Hill the better.

"I'm sorry I lost control," she apologized in a
shaken voice. "I'm sure he's twisting Seth's words."

"He may be. That's why you must listen carefully to
everything he says. He might make a mistake that we
can prove, and then I'll nail him for perjury." More
than anything else, Ian was hoping to ease Marnie's
mind. He knew the old man was much too smart to
leave himself open to a perjury charge.

She nodded, Ian and Rory exchanged worried glances and awaited Judge Greer's resumption of the trial.

"The witness will continue," he said in a bland voice.

Aubrey Hill looked contemptuously at Marnie, then addressed himself to the jury once more. "My son believed she was conducting herself improperly, and it was most embarrassing to him. He had learned of her latest escapade in England, that she was not staying with mutual friends as she'd told him, but rather was keeping company with a reputed international playboy at his country place in Essex. In Seth's very own words, she was shaming him with yet another affair. He said he couldn't tolerate much more, that the only reason he'd put up with her habitual carousing for as long as he had was because of the devastating effect a divorce would have on Sunny and his political future."

Marnie's nails dug into the flesh of her palms. Seth had known very well why she'd visited the "playboy" mentioned. In fact, he'd insisted that she do so. The man in question was a textile magnate with strong labor affiliations in America. Seth wanted labor's vote and her side trip to Essex was meant as a gesture to encourage the man's support.

"Had you any reason to believe he might be imagining his wife's infidelity?" The prosecutor pressed on.

"Quite the opposite. I had every reason to believe it was true. I myself had seen her entice men's attentions and behave outrageously on certain occasions. In the past few years, her name was linked with dozens of celebrated Romeos in issue after issue of those smutty scandal sheets. She made a mockery of their marriage."

"Now, Judge Hill, I want you to be as objective as

possible when answering my next question." Cane withdrew a step, preparing for a climactic ending to his questions. "Would you say that your son was irrationally disturbed by his failing marriage? Is it possible, in your estimation, that he might've been pushed beyond the brink of acceptable anger and somehow instigated the violence that ended in his death? Or may he have been despondent enough to—"

"Absolutely not," Judge Hill answered firmly and a bit indignantly. "My son was disturbed, yes. Irrational, no. And I remind you that this conversation we had took place several months prior to the night in question. Seth did not act hastily or rashly. He wasn't the type."

"One more question, Judge Hill." Cane pretended it came to him in a flash. "After such close association with the defendant, do you believe she would react hostilely to a threat of divorce?"

Marnie raised her head, staring into the eyes of her accuser.

The old judge leered at her before answering. "Threatened by divorce, she most definitely would be desperate. The Hill money and respectability were what enticed her to marry my son, and she would be capable of most anything at the possibility of losing either. I'm convinced she is a ruthless woman."

Ian sprang to his feet with an emphatic, "I object, Your Honor. The witness is again inserting opinion, not rendering fact."

"Sustained. The jury will disregard the witness's last statement, and it will be stricken from the record," Judge Greer instructed. "Continue, Mr. Cane."

"I have no further questions of this witness, Your Honor." Sutter Cane spoke with cocky assurance, believing he had cinched a conviction. He knew very well that Aubrey Hill's remarks could not be stricken from the jurors' minds.

"I prefer to postpone cross-examination until after the noon recess. Court will resume in one hour." He pounded the gavel, then immediately vacated the courtroom.

As the old judge descended from the witness stand and Marnie stood up from her chair, Ian could sense the danger of an impending confrontation. They reminded him of a mongoose and a cobra poised to strike. Purposely he blocked Marnie's view and distracted her attention as the old man passed.

"Let's find that vacant anteroom again," Ian suggested. "I think we should skip lunch. I doubt any of us have much of an appetite."

Only Rory responded. "I don't mean to sound insensitive, but I could use a little nourishment." He, too, grew apprehensive as Marnie turned her head and stalked Aubrey Hill with her eyes.

"Let it pass, Marnie," Ian said firmly. "This afternoon is time enough."

His words reached beyond her anger and pulled her back to her senses. Snatching her purse from the table, she stormed toward the side exit.

Ian conferred with Rory for a second, then followed her into the anteroom down the hall.

She said nothing for a moment. She merely paced like a lithe and leery animal. "He's doing his damndest to convict me," was her only comment.

Ian removed his jacket and slung it haphazardly over a slatted chair. "Yes, he is," he agreed. "But surely his testimony didn't come as a surprise to you,

Marnie. I warned you about the slanderous insinuations that would be leveled against you.''

"Insinuations!" she scoffed. "He's not implying
anything. He's stating it as fact. And he's lying.''

"It's only one man's opinion," he offered.

"Which about ninety-nine percent of a public-
opinion poll would share!" she shouted. "I'm about
as popular as Nazi war criminals at Nuremberg.''

"You're exaggerating a bit.'' He couldn't help but
grin.

"I don't think so. And I'm angry and tired and
scared.'' She came to a standstill, her back to him as
she wiped the frustration from her eyes.

He went to her, gathering her into his arms and
drawing her comfortingly against his warm body. He
pressed his lips to her fragrant hair, murmuring, ''It's
good to be angry rather than resigned. And it's only
natural to be frightened and tired. You're functioning
under a great strain.''

"You've got to discredit that spiteful old man.
They've got to know what a monster he is.'' She
groaned, resting the back of her head on his shoulder
and holding his arms tightly in place.

"You mustn't let him get to you so, Marnie. He
thrives on dissension and preys on the weak. I intend
to use his own tactics against him this afternoon. Once
I expose the fact that he wasn't even aware of his son's
illness, the jury will have no choice but to question the
credibility of his testimony.''

"What if our scheme backfires?" she asked in a
worried voice.

"Think positive, Marnie," he urged.

"I'm trying to, Ian," came the skeptical murmur.

"But when it comes to A. L. Hill, only a fool wouldn't consider the consequences of challenging him and failing."

The trepidation she voiced would later haunt Ian.

COURT RESUMED, Judge Greer giving his permission for the cross-examination of Aubrey Hill to commence.

Ian stood, making the court wait as he removed his jacket once more, and then slowly approached the old man.

"I remind you that you're under oath, Judge Hill," he began.

"I need no reminder," A.L. countered haughtily.

"Oh, I think that maybe you do, sir," Ian said confidently. "As a matter of fact, I think you've been deliberately slanting the truth."

"I object, Your Honor." Sutter Cane sprang to his feet. "Mr. Dunn is badgering the witness."

"You're out of line, counselor," Judge Greer concurred.

"No more so than this witness's prejudicial testimony was out of line, Your Honor," Ian snapped, his hot Irish temper overriding caution.

His impudence was sternly admonished. "One more remark of that nature and I'll find you in contempt, Mr. Dunn." Judge Greer reinforced his warning with a fierce look.

Rory all but groaned aloud. The thing he'd feared the most was happening—Ian was losing his objectivity and temper. He prayed he would remember his painful tutoring and regain himself.

"I apologize to the court," Ian said with mock humility.

Judge Greer nodded. Rory exhaled a relieved sigh. Aubrey Hill glared his own contempt.

"You have led this court to believe that you were extremely close to your son." Ian pressed the hostile witness.

"I merely expressed the truth," came the brusque response.

"You are asking the jury to accept that the senator confided intimate details of his *bitter* marriage to you?" Ian moved in on the witness box.

"My son was distraught and needed my counsel. Yes, he confided in me. It was only natural."

"Yes, only natural," Ian mimicked sarcastically. "But is your jealous vindictiveness toward my client natural?"

"I must adamantly object!" Sutter Cane exclaimed. "The defense is harassing the witness, Your Honor. May I remind the court that Judge Aubrey Hill is not on trial here?"

"Is there some point to this line of questioning, Mr. Dunn?" Judge Greer asked.

"There is, Your Honor. Aubrey Hill is a recalcitrant witness. I wish to show that his claim of improper conduct on the part of my client is in fact biased and speculative."

"Objection overruled," Judge Greer decreed. "Answer the question, Mr. Hill."

"I have no reason to be jealous of, or unduly vindictive, toward *her*," Hill grunted.

"Then you can substantiate your claim, I presume," Ian pursued. "Did you catch her in the act of committing adultery?"

"This is absurd," A.L. scoffed. "She was much too clever to extend me the opportunity."

"Then did you hire a private detective and have her followed? Perhaps document these instances of infidelity?"

"No, I did not. The idea is repulsive to me." The old man fidgeted in his chair.

"So you have no hard facts to substantiate your allegations." Ian backed away, giving the appearance of dismissing the subject.

"I can only reiterate what my son told me. He believed his wife was unfaithful, and he was contemplating divorce," Hill stated flatly.

"He shared his deepest anxieties with you," Ian continued, baiting him.

"Yes. Whenever he was troubled, he sought my support."

"Then you knew of his battle with diabetes and his agony over becoming impotent the last two years?" Ian speared him.

An audible gasp was inhaled by the witness and spectators alike.

Marnie wanted to stand up and cheer her savior. Finally she would be vindicated.

Judge Greer rapped his gavel for order, saying to Aubrey Hill, "The witness will please answer the question."

A.L. hung his head. It seemed he was discredited. But when he raised his glinting eyes to Ian's, the latter realized his gutsy gamble had been a mistake. The old man had been aware of his son's illness. The knowledge was in his eyes.

"I knew," came the affirmation. "My son was afflicted with almost more than he could bear."

Ian stood motionless, unable to collect himself or respond. Marnie went rigid with shock. *He knew! He had known all along! But how could he have?* Her vision was clouded. Her mind was spinning with unanswered questions.

"As I said, my son confided everything in me. I did not mention his illness because he wished it to remain private. He wanted no one to pity him. I assumed he meant in death as well as life."

Ian gathered his wits. He had committed himself and could not retreat now. Frustratedly he ran his fingers through the sides of his hair before asking, "Wouldn't it be fair to say that your son was having to function under tremendous stress? Isn't it possible that his reason was obliterated by manly ego?"

"No; as I stated, he was depressed but not irrational. Moreover, he was appalled by his wife's insensitive behavior during this crucial time. When he needed her most, she deserted him. It was as if his misfortune gave her the license to do as she'd always wished. My son was victimized by her before the fatal shot was fired," Hill boomed, pointing an accusing finger at Marnie. "She destroyed his pride and then eliminated him," came the vehement cry.

Pandemonium broke out—reporters rushing for exits, Marnie dazedly declaring, "No, it's not true. No, no, no...."

Rory fought to quiet her but she was hysterical, a blank expression in her eyes, total disbelief on her face.

"You're risking a contempt charge, Marnie. Say nothing more," the senior partner pleaded, wrestling to contain her in the chair.

"I will have order," Judge Greer decreed, slamming down his gavel over and over again. "The jury will disregard the witness's final remarks, and I will charge your client with contempt of court if there is one more outburst such as this,'' he promised. ''Have you any further questions, Mr. Dunn?''

Ian looked at Marnie. She was lost in disillusionment. It was futile at this point for him to proceed.

''I have no further questions,'' he grudgingly replied. ''Though I reserve the right to call the witness at a later time.''

''The witness is excused. Court will reconvene at 10:00 A.M. tomorrow,'' came the reprieve.

''All rise,'' the bailiff chanted as newsmen dashed out the rear doors to make the late edition.

Ian masked his own disappointment as he returned to the table and went through the motions of consoling Marnie. She wasn't listening—her gaze and attention were fixed on Aubrey Hill. This time Ian and Rory could not distract or subdue her. She jerked from Ian's hold, confronting the old judge before he could escape through the gate.

''You knew all the time,'' she accused him. ''You didn't care,'' she choked. ''Our marriage, his health— it didn't matter, did it? You pushed and pushed and pushed him toward the presidency and over the brink,'' she screamed, bringing back her hand to strike his cheek.

Ian caught her wrist in the nick of time but not before a newspaper artist had sketched the ugly scene.

''You're a despicable son of a—''

''Marnie, stop!'' Ian growled, wrenching her trapped wrist downward. ''This is making everything worse,'' he cautioned.

''I don't care,'' she groaned, struggling against his restraint.

"And you contend that she's not capable of violence?" the old judge scoffed, cocking a brow at Ian. "If you believe that, you're a bigger fool than my son." With an ambiguous smirk, he limped through the gate and disappeared up the aisle, leaving Ian to contend with failure and Marnie. One hurt about as badly as the other.

CHAPTER FOURTEEN

SOMETHING HAD SNAPPED INSIDE MARNIE when the old man admitted under oath that he knew of Seth's illness from the beginning. Oh yes, the devoted attachment and blind loyalty she'd felt for her husband were severed as keenly as a dry twig snapping in two. She had no more illusions about the man she'd protected. He was using her in death as he had in life.

"Do you mind if I smoke?" she asked Ian as his Cadillac passed the city-limits sign.

"Not at all," he answered gallantly, opening his window a bit.

She lit up, leaned her head back and stared ahead, simply saying, "Two years he lived a lie, pretending it had been his choice not to have the surgery...his choice to seek public glory rather than a personal triumph."

"You never suspected?" Ian ventured.

"Only that one weekend after a visit to Rosehill. He was so convincing when I accused him. I believed. Like a fool, I believed." She flicked her ashes, then settled back with a disheartened sigh.

"It's a difficult thing to learn that someone you loved and trusted has deceived you. Difficult but not insurmountable, Marnie," he added, glancing in her direction.

"I know, Ian. Perhaps finding out the true colors of my husband was a blessing in disguise. It's time I quit rationalizing the past and commit to the future. Since I was a child, I've allowed others to manipulate my life. Somehow I always ended up submissively shouldering responsibilities and unquestioningly accepting everyone else's estimation of me. Maybe because I never had a clear picture of who I really was...the last child born of parents who had no desire for another...the model wife to a man who craved an image, not a woman...the fashionable idol on a magazine cover, a glossy illusion with an intriguing caption. Oh yes, I was many things to many people, Ian," she said in a resentful tone, "but never really an individual in my own right."

She stubbed out her cigarette disgustedly. Suddenly smoking became symbolic of dependency and old habits that should have been broken long ago. She vowed to herself to never again be a slave to tobacco. In the broad scope of things, it was a small triumph; but to Marnie it was a major resolution.

"You're being a little hard on yourself, Marnie. All of us comprise many facets."

"But I was only a glittering reflection, Ian—a fake zircon that could dazzle the experts."

"No, angel..." he murmured, reaching out and tightly clasping her hand. "You're a diamond—authentic and precious."

She closed her eyes, bringing his hand to her cheek. "They say diamonds are forever, counselor. I wonder."

"You'll survive this, Marnie. You're strong and resilient," he encouraged.

"What I am is a mother who's terrified of losing her

child," she admitted in a whisper. "If I'm found guilty and sent to prison, Sunny will be abandoned like you, Ian. She's so young and impressionable. It's bad enough that she'll learn the truth in the years ahead: that her mother stood trial for shooting her father. If I'm convicted, A.L. will gain custody of my daughter and poison her mind against me. How do I save her from an obsessed grandfather and still spare her the pain of disillusionment?"

"I don't understand, Marnie." Idly he stroked her cheek, trying to sensitize himself to her moody comment.

She yearned to confide this final secret. How much she needed to unburden herself and seek Ian's advice! But one last charade had to be played—not for Seth but for Sunny.

"I'm rambling," she fibbed, sliding over and resting her head on his shoulder. "I wish we were still eating cheesecake and drinking champagne on the Brooklyn Bridge," came the wistful murmur as she nestled closer.

"We will again," he promised, cradling his arm around her shoulders. "You're exhausted, Marnie, and not making much sense."

"Yes," she agreed, thinking life didn't make much sense. She was doing the same thing as Seth—being deceptive, only for entirely unselfish reasons. Ian was putting his reputation and future on the line for her. And she was, in essence, cheating him out of ammunition he so desperately needed to rescue her from a guilty verdict. Honesty and honor between client and lawyer, man and woman, were being sacrificed in the name of motherhood and for the love of a child.

Forgive me, her heart cried as he drove toward the cottage unsuspectingly. *Should he ever discover my secret, love, unlike diamonds, wouldn't last forever!*

AT HER INSISTENCE, Ian left Marnie supposedly to rest at the cottage. He attributed her odd mood and request for solitude as an understandable aftereffect of the trial. She wasn't herself. But then how could he expect her to be, considering the revelations that she'd been emotionally bludgeoned with today? Her husband was a fraud, and her chances for an acquittal were diminishing by the hour.

He struck the steering wheel with the heel of his palm, cursing under his breath. How in the hell could he rectify the damage? Hold back the gale of retribution that was fast descending on them?

His fears and bleak outlook were the same as Rory's, upon his return to the law offices. The senior partner anxiously awaited Ian. Their day in court had been a fiasco, and this late-evening conference only underscored the negativity.

"Well, what now?" Rory muttered between staccato puffs on a cigar. "The old man's got you just where he wants you. Try to defend her honor and he'll twist your defense to suit his demented purpose. The harder you proclaim her loyalty, his son's unbalanced obsession, the stronger he'll insinuate her ulterior motives," the Irishman stated in a dismal voice. "This angle isn't going to work. You're walking a dead-end street. The D.A.'s going to hack you and her to pieces if you persist."

Ian loosened his tie, unbuttoned his starched collar, and shoved a glass over the desk to his partner. He needed a share of the bottle Rory hoarded.

"Dammit! That old bastard is persecuting her for his sins," came the disgusted retort. "He's the one who had designs on the senator. He molded his son in his own crazed image." Ian's fist pounded the desk in abject frustration as Rory slid back the glass. "What now?" He gulped the potent bourbon. "I'll tell you the truth, Rory. I don't have one glimmer of an idea how to proceed."

This was a first for Rory. Ian always had an angle on the back burner. The utter resignation on his protégé's face truly rattled the rock-steady older gent. "It can get nastier yet," the senior partner warned in a voice this side of doomsday.

"I don't see how." Ian commented miserably.

Rory sighed, blowing a whiff of smoke in Ian's direction as he slumped deeper into the overstuffed chair. "I guess I'd better be telling you a confidence whispered in my ear today."

Ian's features tensed.

"And don't be asking me who. Just listen." Rory cocked a bushy brow, then muttered, "Word is that the old man is bringing a custody suit against her. He wants sole guardianship of his granddaughter. He intends to prove her unfit."

Ian sat motionless, except for the involuntary flex of his jaw. "He's crazy," he said in a tone as deliberate as his flashing eyes.

"He's determined," the bearer of bad tidings grunted, shifting his weight uneasily as he noted the angry flush creeping up Ian's neck.

"Her public humiliation isn't enough for him? He wants to strip her of all that's left of her life? To hell with him! I'll fight him through every appeals court in this land first!" Ian growled.

"That would be a waste of time and effort," Rory cautioned. "The battle's here and now. It's all or nothing. You'd better discover a secret the old man doesn't know, another skeleton buried in the grave with Seth Hill. Or else you'll lose this case and your client will forfeit much, much more."

"There isn't anything else. Marnie would've told me," came the glum reply.

"Are you so sure?" the Irishman challenged. "Because you sleep with her, do you think you share her nightmare?"

Ian's expression grew steely. "Back off, Rory," he seethed. "Who I choose to sleep with is none of your affair. Not another word on the subject," he stipulated. "Not one."

"You're forgetting all I taught you, me boy." Rory rose from the chair and slammed the bottle to the desk. "When a lawyer loses his objectivity, he risks blowing a case. Back away, Ian," he told him, turning and walking for the door. "Get some perspective and take a long, hard look. There are questions you haven't asked her or yourself. 'N' you'll not be finding the answers between the sheets."

The office door slammed shut, Rory stranding Ian in a room filled with doubt and silence. He winced, then leaned back in his chair and rubbed his eyes. Had he lost his objectivity, he asked himself. Was his intimate involvement with the widow jeopardizing her very welfare? Something was amiss. He could feel it as surely as the nagging headache that throbbed at his temples. *Go home. Get some sleep.* Perhaps tomorrow would bring the answers he sought. They were there. Hazy and distant and not quite clear. But he'd search his mind, and his conscience if necessary, until he found the missing pieces to the puzzle. He had to. *"Back away. . .take a long, hard look."* Rory's parting words kept beating in his brain like the headache that the booze couldn't dull.

Ian shoved back his chair and stood. It was futile to sit and ponder and suffer. It was better to trade the bottle of bourbon for a bottle of aspirin and get some much-needed rest. He grabbed his jacket, tossed it over his shoulder and headed for the door.

The phone jangled as his hand grasped the brass knob. *Let it ring. It's after hours and probably nothing.*

His fingers flexed, rotating the knob, and his retreating figure ignored the repeated summons. He was nearly to the front doors of the law offices when something made him turn back and retrace his steps to the receptionist's desk.

The urgent shrill of the phone stilled as he picked up the receiver with an abrupt, "Connery and Dunn Law Offices."

"I realize it's after office hours but it's imperative that I speak with Mr. Dunn." The male voice on the other end sounded courteous yet somber.

"This is he," Ian answered tiredly.

"My name is Justin Hart. I'm with Ansteadt and Associates, Mr. Dunn."

Ian recognized the law firm immediately. He wasn't in the mood to talk shop. This call had better be important.

"How can I help you?" came the standard, though a bit brusque, reply.

"I'd really prefer not to discuss particulars over the

phone, sir. But I can assure you that it's a matter of the utmost urgency. Would it be possible for you to meet me, say in about a half hour, in the club room at the Straton Hotel?''

Ian wasn't sure he liked the man's cloak-and-dagger routine. "It's not my style to conduct business in hotel lounges, Mr. Hart. Surely you can give me some inkling as to what this concerns.''

"The Hill case,'' came the spare reply.

"I'll be there shortly," Ian consented without a second's hesitation.

"I think it might be worth your while," was all the attorney replied before severing the connection.

Ian dropped the receiver into its cradle, pondering the strange call. Had the man's tone been slightly ominous or was he imagining things, he wondered. There was only one way to find out—meet him and discover his link with the Hill case.

Ian made the rendezvous with time to spare. He sat huddled over a drink at the far end of the bar, inspecting each new face that entered. At last he spied an Ivy League type who fitted the voice on the phone—thirtyish and probably from New England. Ian signaled his presence, and the man made his way to the bar stool beside him.

"Justin Hart, I presume?" came the tongue-in-cheek greeting along with an extended hand.

Hart grinned wryly when returning the handshake. "I apologize for insisting on this clandestine arrangement, but this is rather a delicate matter, Mr. Dunn.''

"No problem. I wasn't otherwise engaged tonight." Ian shrugged. "You mentioned that this matter you wished to discuss concerned the Hill case, Mr. Hart. How so?" He quickly pressed for details.

"It's been a long day. Do you mind if I order a drink first?" the young lawyer hedged.

"Of course," Ian obliged, signaling the bartender.

"A very dry martini," came the request before they got down to brass tacks.

"I represent a local official of the Kentucky Transit Authority, Mr. Dunn," Hart began. "He claims to possess information pertinent to the Hill case."

Ian examined his drink before responding. "Claims to have or actually does possess such information?" he probed skeptically.

"Oh, I'm convinced he has vital information. But you see, Mr. Dunn, he's in a very tenuous legal situation himself. I had to advise him that testifying on behalf of your client could very well jeopardize his own case unless he receives assurance of immunity." Hart grew silent as the martini was set before him.

"You're speaking of federal immunity, I take it?" Ian spoke calmly, though he was about to burst with curiosity and hope.

Hart nodded, then sipped his martini.

"And what are your client's chances of receiving such immunity?"

"Procedures are under way. We're trying to strike a bargain with the U.S. Attorney's office, but so far, no go." The Ivy Leaguer paused to pop an olive into his mouth.

"I see," Ian sighed. "So, why are we having this drink together, Mr. Hart?"

"I've been following the trial closely. It's beginning to go sour for your client, isn't it?"

Ian didn't like the fellow's assessment, but he couldn't really dispute it, either. He polished off his drink before bothering to respond. "Let's just say I wouldn't object if your KTA official wanted to exercise his civic duty."

"I don't envy your predicament. This case I'm handling is nearly as complex. I just thought you ought to know there's a distinct possibility that some startling facts could be disclosed about the senator."

"But your client is not willing to divulge his vital information at this time?" Ian tried to disguise the urgency in his voice.

"I'm sorry. Without the federal authorities first agreeing to grant him immunity, my client would be incriminating himself by testifying." Hart cast Ian a sympathetic look.

"What do you feel his chances are?"

"Honestly?"

"Yeah, give it to me straight," Ian insisted.

"Slim," came the disheartening reply. "It's been pending for weeks. Perhaps if you could stall?" Hart suggested.

"I know you're not at liberty to discuss any particulars of the case, but answer me one question, will you?" Ian asked.

"That depends on what it is."

"What's the charge against your client?"

Justin Hart pondered ethics for a moment, then decided to answer what was a matter of record. "Violations of the federal racketeering statutes," was the reply.

Ian exercised amazing restraint in not exposing his absolute shock. Again he extended his hand, saying, "You will keep me apprised, won't you, Mr. Hart?"

"If the federal authorities come through with a grant of immunity, you'll be the first to know," the young Philadelphia lawyer promised.

"I appreciate your cooperation," Ian managed, sliding from the bar stool. "I paid for our drinks in advance. Have another if you like."

"But how did you know what I'd be drinking?" came the astonished question.

"When you've been practicing as long as I have, you'll learn to trust hunches, Hart. Keep in touch." Ian walked from the Hotel Straton's club room out into the hot August night.

He was smothering in his own stupidity. What an utter fool he'd been. It didn't take a genius to figure out the connection between the senator and the Kentucky Transit official—mass transit. And a federal racketeering charge meant only one thing—corruption from a local level on up. . . up to Seth Hill maybe? And was the senator up to his neck in graft? It made sense. The missing pieces to the puzzle were fitting together.

Ian strode thoughtfully to his car, his mind accelerating faster than the speedometer as he cruised the streets to his uptown apartment.

It wasn't until later, when he lay sprawled on his bed in the dark, that another thought struck Ian. Was it possible that Marnie had known of her husband's complicity in the shady scheme? Could she have been concealing the fact all the time?

He lurched up, swinging his legs off the bed and raking his hands through his hair. His mind rejected the possibility, but his heart told him otherwise. Suddenly he recalled all the instances when she'd been evasive, the many moments when she'd become remote and secretive.

Marnie had deceived him! From the very first, she'd deliberately withheld the information that Hart's client possessed. Rory had been right all along—just because he shared her bed hadn't meant he'd gained her trust or respect.

In his entire life, Ian had never been seized by such intense pain. The only analogy he could draw was when Father Pat had died. The loss of someone he loved so deeply had been traumatic. But this was worse. This was a betrayal by someone he'd adored. And it was annihilating.

Marnie had deceived him, used him. She'd turned him inside out and tied him up in knots. The tough punk from Brooklyn had been a sucker for a tarnished angel.

He fell back on the rumpled sheet, staring at the ceiling, remembering her fragile smile, her honey kiss, her lying lips. Flashes of the widow in black, then a vision in an abalone satin gown clashed in his head.

"Marnie," he groaned her name aloud. "Why... why?" he asked for answers to the questions he should have explored.

He swallowed hard. The memories of what they'd shared were bitter. He should never have crossed the line, should never have lost his perspective. *"You're a bigger fool than my son."* Aubrey Hill's taunting evaluation tortured him. Perhaps he was. Perhaps she was as coldhearted and conniving as most everyone believed, he tried to convince himself. Yet he couldn't forget the times she'd swathed him in love while awake, clung to him fiercely in sleep. Who was this enigma named Marnie?

He closed his eyes and gave himself up to sleep. Tomorrow he'd have his answer. Tomorrow he'd confront her. He hated to believe it, but he refused to avoid it—tomorrow their heavenly yesterdays might end.

CHAPTER FIFTEEN

THE FOLLOWING DAY began with a sudden change in weather and a delay in the trial. An unexpected death in Judge Greer's family forced a postponement. Ian was awakened with an early-morning call from His Honor's clerk informing him of the rescheduling. Since Judge Greer had to travel to Montana for the funeral, court would not resume until the following Monday. Normally Ian would've been irritated by such an extensive delay, but after Hart's startling disclosures the night before, he perceived the postponement more like a reprieve. It would give him the necessary time to investigate the new development and adjust accordingly.

He showered, shaved, dressed and was on his way to the cottage within the hour. A bizarre norther had blown in during the night, and the temperature plummeted to the low sixties, putting a nip in the air. It was as if Mother Nature had played a prank, turning August into October as a reminder of how very vulnerable and subject to exterior elements mortals actually were. The freaky weather only enhanced the feeling of ineptness that consumed Ian. His jawline steeled as he turned onto the cottage lane. A showdown between him and Marnie was imminent. This time he would accept no more excuses, hear no more lies. He'd had his fill of the Hills' secrets. Marnie must make a choice between telling the unadulterated truth or finding herself another more gullible champion. He was at the end of his patience, both personally and professionally.

He braked in the driveway, leaped from the Cadillac and slammed the car door. Without any further contemplation or hesitation, he strode to the front door, venting a fraction of his anger by pounding on the weathered wood.

Marnie answered the summons in short order. Though a bit surprised by the early hour of his call, she beckoned him inside with a welcoming smile.

"Can you believe this weather," she remarked, closing the door and following his silent figure into the den. "The cottage was chilly this morning, so I built a fire." He glanced her way, trying not to notice her svelte figure in the clinging velour warm-up ensemble.

"There's coffee in the kitchen, if you'd like some," she offered, starting toward the bedroom. "I'll just make a speedy change and we can be on our way."

"There's no need to change, Marnie," he told her in a flat tone. "Our presentation of a defense is postponed until next Monday."

"But why?" she asked, stepping closer and for the first time noting his grim expression. He looked haggard and thoroughly disgusted. Instinct warned Marnie that another major setback had occurred. "Something's very wrong, isn't it, Ian? Please tell me. I can't stand the suspense."

She stood a few feet away, her polished fingertips anxiously kneading the back cushions of the couch.

"The delay has nothing to do with my foul mood, Marnie," he explained, putting distance between them as he walked to the fireplace and contemplated the crackling blaze. "Judge Greer had an unexpected death in the family and must attend a funeral in Montana. We must wait for his return."

"Then what is it, Ian?" she insisted, growing cold with suspicion as she studied his stern features.

"I had an interesting conversation last night," he stated in a somber voice. "I met with a colleague who is representing a local Kentucky Transit official on a federal racketeering charge."

Marnie paled but said nothing.

"His client claims to have information vital to our case. . . information that implicates your dead husband in a major conspiracy." He met her gaze, analyzing her reaction. She put forth a supreme effort to mask her culpability but failed miserably. Shame flickered in her eyes. Ian was now certain that she did possess knowledge of the link. Still she reverted to her old habits and pat answers.

"I don't know what that means," she said evasively.

Ian's temper flashed. "Hold it right there, Marnie. I've tolerated your omissions, but I won't be deliberately lied to. You do know something about all of this, and I intend to find out exactly what you're concealing."

Her loose and silky hair flounced as her chin snapped up. "It's private. . . something between Seth and me. I don't want or need this mystery witness, whoever he is, to come to my rescue. Decline any and all offers, Ian," she foolishly demanded.

"Like hell I will!" he boomed. "I don't know if you're stupid or just plain crazy, but you're obviously suffering under some grand delusion about your chances of acquittal." He was glaring at her now. He'd reached the limit and she knew it. "Haven't you been listening to what's been going on in that courtroom, lady? Looked at the jurors' faces? We're losing a little more of you each day. You're going to be convicted if I can't salvage something of your character or cast some doubt on your husband's."

"I can't," she declared, her chin trembling. "I have an obligation...."

"To whom?" Ian shouted. "To a husband who was weak and corrupt? A memory that is false and dead? A family who despises you and whose sole objective is to strip you barren?" He verbally assaulted her with the truth.

"To Sunny," she nearly screamed. "My daughter's future is at stake. Can't you understand?"

"Understand this, Marnie," he said in a damning voice. "Your father-in-law, that vicious old man who broke your husband's spirit and manipulated him most of his life, is preparing to steal custody of Sunny. He's already initiated a formal suit challenging your fitness as a mother. You've done everything in your power to undermine your own defense, and now you want to decline a last chance at saving Sunny from a fate worse than Seth's."

His bluntness caused a stabbing pain in her chest. She gripped the back of the couch for support. "Dear God!" she gasped. "He wouldn't... not Sunny... oh, please, not Sunny," she murmured numbly.

Ian rejected an impulse to console her, standing rigid and seemingly unaffected by her pain. "Fight him, Marnie. For Sunny, help me combat him. Tell me what really happened in the bedroom that night," he urged.

She hung her head, a mane of platinum hair spilling around her anguished face. "I wanted to spare Sunny this," she groaned. "She loved him so." Her head lifted and he was struck by the absolute agony in her eyes. "I wanted him to always remain her knight in shining armor, the way he was once to me."

"It's a myth, Marnie—a legacy of disillusionment," he said persuasively.

"I know...oh, believe me, Ian, I know," came the dismal answer.

"Then tell me everything. I can't work miracles. I'm not a David who can defeat a political Goliath with pebbles. And I'm not accustomed to losing, Marnie. In fact, I dislike it intensely."

They stared at each other for a poignant moment, his will vying for supremacy over her loyalty. He won at last. She sighed and released her clutch on the couch, pacing as she spoke.

"I'll tell you the truth to the extent I know it," she said, relenting. "I knew something more was wrong with Seth than just his illness and unfounded jealousies for several months. I suspected he was in some kind of political trouble. The last few months he became paranoid—afraid of phone taps and surveillance, questioning anything out of the ordinary and every contact we had. He was suspicious of everyone, including me. He wouldn't take calls except by specific name. He kept late appointments without disclosing where or with whom. And he became irrationally angry and extremely defensive at my mention of his strange behavior."

"But you had no proof of your suspicions?" Ian asked.

"Not until the night he died," she answered in a direct but resigned manner. "I begged him to tell me. I knew weeks before that Seth was in dire trouble. He could never hide his anxiety from me. I knew him too well. Oh, dear Lord, maybe too well," she muttered brokenly. "Maybe if I hadn't pressured him, perhaps if I had handled the problem differently," she conjectured.

Ian said nothing, letting her continue.

"But I was tired of being his obliging conscience. I knew Seth had let his aspirations lead us to the brink of disaster. I pushed him that night, demanded to know what he had done in the name of the presidency. I couldn't have known...I never expected what he admitted."

"Which was?" Ian kept up the pressure.

"Seth told me that he'd taken a bribe. He'd been approached by an emissary of a Japanese firm that sought complicity in a scheme to sell a monorail system to the Kentucky Transit Authority. In return for his awarding of the transportation grant to KTA, he would receive a sum of money, a contribution to his campaign and a promise of support for his future nomination by those with political clout."

"He accepted the bribe?"

"My husband was desperate to make his bid," she explained. "He thought time was deserting him. He wanted the glory more than—" she swallowed hard "—more than anything else," she finished.

"That night, after the dinner party, you confronted him with your suspicions and he admitted his complicity?" Ian returned her to the crucial subject.

She nodded, sinking in front of the fireplace, curling into a tight ball and hugging her knees.

She looked so fragilely pathetic to Ian, but he remained firm in his resolve.

"He told me that he had reason to believe he'd be discovered shortly. He said he couldn't bear the shame and hoped that with his death the scandal would not be made public. It was when he began begging me to do whatever I must to spare Sunny the humiliation that might follow that I realized his intent. I tried to dissuade him. I told him we could overcome it, promising that I'd find a way."

"But he was determined to commit suicide?" Ian voiced his hunch.

She raised her head from her knees, staring at a memory she beheld in the flickering flames inside the hearth. "'I can't live like this anymore,' he told me. 'Understand, Marnie and—'" she closed her eyes, a solitary tear escaping down her cheek "'—and please forgive me,' he asked." She shivered in response to the memory but continued. "He raised the gun and I grabbed for it. We struggled. The gun went off and he collapsed at my feet. But I remember before he fell the strange, almost serene, look he cast me. As if he were grateful I'd spared him the burden of intentional death."

"So you weren't afraid of him, as you've implied?" Ian sank to a chair beside her, raking his hands through his tawny hair.

"No," she sighed. "I never feared for my own life, only his."

He cradled his head in his palms. She rested her forehead on her knees. Only the sounds of popping cedar and their laborious breathing filled the room.

"You've done yourself and me a great disservice,"

he finally said. "And for nothing, Marnie. You've only managed to insert more confusion into an already complex affair."

"I did what I thought best."

"Without thought of the consequences?"

"Oh, believe me, Ian, I realized. I just didn't feel I had a choice."

"Did you honestly believe that the truth would die with him? That the corruption wouldn't be traced back to the source? You can't be so naive."

"Maybe I was more desperate than naive. I'd hoped—" she choked, then cleared her throat and amended her statement "—I prayed this scandal wouldn't come to light."

Again, silence fell on them. Ian stood, drawing a deep and expressive sigh. No more was he angry—only disillusionment glimmered in his hazel eyes. "I wish I understood you, Marnie," came the painful confession from deep within him. "I wonder which you really are—self-serving or self-sacrificing?"

Her head jerked in his direction, defiance and need mingling in her steadfast gaze. "Don't you know by now?" she asked of him.

He looked away. "I know I loved you. And you were the only one who ever made me want to risk all that that implies. But now I can't help questioning your motives. Why did you become intimate with me, Marnie? To ensure my devotion to your cause? Or have you been involved in manipulative games so long you can't tell the difference anymore? From the very start you weren't honest with me. Love means implicit trust. As far as I can tell, angel, only one of us truly loved." He dismissed her clinging gaze and walked for the door.

"Ian?" His name trembled on her lips. He glanced back. "Are you walking off the case?"

"No," he assured her with a taut, sad smile. "I'm walking out on you. See you in court Monday."

Never in his life had an exit been harder or the slam of a door more symbolic. He refused to look back, striding purposefully to his car and then peeling out of the driveway onto the lane. He hadn't gone a mile when he missed her terribly, hadn't reached the city-limits sign when he was forced to wipe away her memory like the alien moisture that collected in his eyes and blurred the road.

At the slam of the door, Marnie's head sank to her knees. She had retained her lawyer yet lost her man. No matter what the extenuating reasons were, Ian wouldn't forgive her for the choice she'd been forced to make. He was so extraordinarily honest that deceit of any kind was repugnant to him. She had gambled and lost. And no one was to blame but herself.

Marnie sat paralyzed before the fire, remembering and regretting. She hadn't intended falling in love with Ian. She hadn't meant to hurt him. There was no earthly way she could've predicted or thwarted the chemistry between them. No more than she could make amends for the unintentional pain she'd brought to him. She knew how sensitive he was about his child-hood and the rejection he'd suffered. And she realized he perceived her lack of trust and candor as a final rebuff. Dear God! If he only knew how badly she wanted and needed to confide in him, how hard it was for her to exclude him. But she'd believed it was the one way to protect her daughter: to say nothing and keep the secret of her husband's shame.

She struggled to her feet and stumbled aimlessly about the cottage—Ian's cottage—the haven they'd created in the midst of a nightmare. Memories lurked everywhere, reaching out and tangling around her heart, strangling her with despair. *"Why did you become intimate with me, Marnie?"* His words mocked her.

Didn't he understand? Wasn't it obvious, her tortured mind asked. But her love for him was shadowed by a haunting past and tempered by an uncertain future, while his knew no bounds or tanglements. He could love freely and without the shackles of having loved before. She could not. It was that simple; that complex; that heartbreaking.

Ian was pledged to defend her publicly, but privately he condemned her. It seemed Marnie Hill was born to have, to hold for a precious while, then to lose forever.

Once again she collapsed in front of the fireplace, hugging her knees to her chest and rocking to and fro. She tried not to give in to self-pity, tried not to cry. But her will broke along with a muffled sob, and she bent her head and wept—wept bitterly—and for no one but herself.

THE MASSIVE DOORS OF ROSEHILL swung open, a pair of unfamiliar eyes assessing the casually clad woman on the doorstep.

"May I help you?" the recently hired staff member asked in a haughty tone.

"I'm here to see Judge Hill," Marnie informed the snooty maid.

"I'm sorry. He's not receiving any visitors today," came the curt comeback as the door began to close in Marnie's face.

She braced it open with a hand, asserting, "He will see me," as she barged inside.

"I beg your pardon!" the maid huffed indignantly. "I told you he's seeing no one today. I must insist that you leave."

Marnie stood her ground, bullying the domestic with an imperious look. "Inform him that his daughter-in-law awaits his company in the parlor. Tell him I will not budge from this house until he consents to see me."

"But he's napping," the aghast servant whined, wringing her hands.

"I'm afraid you'll just have to disturb him," was all Marnie replied, turning on her heel and marching into the adjacent parlor.

She tossed her purse on the brocade settee, then paced around the elegant room. Her posture was rigid and the expression on her face was implacable. Atypically, her hair was drawn smoothly back and twisted into a loose knot atop her head. The sleek coiffure accentuated the severe look on her gaunt face and the fierce blue of her eyes.

"Miss Marnie?" Nadine inquired from the doorway. "The maid told me you were in here," she explained.

The former mistress bestowed a faint smile on the housekeeper. "I was a bit rude to her, I'm afraid. How are you, Nadine?"

"Well, Miss Marnie. And yourself?" Nadine asked, noting that her ex-mistress was visibly thinner and decidedly upset.

"As well as can be expected, under the circumstances," came the vague reply.

"Excuse me for saying, but you look as if you've been crying, Miss Marnie," Nadine boldly venture. "Is there anything I can do?"

Marnie's fingertips brushed the puffiness beneath her eyes that even the expertly applied makeup could not conceal. Then, walking over and taking Nadine's hands gently in her own, she shook her head, murmuring, "It's kind of you to offer, but my troubles are my own, Nadine. And I must deal with them alone. Perhaps if I had acted more assertively long ago, some of my problems could've been avoided."

"You're speaking of Mr. Seth, aren't you?" Nadine searched her mistress's forlorn face.

"In part, yes," she admitted, releasing the housekeeper's bony hands and walking to the window. "After all the years you spent with him, I'm sure I don't have to tell you that Seth wasn't the strongest man, Nadine. He was too easily influenced. But I closed my eyes to his faults because I thought that course was the lesser of two evils... believed it was much more harmonious to excuse his weaknesses and, when that became impossible, to cover his tracks. I made a wrong decision and now I am reaping the repercussions of my mistake."

"You mustn't be so critical of yourself, Miss Marnie. I know one thing for certain—he was the happiest in your company. His life was enriched by you."

Marnie smiled sadly at the loyal servant. "It was special at first, wasn't it? Almost like a fairy tale," she sighed. "But like Cinderella and Prince Charming, we stayed too long at the ball, Nadine. We never even heard midnight strike."

Marnie's fatalistic mood distressed Nadine. She

yearned to say something wise and consoling, but instead all she could offer was some tea. "Perhaps some herb tea will pick up your spirits a little?" she suggested.

"I doubt I'll be staying long enough for tea," was the only reply.

"It's no bother." The savvy housekeeper pretended not to catch her meaning. "I'll see to it myself."

Before Marnie could stop her, Nadine withdrew from the room. She smiled to herself. Nadine had always been a step ahead of her around Rosehill. Aimlessly she strolled back to the window, gazing down on the gardens below.

"You have more gall than sense, madam!" The old judge's raspy voice startled Marnie. She stiffened and turned to face his searing gaze. "How dare you barge into my home and make demands."

"I wanted to speak with you." Her tone was icy.

"I didn't think it was a courtesy call," he scoffed, limping nearer. "Well, say what it is that's so urgent, and then get the hell out," he croaked.

"I understand that you're contemplating bringing suit to gain custody of my daughter," she challenged, her voice as steady as her gaze.

His coarse features hardened even more. "It's only a precautionary measure, I assure you. I have the utmost confidence that you'll be convicted and this legal action will not be necessary."

"Drop the suit, A.L.," she advised him, her blue eyes glinting like sapphires.

He smirked, leaning his palms on his walking stick. "Is that a threat, madam? And if I refuse to do as you wish, do you intend to eliminate me, too?" His acid remark was meant to make her cower.

She did not flinch or even blink. "Actually, A.L., you might prefer a quick death over what I have in mind."

He quirked a brow, his gnarled fingers tightening around the ivory handle of his cane. "Do you think I can be intimidated by idle threats from a little mouse like yourself? I didn't build a political dynasty by docilely submitting. No, not at all, madam. Others have tried to outwit me and failed. Do you believe you can accomplish what men of means and clout have attempted throughout the years? To best me? You are presumptuous!" he sneered.

Her shoulders squared and her pulse quickened. "I possess something they did not," she retorted.

"Ahh, I see," he responded in mock contemplation. "And what is this secret weapon that you foolishly think can deter me?"

"Blackmail," she answered in a word.

His eyes narrowed but he feigned nonchalance. "There seems to be no end to your transgressions—adultery, murder, now blackmail. You are an enterprising woman."

"I lived under the same roof with a master. Some of your perversity was bound to rub off." She cast him a spurning look.

He veiled his surprise beneath drooping lids, limping to the brandy decanter and pouring only one drink. Slowly his lame body eased into a chair beside the Country French table, pregnant seconds passing as he sampled the aged brandy, then glanced up and grinned crookedly.

"Could I have underestimated you all these years, Marnie?" Except on the rarest occasions or when in the company of others, he did not address her by her given name.

She slanted him a suspicious look, refraining from answering.

He pursed his lips, scrutinizing the amber brandy. "I wonder?" he said in an assessing tone. "You were always a bit stronger than I gave you credit for, you know? I never liked you, but I did respect that tough core of yours. You don't give up easily."

"Oh, but we both know how hard you tried to discredit and banish me from your private kingdom, don't we, A.L.?" Her chin lifted defiantly.

His answer was a salute of his glass. "It's a secret we share. Unfortunately for you, madam, my animosity cannot be proven."

"But I know other secrets—ones that can be proven," she warned him. "Seth didn't only confide in you. You see, A.L., I know dates and places and names; I know about behind-closed-doors trades and under-the-table payoffs; I know how you built your precious dynasty and nearly every corrupt move you made. You poached your power and ruined men whose families still carry a grudge. I'm in a position to set the hounds on your heels and I'll do it, A.L., if you push me."

A crimson stain suffused his saggy cheeks. For a moment, Marnie feared he would suffer a stroke, and she'd be blamed for his death, as well.

Nadine chose this inopportune moment to appear with the tea. She had only to step into the room to realize the strained and explosive mood between the two.

"I, ah, have your herb tea, Miss Marnie," she stammered, trying to be as inconspicuous as possible as she set the tray down.

The old judge's rebuking eyes nearly snapped the housekeeper's composure.

Marnie felt compelled to intervene. "I'm sorry to have insisted, Nadine. I forget that I'm no longer in a position to make requests at Rosehill. Thank you for indulging me."

"It was my pleasure to serve you again," Nadine answered sincerely, grateful to Marnie for rescuing her dignity.

"That'll be quite enough, Nadine," the old man barked.

"Yes, sir," she acquiesced, quietly slipping from the room and shutting the parlor door.

His glare stabbing like a knife in her back, Marnie wasn't certain she could pour, let alone swallow, the tea. *"He thrives on dissension and preys on the weak."* Ian's words gave her the strength to continue the battle. Her hand was steady as she carried off the tea ceremony.

"You truly are trash," he growled. "Drinking up my imported tea while blackmailing me. Is there no limit to your crassness?"

"Let's not resort to slander, A.L. It's really beneath you," came the sarcastic gibe.

"If you think I'm impressed by your threats of blackmail, you're greatly mistaken," he said menacingly. "Do you think claims like yours haven't been made before? You're bluffing."

"I assure you I'm not, but it's your prerogative to dismiss my claims and disregard my warning." She shrugged, then sipped the tea. "But I promise you that if you continue with this suit to take Sunny from me, I'll call a news conference within a few days and divulge everything I know about you. The press will be more than happy to accommodate me. They've been hounding me for months for an interview. I'll provide them with smut enough to keep you in the limelight for months. Since my reputation has already been smeared from coast to coast, what have I got to lose?''

Aubrey Hill struggled to his feet, his face ashen, his reason obliterated by rage. He raised the walking stick to strike down this woman he detested.

Marnie dodged his thrust, the cane smashing into the table, shattering china and sending the tray toppling. Quickly she sprang at him, but he clutched the walking stick and held it above their heads.

''A thrashing would've been kinder than the abuse I've endured from you,'' she spat in his face, wrenching the stick from his hand and sending it crashing against the marble fireplace.

His arthritic fingers seized her arm. ''You wouldn't dare instigate such a scandal! Not even you would wallow in such swill!'' he snarled through gritted teeth.

She jerked free of his grasp, feeling a rush of gratification at besting him for once. ''Try me, A.L. I promise you, you'll regret it.''

''Get out! Out of my home...out of my sight,'' he bellowed like a wounded bull.

''Gladly,'' she consented, grabbing her purse from the settee and storming out of the parlor.

''You'll be convicted. I'll have Sunny in the end!'' His tirade followed her down the foyer.

Nadine stood by the front doors, swinging them open as Marnie approached with purse tucked under her arm, head held high.

''I enjoyed the tea, Nadine.'' Always gracious, Marnie brushed the housekeeper's ebony cheek with a farewell kiss, then swept past her to the outside world.

"The good Lord keep and protect you, Miss Marnie," Nadine murmured, closing the door on the gloom of Rosehill behind the regal figure of her former mistress.

CHAPTER SIXTEEN

TUESDAY BROUGHT A RETURN of seasonal weather and a strong tailwind to propel the jet that took Ian to Washington and the U.S. attorneys' offices. He had a hunch to follow and an old law-school chum to look up.

He explored the building's maze of terrazzo corridors, scrutinizing the black lettering on rows of office doors. Finally he found the office that supposedly Jake Dittman occupied. His intrusion went virtually unnoticed. Barely did the staff look up from the legal volumes they pored over or take time out from the miniconferences being conducted in hushed tones. He spied Jake's balding head above a mound of paperwork stacked on a desk in a corner.

"And here I thought assistant U.S. attorneys had cushy setups," Ian said, greeting his old friend with a broad smile.

"Well, I'll be damned. If it isn't the Kentucky boy wonder himself. How the hell are ya?" Half rising from his stool, Jake stuck out a welcoming hand. "Sit down, sit down," he muttered, gesturing to an antiquated chair beside his desk.

"A little older and a lot more cynical," Ian replied, settling on the uncomfortable wooden object. "Do they pay you enough to wade through all that crap?"

he mused, noting the clutter his old chum was shoving aside.

"Hardly." Jake grinned, taking off his glasses and dropping an empty Coke can into the trash. "But it beats chasing ambulances. I hear you're making a name for yourself. Some say you're a real-life Perry Mason. Of course, taking on cases like the Hill fiasco tends to add substance to the rumors," came the friendly barb.

"I'm eking out a living," was the spare reply. "How're Sally and the kids?"

Jake glanced away, fumbling with his rolled-up shirt sleeves. "Sally divorced me a couple of years ago. Last I heard she remarried a Pennsylvania truck driver and was living somewhere outside Scranton. I got a Father's Day card from the kids last June."

Instantly Ian regretted bringing up the subject. "That's tough, Jake. I'm really sorry to hear of your breakup."

"Yeah, well, I'm adjusting. I miss the kids, though," he sighed. "Hell!" he exclaimed. "If the truth be known I miss Sally, too. God only knows why. All she ever did was gripe about me putting in so many hours at these tombs. She thought I should've been appointed attorney general by now. She always did fancy herself a wife to a big man. Geez! It makes no sense, ya know? She married a truck driver, for God's sake!"

"I'm beginning to think not much between the sexes does make sense," Ian commented wryly.

"You married yet?" Jake asked.

"No," came the monosyllabic reply.

"Got a special lady in your life?"

Ian tried to blank the picture of Marnie from his mind. "There was, but things just didn't work out."

"Your fault or hers?" Jake pressed.

"Are you planning on writing my biography?" Ian covered his sensitivity with a phony grin.

"Maybe. Assistant U.S. attorneys have a reputation for moonlighting." Jake studied his friend, noting his sullen expression.

"Well, find another subject, my friend. My life story would make dull reading material." Ian fidgeted in the chair.

"So, what brings you to Washington? I'm sure you didn't travel all this way just to shoot the breeze with me." Wisely Jake dropped the touchy topic.

Ian glanced over his shoulder, scouting out the probable eavesdroppers. Washington wasn't only renowned as the national capital; it was also a vipers' pit of gossip. "I happened to be in the neighborhood and thought I'd drop by and see if you were free for lunch," he hedged.

Jake slanted him a disbelieving look as he stood up from his stool and unrolled his shirt sleeves. "Sure, I'm game. I seize any excuse not to have to brown-bag it. By the way, you are picking up the check, aren't you?"

"Didn't I always?" A devilish spark lit up Ian's hazel eyes as they strode out of the dank and musty office.

A PERT LITTLE WAITRESS cleared the plates, then refilled their coffee cups. On the prowl since his divorce, Jake was engrossed in the slinky rotation of the woman's hips as she moved away.

"I'm up against it on this one, Jake. It'd take weeks for me to circumvent the miles of political and legal red tape surrounding this transit scam. I need this favor," Ian explained in a somber tone.

The urgency in his voice regained Jake's attention. He mulled over the request while creaming his coffee. "The case is hot, Ian. . . strictly hush-hush. No one's supposed to leak any details."

"I know I'm asking a lot and I don't want you to compromise yourself," Ian said in a defeated voice, thinking his trip to Washington had been a lost cause.

Jake sucked the inside of his cheek, weighing his allegiances. Then, setting down his coffee cup, he simply said, "I owe you, Ian. Hell, I wouldn't have made it through law school without your help. I'll fill you in on what I know. Keep in mind that I only worked on the preliminary investigation, but I've heard bits and pieces since." Jake drew a deep breath, then tasted his coffee.

"Whatever you can give me will mean a great deal," Ian assured him.

"Yeah, well, for openers, your colleague in Lexington wasn't feeding you any bull. The senator was implicated, all right. He was in the scam about as deep as you can get."

"Go on," Ian urged, leaning closer and speaking in a low voice.

"Hart's client was dealing with an undercover agent on the local level. It was a slick setup and it worked beautifully. The investigation took months, but finally the graft was traced back to the illustrious senator. The evidence is overwhelming—irrefutable and as incriminating as hell. We have a solid case linking a

Japanese firm by the name of Mitsuki International to the mass-transit committee the senator chaired.''

''How solid?'' Ian quizzed.

''Tight enough to squeeze the big boys,'' came the convincing answer.

Ian was impressed. ''You fellas do neat work,'' he admitted.

''When you intend to step on some influential toes, there's no margin for error.'' The smile dwindled from Jake's lips.

''How about the immunity for Hart's client, Jake? What's your guess? Will it come through?'' Ian held his breath.

''Don't count on it. I think it's unlikely,'' was the deflating answer.

''Are you sure?'' Ian persisted.

''About as sure as one can be about anything in Washington. That's why we use terms like 'possibly' and 'unlikely.' The first rule in this town is to cover your butt.''

''Is there anything else you can give me, Jake? I'm working blind.'' Ian was trading on their friendship.

''I can give you a name—Copeland, Charles Copeland. He's the man your case hinges on—Hart's mystery client. And there's one more lead. If I were you I'd probe into Hill's private-practice files. Conclusive proof of his complicity might be found. The scuttlebutt I've heard is that the payoffs were laundered through the firm via dummy legal transactions between Hill and Mitsuki International.''

''I owe you, Jake.'' Ian's expression was one of gratitude.

"You sure do." His college chum shrugged off the debt. "I believe you agreed to pick up the check?"

A LATE-NIGHT FLIGHT back to Lexington and a snatch of a few hours' rest and Ian began to track Jake's tip to Seth Hill's private law offices. Only after Ian insisted on speaking with Forbe Hendricks, the senator's law partner of many years, did a dour-faced secretary grudgingly escort Ian into a swank office with an assurance that Mr. Hendricks would meet with him shortly.

"Shortly" turned out to be an hour and a half later, and Ian was hardly in the mood to observe amenities.

"Sorry to keep you waiting," Hendricks mumbled insincerely, then seated himself behind the desk without so much as a handshake. "My secretary tells me you were most insistent upon speaking with me. I'm afraid I haven't much time, so please be brief."

Ian controlled an urge to yank Hendricks over his fancy desk by his Halston lapels and punch the smug grin off his arrogant face. "I'm sure you know I'm representing Marnie Hill," he stated in a curt tone.

"I'm aware." Hendricks smothered a bored sigh.

"I have reason to believe that your deceased partner was a coconspirator in a transit scam and this law firm was used as a front." Ian hit him hard and head-on with the ammunition he now possessed. "Since you've impressed upon me how invaluable your time is, I won't mince words, Hendricks. Because of your former partner's unethical conduct, this firm and, most especially, you are in a hell of a mess."

Forbe Hendricks leaped to his feet. "See here. You can't just waltz into my office and make unfounded accusations such as that."

"I not only can, but am," Ian countered. "Whether or not you were in fact a knowing accessory to your partner's wrongdoing, you are just as guilty by default."

"You can't prove one word of these preposterous allegations," Hendricks huffed.

"Don't waste your breath or my time, Hendricks. Either you cooperate willingly or I'll subpoena the records and drag you and this firm through an ugly court appearance," Ian threatened.

Forbe Hendricks sank back into his chair. He was torn between incurring Ian's or Aubrey Hill's wrath. He'd known of his partner's unscrupulous association with Mitsuki International and the payoffs that had been accepted. Further, he realized the firm's records would substantiate Ian's claim. Sweat broke out on his brow as he met the determination in the impassioned defense counselor's eyes.

He cleared his throat and amended his prior tone when he responded. "For some time I was aware of Seth's—" he paused, searching for the proper words "—shall we say, dubious business transactions. But I swear I never participated in the scam or accepted one dime of the bribe." He removed a handkerchief from his pocket, wiping his clammy palms, then dabbing his forehead.

"I want your permission to examine the firm's records." Ian stated his terms.

"You're putting me in a most indelicate position," Hendricks sputtered. "Judge Hill will be displeased, to say the least."

"Do you honestly believe I give a damn, Hendricks?" came the sharp retort.

One glance at Ian's granite features was sufficient. Hendricks had no doubt that Ian would take him to the limit and into court. He pressed the intercom button, grudgingly leaving instructions with his secretary for Mr. Dunn to be given a free rein and access to Seth Hill's private files.

"Is that cooperative enough for you, Dunn?" Hendricks stood up, looking down his nose disdainfully. The crass counselor and his crude tactics were repugnant to the high-dollar attorney.

"One more thing, if I may?" Ian purposely goaded his stuffy colleague. "When you make that phone call to Aubrey Hill, I wouldn't mention the fact that you panicked under fire. He strikes me as a man who's intolerant of quitters."

Hendricks went white at the insult. "I find you offensive, Dunn."

"The feeling's mutual, I assure you," Ian snapped, standing from the chair and turning his back on Hendricks. "Don't bother to show me to the senator's office. I can follow the stench."

IAN SWITCHED ON THE DESK LAMP. He'd been so engrossed in Seth Hill's private files he hadn't noticed the gradual descent of evening's darkness. He pondered the incriminating document before him, his palm idly scraping the five o'clock shadow forming on his cheeks.

Supposedly the senator had not been practicing during his Senate terms, as that might have been viewed as a conflict of interest. Yet behind the scenes he was very much involved with one particular corporate client. After a thorough examination of the books and files,

Ian discovered that Seth Hill solely represented an American firm by the name of Argus Incorporated, a manufacturer of foreign car parts. Further, the fees paid him for his representation were exorbitantly out of line for the services rendered.

Feeling that he was on to something, Ian probed deeper. After cross-referencing the American company, he found the link. Argus Incorporated was a subsidiary of Mitsuki International. He now had the proof of unethical conduct and the Japanese connection.

He gazed at the open files spread on the desk, drew a deep breath, then stood and stretched. He had nearly everything he needed except the substantiating testimony of Charles Copeland. Seth Hill's death had accomplished what the bastard had intended. A dead man couldn't be named in an indictment. Ian knew he could allude to the senator's complicity but without Copeland's essential corroboration, Hill's guilt could not be conclusively proven.

His hands were tied by legal loopholes. Everything hinged on Hart's client receiving the immunity that would allow him to testify. Damn! Was nothing going to break in this case?

"We're all going to go down the sewer." Rory's prediction beat in his brain. Wasn't it ironic? The affluent scum would come out clean once more. Ian found himself questioning the system. It was wrong, wrong, wrong that men like Seth Hill could find shelter in the arbitrary character of the law.

He slammed shut the files, his blood pressure elevating at a faster rate than his diminishing hope. *Outsmart them,* his mind badgered. *It's a chess game.*

Who will overanticipate, undercalculate...check-mate? This was the question that he took to Rory after thanking Hendrick's dour-faced secretary for her assistance and leaving Seth Hill's sanctuary.

IT WAS BEYOND THE SHANK OF THE EVENING when Ian pounded on Rory's door.

"I have to talk to you," he wheezed, after climbing the endless steps to the dwelling.

Clad in a faded bathrobe and barefoot, Rory muttered under his breath as Ian barged past. "Had the thought ever occurred to you that I might be wishing a little privacy tonight?" Rory groaned.

It was too late. Ian was already into the living room and face to face with a pleasant-looking, though a bit rotund, lady whom Rory had been entertaining.

He nearly exploded into embarrassed laughter, but instead recovered himself and smiled apologetically. "I'm sorry. Am I interrupting?" he said contritely.

Rory rolled his eyes, then made the necessary introductions. "Mrs. Garraty, I'd like you to meet my partner, Ian Dunn."

Her rosy cheeks flushed a shade more crimson as she replied, "It's pleased I am to be meeting you. And, no, you're not interrupting. I just dropped by to bring Rory some of my Irish stew. I try to look after his needs now and then." Her explanation was accentuated by a plucky grin.

Rory's needs were evident beneath the tattered bathrobe. "Sure 'n' she's a blessing," he blustered. "I will savor your kindness with each spoonful I devour."

The lady friend lowered her twinkling eyes demurely. "Then I'll be on my way," she chirped. "Should you want the recipe, you know my number."

"I'll be in touch, to be sure," he assured her, escorting her to the door.

At the slam of the door, Ian collapsed into uproarious laughter and onto the couch. "Irish stew, my eye!" he taunted as Rory stomped back into the living room.

"Mrs. Garraty is a dear friend. Get your mind out of the gutter and that glint out of your eye." Rory walked to the liquor cabinet, snatching a bottle of bourbon he'd been saving for the priming of Mrs. Garraty.

"You're going to sulk. I can tell." Ian tried to stifle his amusement.

"Don't be absurd. Do you want a hit 'o' this or not?"

Ian nodded, straightening his sprawled body and composure. "I really am sorry if I messed up things, Rory," he apologized.

"Mrs. Garraty will understand. She's a remarkable woman."

"Remarkable," Ian agreed, still astounded by finding her there.

Rory passed him a stingy portion of bourbon, then dropped into a chair. "Well," he grunted. "I'm supposing your impromptu visit has something t'do with your mysterious disappearance for two days," he shrewdly surmised.

"Mmm," Ian murmured. "Things broke loose so quickly, Rory, I hadn't time to consult you. You'd better sit back and take a deep breath. I've got a lot to fill you in on."

Ian proceeded to bring Rory up to date—starting with the phone call from Hart and ending with the contents of Hill's private files.

Thirty minutes and several drinks later, Rory expelled an astonished whistle. "I suspected there was more to all of this but your tale is even wilder than I imagined. Blessed Mary! What a can of worms!"

"The worst of it is, I'm no better off knowing the truth than if I'd never found out. I can't prove a damn bit of it...not without Copeland's testimony."

"There's always the chance that immunity will be granted." Rory tried to uplift his spirits.

"Well, the way it stands right now, it doesn't seem likely." Ian quoted Jake Dittman's pessimistic opinion, then leaned back his head and sighed. "I can't remember feeling more inept. It goes against my grain, Rory. If only I could take the initiative...break everything wide open."

"I know its hard to curb that aggressive streak of yours, but you've no choice on this one. You've got to pace yourself, Ian. You must stay abreast of the developments and not prematurely tip the balance of things." Rory offered his seasoned wisdom.

"I don't want to lose this case, Rory," was the only reply.

"Is it the widow's welfare or your own pride that torments you?" came the poignant query.

There was no response as the astute Irishman finished his drink, then set aside his glass. "You're blaming her for not taking you into her confidence from the first, aren't you, me boy?"

Still there was no reply as Rory hauled his bloated body from the chair, then searched atop the mantel and found his "emergency only" cigar. He lit up, taking deep, lazy puffs. "You know I care for you like my own son, Ian," he said between puffs. "So I feel I have the right to say what's on my mind."

Ian's head lifted, drawn by the soberness in his partner's voice. He stared at the elder gent as he paced around the couch.

"You're a fine man in many ways, me boy, but you're also an emotional cripple. I've held my tongue all these years because I believed you'd eventually realize that it's futile to measure tomorrow by yesterday's yardstick. But you've yet to admit your flaw—that you have no capacity for commitment or forgiveness. You're a modern-day martyr, and sometimes you can be as obnoxious as hell."

Ian was flabbergasted. Never had Rory talked to him in such a manner. "I'm not in the mood for this tonight," he snapped, making a move to rise from the couch. Instantly his shoulder was trapped by an iron grip and his weight shoved firmly back down upon the cushions.

"In the mood or not, you'll hear me out," came the gruff command. "It's time you quit avoiding consideration of the future and a debt you owe yourself. No one's perfect...not even you. Might it be your fault that she disappointed you? You idealized her, tending to forget that she's human like us all."

"She deliberately deceived me." Both agitation and bitterness registered in Ian's voice.

"Did she now?" Rory mocked. "And why would she do such a thing? To protect her little girl from life-long scars," he reasoned. "As a mother, she had to consider the child, had to conceal the truth. And you condemn her for that? Who gave you the right?" Rory challenged.

Ian bent his head, rubbing his tired eyes. "I hadn't looked at it quite like that," he murmured ashamedly. "But I can't retract what's already been said."

"Sure you can. You simply say, 'I was wrong. I'm sorry,'" Rory offered, patting his partner's slumped shoulder.

"I haven't much experience in matters of the heart, Rory. I'm a clumsy ox with no confidence or tact."

"There's no amateur or pro rank in such matters. No one's keeping score or awarding blue ribbons for an outstanding performance." The veteran of many intimate campaigns shook his dulling red head bemusedly.

"She did run me in circles for months. I've got my pride, too, you know?" came the deep, troubled reply.

"Sure 'n' I know you do," the Irishman commiserated. "I guess you just have to decide which it's to be—keeping your pride or baring your heart."

"Why are you so fiercely defending her character now when it was you who was skeptical of her from the first?" Ian was truly baffled.

"She's not an easy woman to understand, I grant you. But I've come to believe that she's a kind and incredibly brave lady. I admit when I'm wrong. 'N' I'm thinking that if you're ever to find any peace in this world, Ian, you must learn t'do the same." He gazed sympathetically at the hurting young man, then cleared the emotion collecting in his throat. "Men on death row look less discouraged than you. I suppose you've not slept in days," he grunted. "''N' when's the last time you had a decent meal?"

"I don't remember. Lunch yesterday, I think," was the numb answer.

"Come on," Rory urged, inclining his head toward the kitchen. "It just so happens that I have a pot of tasty Irish stew to share."

Ian couldn't help but grin. "You're sure Mrs. Garraty wouldn't mind?"

"I'll be sure to extend your compliments. The woman thrives on flattery." Rory winked rascally, then clamped a brawny arm around Ian's shoulder and ushered him into the kitchen.

CHAPTER SEVENTEEN

THE FOLLOWING DAYS were anxious ones for Marnie and Ian. They each awaited a phone call. She yearned to hear from him; he prayed to receive word that immunity had been granted Copeland. Neither call materialized, and by late Sunday night they both were consumed by resignation.

Marnie tossed aside the best-seller she'd been trying to wade through. For the last two chapters the printed pages had been no more than a blur. She eased to the edge of the bed, pulling back the tumbled hair from her eyes and staring at the phone. *Ring! Damn you! Ring!* her heart willed. But to no avail. The deafening silence roared in her ears.

She sighed and fell listlessly back on the rumpled covers, trying to regain her dignity, trying to forget. *"Take my hand, Marnie."* The sound of Ian's long-ago plea echoed in her mind. *"I've a firm grip and I'll hold on tight. I promise."*

It was a promise he had broken, just as he'd broken her heart. Her objective self understood his reasons, but his rejection hurt even more deeply than Seth's betrayal. He had become as necessary as each breath she drew, as vital to her existence as food or water. And now denied him, she was smothering in the memory of him, starving, thirsting for his nourishing presence.

She draped an arm over her eyes, trying to block out haunting images of the wind ruffling through his hair as he'd embraced her that starry night on the Brooklyn Bridge and the golden promise in his eyes as they'd made love in the warmth of the afternoon sun and the cool of a brook. For even though their affair had been brief it was also unforgettable...torridly so.

Perhaps, like a flaming comet falling from the heavens, they'd burned themselves out and disintegrated into nothingness, leaving no trace of the spectacular phenomenon but a mark left on the heart and ashes of regret.

She rolled onto her side, her thoughts thrashing. Not only was she wrestling with recollections of Ian, but also worrying over a long-distance phone conversation she'd had with Sunny a few hours earlier. Several times during their talk she'd nearly lost her composure entirely.

"You must never forget how much I love you, baby," she'd choked.

"I miss you, mama. When can I come home?" Sunny had begged.

"Soon, honey. We'll be together again very soon." She'd avoided the touchy question while attempting to reassure her daughter. "Perhaps we'll take a trip... just you and I. Would you like that?"

"I guess," Sunny had replied, an odd hesitancy creeping into her voice. "Only...." Her attention had wandered.

"Only what, baby?" Marnie had pressed.

"Well, grandpa says he wants to take me on a trip, too. I'm not supposed to tell. He said it was a secret."

Marnie's heart had stilled in her chest. She fought to

keep the panic from her voice. "You're not to go with your grandpa without my permission, Sunny. Do you understand?"

"But why, mama?" Sunny had argued.

"Because I say," Marnie had snapped, then instantly regretted her lack of diplomacy. "And because I miss you so terribly much and want you with me just as soon as it's possible, sweetheart. You can travel with Grandpa Hill later, all right?"

"Don't tell him I told you about the secret, mama." Sunny's only concern had been that she not be caught in the act of betraying a trust.

Marnie feared much worse consequences—that A. L. Hill was making long-range plans for the abduction of Sunny. "I'll keep the secret, Sunny, if you promise to call me immediately if your grandfather insists on taking you on this trip."

"I promise," Sunny had obediently agreed. "I love you, mama. Come for me soon," she'd pleaded.

"I will, sweetheart. It shouldn't be much longer. Hugs and kisses and sweet dreams," she'd bade her before hanging up.

Her first inclination had been to call Ian and once more rely on his coolheaded assertiveness. But she refrained, mostly because of pride. She didn't want him to think her incapable of handling the crisis or misinterpret her motives. He might assume she was using the incident as an excuse to reinstate herself. Should he decide to discuss the matter in person, she knew he would only have to look into her eyes and her longing for him would be apparent. It would be too humbling. She wouldn't risk the pain of yet another rejection.

Caught in the cross fire of concern for her child and

false pride, Marnie groaned aloud and lurched from the bed. Her hand gripped the phone's receiver, but then her fingers relaxed and she backed away, cursing as she slumped to the edge of the bed and buried her head in her hands.

"Spare me this concession, Ian. Call! Please, please call," she implored.

IAN SNAPPED ON THE RADIO, continuing to pace the length of his moonlit bedroom. The music was soft, the lyrics sad; the melancholy the tune provoked was becoming suffocating. He lashed out, striking the wall with his fist, then staggering backward and groaning in agony as he rubbed his smarting knuckles.

Damn Marnie for making him crazy, for making him walk the floor and ram his fist into a wall like some blithering idiot. She was driving him to distraction, reducing him to a mooning lunatic.

Why couldn't he dismiss the memory of her? Why wouldn't she fade like the pain that had begun to recede from his knuckles?

"Simply say, 'I was wrong. I'm sorry.'" Rory's advice haunted him. He grimaced at the thought. Ian Dunn apologized to no one! But then except for Father Pat and Rory no one had ever really mattered enough to warrant such a humbling.

Ian raked his throbbing fingers through his hair. If only he could shut off his thoughts, blank Marnie from his mind. She was there in that room, her spirit in his heart. She filled every inch of space and the immeasurable reaches of his soul. She was so vivid, so compelling. He was utterly confused, totally miserable.

He could call her, disguising his need with a pretext
of reminding her about the resumption of court tomorrow. It was a flimsy excuse but plausible. Since
he'd been shuttling her back and forth between sessions, he could legitimately coordinate the morning arrangement. But what would he accomplish really, he
asked himself. She'd be polite; he'd be noncommittal.
In the end, they'd hang up and then analyze the futility
of the call.

No! A few minutes of hearing her voice wasn't
worth the strain. It was better to leave things as they
were—indefinitely indefinite.

He threw himself onto the bed, folding his arms
behind his head and staring up at the ceiling. Hadn't
he once made the observation that Marnie was as
resilient as a diamond? She was practiced at coping.
He felt certain that she'd resolved their relationship in
her mind, found a way of separating herself from the
intimacy they'd shared. After all, she'd tried to dissuade him from becoming involved—tried to warn him
that her past could not be ignored, that it would come
between them eventually.

Perhaps he should've taken heed; perhaps he should
not have crossed the boundaries she'd drawn. And
yet. . . .

Lightning flashed in his mind and visions of Marnie,
writhing and clinging and desperately needing, crystallized. Was he imagining a responsiveness that had
never existed? he wondered. Or was he recalling an
urgency, a mutual dependency, that was both real and
significant?

He rose up, his eyes searching out the phone. Dare
he chance it? Should he call?

FAR, FAR AWAY in the remote and secret valley, a sudden breeze stirred the wild rose, its opiate scent rising on the wind and carrying a message over hundreds of miles to Lexington. *Disregard pride... transcend petty strife and reach out for love. Declare! Declare! Declare!*

TWO LOVERS REACHED FOR THE PHONE at precisely the same moment, dialing and never realizing their decision had been inspired by fate. A busy signal buzzed. They each hung up. It would now be a matter of who got through to whom first.

"Marnie," Ian's voice tripped over the line. "I realize its late. I hope I'm not disturbing you."

"Not at all," she eagerly responded. "I had just tried to reach you."

Her admission soothed his manly ego. "I wanted to remind you about court tomorrow," he said with a believable degree of nonchalance.

"I've been thinking of little else," she sighed. "It's our turn now, isn't it?"

"Yes, and the witnesses I plan to call ought to help repair some of the damage Cane has inflicted."

"I just want it to be over, Ian. This trial is taking a toll on us all." She subtly hinted at the rift between them.

"Shall I pick you up as usual?" he asked, leaving the door she had opened ajar for the future.

"If it wouldn't be an imposition." His offer was encouraging; her acceptance was spontaneous.

"I'll be there by nine," he replied, fighting to keep his tone strictly professional.

"There's something else we should discuss, Ian." She swallowed her pride.

His heart pounded. "Yes?" he prodded.

"It's about Sunny." She dashed his spiraling hopes.

He quickly adjusted for his miscalculation. "Is there a problem with your daughter?"

"I think maybe my father-in-law is planning to abduct her. Sunny confided in me that her grandfather had mentioned a trip they might soon embark on. What's really suspicious is that he swore her to secrecy. I don't like the sound of it at all, Ian."

"Neither do I." Ian instantly forgot his personal needs, concentrating instead on his professional duties. "More than likely he'll try to take her out of the country. I think we should initiate a precautionary measure. I'll see to it that the proper authorities are alerted and no passport is to be issued to Sunny without our being notified in advance."

"Thank you, Ian. I hated to bother you with this, but I am concerned." Her voice was husky with gratitude.

"I know how much your daughter means to you, Marnie. I'll do everything in my power to safeguard your rights over her."

"I appreciate everything you've done for me, Ian. No matter what the final outcome, I'll be forever in your debt."

He clung tighter to the receiver and to her every word. "Try to get some rest, Marnie. I'll be by at nine sharp." He was afraid to pressure her—to claim her for his own.

"You should do the same," she murmured. "Good-bye, Ian."

"Not goodbye, just good night," he whispered when dropping the receiver to its cradle.

She only heard a severing *click*. Perhaps in time he could find it in his heart to forgive her, she fervently hoped. He hadn't let go of her hand completely. They were hanging on by their fingertips but, nonetheless, still keeping in touch. After everything that had passed between them, it was incredible . . . incredible and at the same time indelible.

THE WIND IN THE VALLEY CEASED; the petals of the wild rose slowly folded closed. The chosen ones were stubborn and prideful, but not without faith. Time and fate would bring them together. The Indian prophecy would soon be fulfilled, and the sweetest flower of all would bloom no more in the valley. For its essence would take mortal form, existing in the hearts of the chosen.

CHAPTER EIGHTEEN

ANOTHER FULL WEEK PASSED. The pressure on Ian was immense as he valiantly defended his client's tarnished reputation. A parade of witnesses took the stand on Marnie's behalf, offering opposing views of her character and expert testimony about her husband's illness and mental state. Yet by Friday it was evident that Ian was stalling. Sutter Cane was becoming surly, Judge Greer testy, and the jury fidgety.

"Your Honor," Cane addressed the bench in an exasperated tone, "this testimony of yet another expert witness is becoming redundant. I urge the court to expedite the process. If my colleague has his way, we'll still be trying this case in the coming year."

Though Ian realized the D.A. had every right to make the challenge, he pretended to be indignant. "Am I to be timed by the prosecution's stopwatch, Your Honor? He certainly had ample opportunity to present the State's case."

Judge Greer removed his glasses, pinching the bridge of his nose thoughtfully as he considered both arguments. "I feel you've had ample opportunity, also, Mr. Dunn," he said in a weary tone. "I shall allow you to conclude your examination of this witness and then court will adjourn for the weekend. But upon resumption on Monday, I strongly suggest that you not waste the court's time on repetitious and unnecessary testimony. I will tolerate no more delays or rhetorical questions. Am I making myself understood, Mr. Dunn?"

"Perfectly, Your Honor," Ian responded in a sufficiently respectful tone.

"Then continue," Judge Greer sighed.

"I have no further questions of this witness," Ian stated with semibelligerence, turning his back on Judge Greer's incredulous expression and ignoring Sutter Cane's agape stare as he strode back to the defense table.

"Was that necessary?" Rory muttered under his breath as Ian seated himself and began to stack his notes neatly.

"It sure as hell made me feel better," Ian snarled through gritted teeth.

"The witness is excused." Judge Greer whacked the gavel down. "Court will resume Monday morning," he barked, strutting from the bench.

"All rise!" the bailiff chanted, bringing the people to their feet.

"You think you're pretty clever, don't you, Dunn?" The snide remark came from Sutter Cane who tarried at the side of Ian's chair.

"All's fair in love and murder trails," Ian quipped, never deigning to glance the prosecutor's way as he stuffed papers into his attaché case.

"If you try to drag this out any more, I'm going to—"

"Ask for a mistrial, I hope," Ian rudely interrupted, smiling to himself.

"Expose you for the shyster that you are," Cane

completed his threat. "Slick-trick lawyers like you leave a nasty taste in my mouth," he growled.

"Save your assumptions for the jury, Cane." Ian dismissed the insult, placing a hand on the D.A.'s pompously swelled chest and brushing him back a step as he passed.

Marnie and Rory awaited him at the side exit. A shiver ran over Marnie's shoulders as she noted the utter contempt in Sutter Cane's eyes as he watched Ian from across the room.

"What was he saying to you?" she whispered.

"Would you believe he was commending me on my courtroom finesse?" A rebel grin broke across his handsome face.

"Hardly." She couldn't help but smile at his wit. "He looks as if he's positively seething."

"We can always hope he'll have a stroke." Ian winked at Rory before holding open the door. "Shall we go?"

The threesome went into the corridor, Marnie walking between her two lawyers. "Will I be seeing you back at the office tonight?" Rory's request sounded much more casual than it was intended. Ian picked up on his pragmatic tone immediately.

"Yes, I think it might be best if we compare notes later." For Marnie's sake Ian disguised his own concern. "I thought I'd take Marnie for a bite to eat before driving her home. Want to join us?"

After he had spent a week in their strained company, the last thing Rory wished to do was accompany them to dinner. "I've been counting calories lately. I'd better decline."

Ian cocked a dubious brow. Counting calories indeed! Rory hadn't considered his weight since age thirty. "Then I'll meet you at the office around eight."

"Enjoy yourselves," Rory said, leaving them on the rear courthouse steps.

"Have a nice weekend, Mr. Connery," Marnie called after him, before warily turning back to Ian. "I wasn't aware that we were stopping for dinner," she said in a tight voice.

"Have you some objection?" he inquired.

"No, I'm just a little surprised, that's all. We haven't exactly been social lately."

He took her arm, politely aiding her descent of the steps. "Whose fault is that—yours or mine?" he responded in an amiable tone.

"Maybe it's neither of our faults, Ian," she said. "Perhaps it's just the strain of our situation."

"I hate this civility routine we're using with each other, Marnie. After all we've shared, at least we should be friends." His hand lingered on her arm, his eyes on her lovely face.

She dropped her gaze, unable to stand the intensity radiating from his eyes. "Yes, at least," she murmured, a sad smile touching her lips. At least he didn't despise her for purposely misleading him. At least he wasn't rejecting what they'd once meant to each other.

For an instant his fingers tightened on her arm and his gaze took on that passionate glaze she remembered so well. But then he released his hold of her, his expression changing and his tone becoming cooler as he opened the Cadillac's door. "What are you in the mood for? Chinese, Italian, seafood, steak?" he rattled off.

"I'll trust your judgment," she said, deferring the decision and drawing her shapely legs into the car.

Her long limbs captured his attention. He drew a deep, silent breath, then simply said, "You may regret those words, Mrs. Hill."

"Not nearly as much as I regret some other things I've said and done," she confessed, never daring to meet his eyes.

Without comment he slammed the door shut.

THE DINNER THEY SHARED had been tasty, the conversation cordial, but when he'd dropped her off at the cottage there was a difficult moment as a wordless exchange passed between them. If their body language could've been interpreted into words, Marnie was saying: If I knew positively how you felt, if I thought you'd accept, I'd invite you in and ask you to stay the night. Ian was answering: If I believed for a second that taking you to bed would resolve this dissension between us, I wouldn't decline the invitation.

The declarations remained unspoken. Instead she thanked him for dinner, and he responded by saying that it had been his pleasure. It seemed they were destined to be lost in limbo somewhere between lovers and friends.

Ian drove at a reckless speed. Not that he was late to keep the appointment with Rory but because he was furious with himself and with the world. Words that should've been simply and honestly said were not, feelings that should've been candidly expressed were not. And why? Because the sexes are born with an ingrained mistrust of each other; because seldom can lovers be friends or friends become lovers; because pride sets apart men and women, creating a wariness: what would be perceived as tenderness with their own kind could easily be suspected of containing ulterior motives by members of the opposite sex.

He accelerated faster as the ridiculous truths stormed his mind. What sort of asinine sense did this make, he wondered. Here he was driving the highway at ninety miles an hour and cursing to high heaven his prideful escape! Who in the hell made up these absurd rules that men and women play the game of love by? What an absolute waste of emotional energy it was!

He arrived at his office in record time, without any recollection of having driven the last twenty miles. He'd cut off two pickup trucks and nearly rammed the back of a tractor-trailer, but the nearly calamitous incidents were only hazy blurs in his mind.

Rory was finishing off a deluxe burger and jumbo malt as Ian joined him. "Well, have you kissed and made up?" the Irishman asked, smacking his lips.

"Yeah, just like you're dieting," Ian grunted testily, opening the secret compartment of the bookcase and retrieving his private stash of bourbon.

"I take it that you and the widow are still fighting the battle of the sexes," Rory ventured, aiming for the trash can with his wrapper and missing.

"It's a standoff, Rory. No matter how much we wish otherwise, it's just not going to work out." Ian sighed, the desk chair groaning as he all but slammed his body into it. "I swear I don't understand myself or her." He unscrewed the top and poured a hefty glassful. "Do you want a drink?" came the afterthought.

"I never mix my poisons." Rory swigged from his malt.

"Well, let's get after it," Ian said in a disgusted voice, undoing his tie, slipping off his loafers and bracing his stocking feet on the desk. "Throw out our options."

Rory wasn't sure he cared for his partner's attitude. From his objective point of view, things were going to hell in a hand basket. He sucked the straw for a second, then offered his opinion. "We're down to the wire, Ian. Since it doesn't look as if the immunity is going to come through, you'll have to put her on the stand and present the suicide theory without corroboration. Then you'll have a basis to delve into the Mitsuki connection."

Ian sipped the bourbon, mulling over Rory's advice. "It might be interpreted as a last-ditch effort to smear the Hill name. It could backfire," he reflected.

"What other option do you have? Unless...." Rory grew pensive as he struggled to his feet and sucked again on the malt. Finally he turned to Ian, a curious gleam in his eye. "We both know by now that Judge Hill has been warned by Hendricks. What if you bluff to expose the firm, the senator and the Hill name? That might rock the old bastard! What if he wants to preserve the image he worked so diligently to contrive more than he wishes revenge? We call him. Make a deal. If he'll testify to his son's deteriorating mental condition brought on by his waning health, the possibility of his suicidal tendencies, we'll agree not to explore the senator's unethical conduct and spare the family the inevitable notoriety."

Ian sat a little straighter in the chair. "And why would be consent when the federal case against Charles Copeland will expose everything eventually?"

Rory's ruddy features took on a smug look. "Because the old man's still got immense power in high places. He may feel he can squelch the indictment of his son's character. You know how it works, me boy. Trade a political favor for a concession of silence. Burn the local boys and bury the scandal along with their ashes. It's been done a hundred times, by ingenious ways. Cover-ups are expensive, but Aubrey Hill can afford it. What he can't afford is a mention of the dirty affair before he can clean it up. If that happens, he won't have a chance to trade at all."

Rory's enthusiasm was infectious. For the first time in a long while, Ian began to feel encouraged. "It just may work!" he exclaimed, gulping a fierce slug of the bourbon. "We could recall him to the stand. His supportive testimony would carry a lot of weight. If he could be convincing enough, instill sympathy for both his son and Marnie in the jurors' minds, make them realize it was a tragic set of circumstances, we may have our most equitable solution. But he must also agree to drop any and all claims on Marnie's daughter," he stipulated.

Reservation creased Rory's forehead. "You're pressing your luck on that point. He may trade her life for Seth Hill's reputation but not his only chance at restitution. He'll not relinquish his granddaughter."

"Marnie has no life without that little girl, Rory. Either he agrees to both conditions or we attack the Hill name. It's the only way I'll deal."

Rory pondered the sensitive issue for a moment, pursing his lips and drawing greedily on the straw. The empty malt cup gurgled, the sound driving Ian to distraction.

"For pete's sake, will you quit sucking air," he complained.

Rory complied, scooping up the burger wrapper

from the floor and discarding it along with the cup in the trash can. "He'll know you can only insinuate the senator's complicity. He's shrewd enough to realize you can't substantiate the claim without Charles Copeland's testimony," he put forth.

"So the question is, will he succumb to the bluff or tell us to go to hell?" Ian summed up their prospects.

"There's only one way to find out." Rory walked to the desk and lifted the receiver of the phone, offering it to Ian.

Ian looked thoughtfully at his partner, then declined with a shake of his head. "I don't want to be hasty. It might be better to sleep on this and deliver the ultimatum tomorrow. I want that old man to know I'm dead earnest when I make the proposal. Then maybe he'll be convinced of how far I'm prepared to go."

Rory dropped the receiver onto the cradle, asking, "And are you committed to these drastic lengths, Ian? Will you proceed with so much at stake and without corroborating evidence?"

"Have you any other alternative to suggest?" came the poignant question.

Rory's glaring silence rendered the decision. The intuitive Irishman sensed Ian's mood. He offered one last suggestion as he left the room. "You'll need your wits tomorrow. I know you're disturbed over the widow, but I'd refrain from drowning my sorrow in a bottle, were I you. Get some sleep, Ian. Sure 'n' you'll be needing it."

Ian didn't even have a chance to thank the old gent before Rory vanished like a ghost from the room. He drained his glass and then strongly contemplated having another.

What the hell, Ian figured as he poured. The whole damn situation was up for grabs, anyway. He had the feeling of being perched on a high precipice, his footing tenuous. Below was a bottomless pit and one careless slip meant sure, sudden death. What he couldn't distinguish was whether it was a professional termination or an emotional one.

He shrugged off his thoughts, deliberately and defiantly sipping the bourbon. In all the many drink fests he'd participated in with Rory, he'd never gone over the brink, never become fuzzy headed or incapacitated. He had a strong, strong urge to do so tonight. Alone and angry and rebellious, he was enticed by the bottle of bourbon. There was so much he'd like to forget. He gulped again of the liquid anesthetic. It was Marnie he wished to obliterate from his mind. The poised and so damn alluring widow was making him think things he shouldn't and want things he couldn't have. They were opposites—a mix that didn't blend—like water and oil—a crass Brooklyn punk and an ever-so-refined lady.

Ian rolled the cool glass against his cheek. Marnie was so very special—a one and only—an original. Even Michelangelo's labors on the Sistine Chapel ceiling did not capture an angel's essence—not the way Marnie projected it.

His mouth curved in a bitter smile. Perhaps the booze was going to his head. Why else would a grown man sit, contemplate art and have the sensation of plummeting from imaginary precipices? He shoved aside the glass, truly afraid what craziness he might contrive were his mind set free on ninety proof.

Marnie needed a guileful lawyer, not some ogling

fool. He stood and replaced the bottle. *No more. . . no more tonight,* his befuddled mind warned him. *Ninety proof and rescuing tarnished angels don't mix, either.*

He headed home. Perhaps tonight this dull ache would disappear and he might drift into an easy sleep. And, as Shakespeare said, "Perchance to dream."

CHAPTER NINETEEN

By MIDDAY SATURDAY, Ian had contacted Judge Hill, hinting at his intent, convincing him of his earnestness, and arranging for a summit meeting between them at an out-of-the-way roadhouse beyond the city limits. Since they each were suspicious of the other, the selected site filled a dual purpose—being low-profile and neutral. And as the "hour of reckoning" drew near, the two mentally prepared themselves for the confrontation ahead.

At sundown on Sunday the real-life chess game proceeded. Judge Aubrey Hill and Ian met and engaged in a duel of theoretical moves. One man was dedicated to Marnie's obliteration, the other determined to rescue her. The savvy counselor did not underestimate the judge's cunning; the old man did not fail to respect his adversary's ability. Yet though the judge perceived skill, he also recognized an impassioned man. And though Ian realized the power the old man wielded, he did not discount the obsession he exuded. Impassioned men make brash mistakes; obsessed ones were susceptible to miscalculation.

"So you have intentions of blackmailing me, also," A.L. surmised, leaning back against the slatted chair and assessing Ian through dull eyes.

"Blackmail's a harsh and incriminating term, Judge

Hill. I prefer to call this matter between us a trade. By the way, this place is celebrated for its cherry cobbler. I recommend it highly." Ian signaled the waitress, placing his dessert order, then raising a brow to the judge.

"Just a little more coffee for me," he instructed, refusing to follow Ian's suggestion.

At the waitress's departure, Ian braced his forearms on the table and continued their conversation in a hushed tone. "I'm sure you're already plotting a way to squelch the evidence against your son. But you need time to call in your political markers, time to sweep the family dirt under the rug. Not even *you* can cover up something of this magnitude overnight. And since I plan to put Marnie on the witness stand tomorrow, that's exactly what you'd have to do." Ian stressed his threat with a steely look.

"And if I concede to your demand to take the witness chair in her stead tomorrow, to perjure myself on her behalf, you'll refrain from mentioning the alleged bribe?" Though the old man's face remained expressionless, his tone was baiting.

Ian held his answer until the waitress had served the cobbler and retreated. "You perjured yourself the first time around. I'm only asking that you tell the truth— admit that your son was a very sick and depressed man and that the possibility of his taking his own life existed."

Hill's reply was preceded by a snort. "Amazing. . . ." he said in a cynical voice. "Can it be you actually believe that absurd suicide alibi she's concocted? I thought you brighter, Mr. Dunn." The old man mocked him with a patronizing smirk. "Like my son before you, perhaps you've fallen under her spell, also? She's a witch who bedevils men's minds," he spat.

"I think you exaggerate her power, sir." Suddenly losing his appetite for quibble and cobbler, Ian shoved aside his plate.

"And I think you underestimate her devious nature," Hill retorted. "She's ruthless and guilty as hell. I wouldn't spit on her if she were on fire, let alone strike any bargain that would abet her escape from justice."

All traces of amity promptly terminated between them. Ian's expression grew stony. "If I were you I'd reconsider. I assure you I'm not bluffing. Make no mistake, if you leave me no other recourse, I will expose your son's corruptness."

They glared at each other, trying to measure the determination in the other's eyes. "You may insinuate it, but you cannot prove it. You think yourself very clever, I'm sure." The judge arched a bushy brow. "And from the inquiries I've made, it's been established that you are daring," he went on. "But I wouldn't be too smug were I you, sir. I'm still the wizard of upsets. My reach is long and I've an iron will." He leaned closer over the table, his eyelid ticking with repressed rage. "If you dare even intimate my son's complicity in this shabby affair, I'll spend my last dime and devote whatever years I have left to securing your disbarment," came the raspy vow.

The amber flecks in Ian's eyes flashed. "Times have changed, Judge Hill. Like the dinosaur's, your days of supremacy are over. You can't tamper with me or the jury. I urge you to accept my terms and amend your testimony. Otherwise you leave me no choice. To save my client from an unjust sentence, I'll have to sacrifice your dead son's reputation."

The old man's posture went rigid as he abruptly

stood. "This night and conversation will haunt you in years to come, sir. You've foolishly misjudged both my influence and utter contempt for that woman. Prior to this meeting I had only one last coup de main to achieve—my daughter-in-law's conviction." His gaze traveled over Ian in an imperious manner. "Now I have a second, maybe even more compelling, reason to defy death. I shall make you regret your impudence, counselor. You will learn a healthy respect for dinosaurs like myself."

Slowly Ian rose from his chair, standing tall and unintimidated before the iron-willed old man. "You're obsessed," he challenged.

"Perhaps," Hill conceded. "But you, my young and reckless friend, are bewitched." He took a dismissive step, then turned and captured Ian's attention with a slight poke of his ivory-knobbed walking stick against the younger man's ribs. "Do what you must, Mr. Dunn. So shall I. But a word of advice, sir. My son forfeited his life for that Jezebel. What price are you willing to pay?"

His eyes were fierce, his tone ominous. Before Ian could respond, Judge Hill turned his back and limped away. The question lingered in his absence. *"What price are you willing to pay?"*

AFTER THE DISASTROUS MEETING, Ian drove the back roads in aimless pursuit of an answer for hours. His clash with the old man had gone badly. Not only had his bluff backfired but now he had doubts about his entire handling of the case thus far. Should he have pressed harder when he had the old man on the stand? Might he have approached his defense of Marnie differently if he'd been apprised of all the facts in the beginning? He was losing the most important case of his life. The tough Brooklyn punk whose uncanny ability to second-guess had won him fame and fortune was suddenly without option or confidence.

Tomorrow he must put everything on the line. And he was unsure. Damn! He was stumbling like a blind man. A woman's very life was hanging by a thread, depending on his expertise, and he was scared senseless.

He found himself questioning his own motives. Had he really believed in her? Or was it more, as Hill had said, that he was bewitched by her? He wondered. Oh, dear Lord! How he wondered! At this stage, the question was crucial. Was he an attorney convinced of a client's innocence or an infatuated man?

The Cadillac balked at his reckless abuse, skidding on the gravel road and fishtailing wildly. He snapped to and gained control of the swerving vehicle. At this rate he'd be making final arguments in a body cast. And regardless of his doubts, the last thing he wanted was to be relieved of the obligation he felt toward Marnie. Of that much he was certain.

He braked, draping his arms over the steering wheel and collapsing with his head on his forearms. One firm fact remained clear in the midst of his muddled thoughts. He was the widow's only hope. Yes, he was fascinated by her; and yes, he was devoted. His body told him he was—it longed for her. His heart concurred—it ached for her. Yet his mind, his intellect, fought the conclusion. Ghostly memories, phantom loyalties stood between them, maybe never to be exorcised. He was a man of immense pride who had no wish to compete with or wither under another man's

shadow. A choice had to made—not his, but Marnie's.
Should he force it? Admit that he loved her and demand
that the mourning widow bury Seth Hill more than six
feet under? Would she turn *to* him or *on* him? Did he
care? Perhaps he was only looking for an excuse to
behold her, embrace her, make love to her a last time.
For should he go to her tonight, should she accept him,
it very well might be their final moment together. God
help him! What if his attempt to pressure Aubrey Hill
had been a mistake? What if in doing so he'd condemned Marnie to life imprisonment? He rolled his
head in anguish. He was so afraid of tomorrow. What
price was he willing to pay? His heart, his soul, every
ounce of honor and strength, every shred of pride he
possessed!

MARNIE STOOD IN THE DOORWAY of the cottage, restless,
unable to close her eyes. Only taunting memories
waited her in sleep, only ghoulish predictions of her
final fate. She was remembering so much, regretting a
vast portion of her life. Tomorrow she must face more
than the paramount twelve who would decide her fate,
she must face the judgment of the world. It struck her as
ironic that even the man who so passionately defended
her in public held grave reservations about her character. His private rejection did little to bolster her
waning confidence.

   She leaned her head against the doorframe, listening
to the crickets chirp and the bullfrogs croak their
mating call. Unlike the night creatures', her cry for love
was silent. She wondered when exactly it was that she'd
fallen in love with Ian. It was unclear, unpremeditated.
When a woman has loved before, the second time

around is more subtle, less erratic. Somewhere in the midst of her despair and confusion, he'd materialized as a man—a handsome, sensitive and magnificently compelling man.

She sighed, her hand reflexively finding, then clutching the St. Jude medal nestled at the divide of her breasts. The present of "faith" Ian had given her in New York comforted Marnie. Miracles happen— juries can acquit, a lover can forgive, she told herself. Unlike Seth, Ian wasn't a whimsical Prince Charming made of pretty words and fragile pipe dreams. He was a man of substance, earthy and permanent. And the same as the wind leaves an impression on the land, for- ever altering the bend of hard oak trees and eroding granite cliffs that stand in its path, Ian left his mark on one's soul. For he, like the wind, possessed an invisible force whose touch eroded long-standing defenses and altered the course of a heart.

Marnie Hill had come to love her champion more deeply than she ever thought possible. Seth was gone, lost to her long before the accident. Her commitment to him and all that it had entailed was over. She had been a good wife. After his death, she'd done all that was humanly possible to protect him. But he and the obligation she'd felt toward him were beyond her now. It was time to try to salvage something of her life. The jury would decide how much time was actually left her. *Dear God,* her heart cried. *It mustn't be too late. I want more than mere days to spare! I want time, pre- cious time, to watch my daughter grow into a wom- an...time to make peace with Ian, years to make love to him.* Her fingers tightened around the St. Jude medal and the wind heightened, rustling the leaves and billowing her filmy gown. A queer scent assailed her senses. She closed her eyes and breathed deeply of the sweet essence. Wild roses. She was inhaling the scent of wild roses. How odd. She hadn't noticed any fields on her many walks.

As Ian and Marnie explored the caverns of their minds, he'd unknowingly traveled the road to the cottage. It was too late when he realized his course. Afraid he'd awaken her and she'd think him mad for appearing on the doorstep at this hour, he turned off the Cadillac's lights and coasted to a stop a discreet distance away. No light beckoned from within the cottage, but nonetheless he got out of the car, softly shut the door, slipped his hands into his jeans' pockets and sauntered toward the bungalow. He really didn't have any intention of waking her. As a matter of fact, he really didn't know what the hell he was doing wandering the grounds. But then he spied her, braced in the opened doorway, adorned in a gossamer gown. She looked like the angel he had always imagined—the vision of his boyhood fantasies. His breath caught, his heart accelerated the way it had when he rode the roller-coaster as a kid and was about to take that first, awesome plunge down the tracks and experience a lickety-split thrill.

A twig snapped under his boot. Marnie's eyes blinked open, spotting his familiar form a few feet away.

"Hello," he said dumbly, stepping nearer, feeling absurd. *What should I say? I just happened to be fifty miles out of my way and hell-bent on a midnight stroll? Dammit! What an ass I'm making of myself!*

She smiled warmly. Her tone of voice was knowing as

she simply said, "I was looking at the full moon and smelling wild roses."

He rested a foot on the bottom step, glancing up at the opal moon. Strangely, he recalled all the romantic clichés that had been attributed to the luminous sphere. The man in the moon was supposed to be privy to lovers' secrets...supposed to make magic and cast forgiving spells. It was nonsense, he knew. But how he wished!

"You're dreading tomorrow," was all he answered, astutely guessing her mood.

"I couldn't sleep," came the honest reply.

He moved nearer—too near. He could smell perfume, not wild roses. "I understand," he sighed.

"There's still some brandy inside. Do you want to indulge?" She moved slightly, the moonlight spilling across her beautiful face. Never had she looked more desirable; never had he been more susceptible.

"Maybe we should. Tomorrow's going to be difficult," he said, hoping the drum roll of his heart couldn't be distinguished.

"You're going to put me on the stand, aren't you?" she asked, knowing the answer but seeking confirmation.

"Yes," he admitted, his hand raking through his hair, as was his habit when he was disturbed.

"Then by all means let's have that brandy. We'll need it." She turned from him, her slender form swallowed by the shadows within the cottage.

Ian followed her inside, his eyes still trying to adjust to the lack of light. He could hear the clink of a bottle and glasses as he followed the streaming moonlight to the floor pillows by the fireplace.

A drink was extended to him, then she chose a pillow seat beside him and settled like a cloud. They sipped in the moon-washed room in silence, in absoluteness.

Finally she spoke. And at last he truly heard. "I want to drown myself in something tonight," she whispered. "I don't want to think, or remember, or give a damn."

His entreating hand covered hers. "Neither do I, Marnie," he concurred.

Instantly, significantly, she set aside her drink, reaching out and slinking her fingertips through his tawny hair. "I'm not going to apologize for being mortal, Ian," came her emotional confession. "I've spent too much of my life saying I'm sorry," came the ache from deep within. He, too, deserted his drink, circling her petite waist with a trembling arm and pulling her nearer. Her lips caressed his ear as she nestled a cheek to his, murmuring, "But I will tell you I regret the timing, the circumstance we share. If fate had been kind, we might've been spared. Accept me as I am," she begged. "I can't help that I loved before you."

It was too much, too sudden, too sad. His arm tightened about her slim body, his yearning lips drawing along her cheek to her honey mouth. "No more than I can help adoring you," he groaned, capturing her sweet, sweet lips and kissing her desperately. Why? Why had he rediscovered her so late, only to perhaps lose her to an injustice? "I love you, Marnie," he moaned passionately, guiding her to the plush carpet, untying the satin ribbons at the bodice of her gown. "So much... I've missed and love you so much," he confessed, shivering at the contact of his hot cheek against her cool flesh.

Dawn could wait. The verdict could wait. He

couldn't! He needed one more heavenly moment with his tarnished angel. His lips trailed her neck to the hollow of her throat, to the soft swell of her breasts. "Make this night special, Ian," came the urgent request as her wondrous hands slid beneath his shirt, stroking his muscled back and beckoning him onward.

With a lusty moan, he undressed her. With runaway desire, she reciprocated. And it was then, once stripped of their garments, their pride, bared of all but their personalized senuality and mutual love, that they enacted the most sacred ritual between man and woman—a union not just of passion, not just of need, but of faith. He kissed her deeply, explored her wantonly, then claimed her sincerely. She embraced him covetously, stroked him preciously and accepted him unequivocally.

It was a moment more infinite than the starry cosmos, more splendid than the Northern Lights, more melodious than a nightingale's song, sweeter than blackberry wine and softer than a lullaby. It was a moment beyond description, a moment when a man who'd never cried shed tears and a woman who'd wept more than her share found peace—sweet, elusive peace. And at the ultimate second, when his body went rigid with ecstasy and he sought refuge, reassurance, rebirth in her kiss, when her hips arched and she searched for release, respite, reincarnation through him, there was gold at the end of the rainbow; there was heaven in the midst of hell; there was a brief, shining moment in Eden for two who had paid the dear, dear price—sacrificing self for love of the other.

Ian eased atop her, satiated. He snuggled her cheek, draping grateful kisses from her forehead to her chin, from dainty ear to ear. "Nothing...no one can take you from me, Marnie. I've waited a lifetime to share this love I've stored." He braced himself above her, staring deeply into her misty eyes. "Aubrey Hill and Sutter Cane be damned. You're mine," he vowed.

Her arms entwined his neck, her willowy body going with him as he collapsed on his back, drawing her with him. "Ian, I must tell you something," she whispered in a strained voice. "I have to, dear heart, and I pray you'll understand."

Her long platinum hair gleamed in the moonlight, cascading over her shoulders to his and partially hiding her delicate face.

"Anything, Marnie," he murmured. "You can tell me anything," he encouraged, smoothing the spilled hair from her flushed cheeks.

She buried her head in the bend of his shoulder, her palm soothing the irregular beat of his heart. This was difficult for her—difficult but necessary. So long she'd carried this guilt; so long she'd wanted to confide this final secret.

His fingers combed through her hair; his chest rose and fell—waiting, anticipating the admission she so much wished to voice.

"I'm not sure anymore, Ian," she confessed, a shudder running through her. He felt her steel herself against the dark thoughts that had claimed her silence and demonized her for months.

"Not sure of what, angel?" he prodded, stroking her, loving her no matter what.

"I don't know for certain if the gunshot was accidental or intentional," she blurted. "Crazy, isn't it?" came the tormented question against his furred chest. "All through this ordeal I was so sure I wasn't at fault. Now. . . looking back. . . ."

He felt her misery, hugged her close. "It's the stroke of never, Marnie. Whatever you say is between us only. I promise. Trust me," he pleaded.

She exhaled a fraction of the ache, begging, "Help me, Ian. I'm afraid." Her arms entangled him. He breathed every labored breath she drew.

"Say it! Once and for all, say it, angel," he implored, holding her fast, absorbing the shockwave of the sob that racked her body.

"I was so disgusted at his betrayal of everyone who'd ever believed in him. I wonder. Ian, I wonder," she choked. "Both our hands were on the gun. It took such a little pressure on the trigger. Was it mine? God help me! Was it mine?" She clutched him fiercely, relied on him wholly. It was a question of faith. *Tell me... please, please, tell me—am I guilty?* the press of her body pleaded.

He melded her against his steadfast length, his fingertips entwining in her hair, a binding arm embracing the small of her back. "I've never had any doubt about your innocence, baby," he soothed. "You aren't to blame, Marnie. You didn't do it!" he assured her.

"Didn't I?" She rocked miserably against him. "I could've, you know?" she moaned. "I swear for a split second I was capable of it. Maybe I'm the way they say... maybe I'm horrid and spiteful and...."

He captured her lips, smothering her doubts and stilling her terror. "You're confused and frightened and sweet, Marnie. You were once more conveniently used by your husband. He wanted out—finally out. And you gave him the means—the argument. Don't do this... don't give him what I so cherish. I love you, Marnie. Be strong—resist him and exist for me." He clutched her so tightly that Seth Hill had no more space, no more domination over the widow.

"I want to be with you always, dear heart. But should it go badly and against us tomorrow, I wish to savor this night with you in the years to come." She raised her head from his shoulder, gazing adoringly at his handsome face. "Love me till dawn," she murmured, slowly tracing the sensuous curve of his bottom lip with a tapered nail. "Make your words memorable—" she inched closer, a strange, almost ethereal expression in her blue eyes "—your touch unforgettable...." She sighed resignedly, whispering, "I want to remember us as inseparable," a second before claiming his mouth with a bittersweet kiss.

With surging urgency, Ian clasped her as if he were holding on to life itself, ravished her mouth as a famished man consumes a banquet. Body and soul, he was hers—not just for tonight but for always. "We are inseparable, Marnie," he vowed, kissing her again and again. "You mustn't be afraid. Angels are immortal," came the fervent prayer before he granted her one and only wish.

They had tonight; they had each other; they had the glory of Eden till the first faint light of dawn.

CHAPTER TWENTY

"ARE YOU DAFT?" Rory mumbled, wrestling with the bed covers and rubbing his sleep-puffed eyes. "Damn birds aren't even flying at this hour and you want me to make a trip to Vicksburg!" Awakened out of a sound sleep, the grumpy Irishman was not in a co-operative mood. "'N' why are you so certain he's going to make a move to abduct his granddaughter in the next few days?"

Rory scratched his head as he listened to Ian's incredible explanation. It was all he could do to control his temper and not slam down the receiver. "A premonition, eh? I'm supposed to go trooping off on some wild-goose chase to Mississippi because you've a hunch the old man has pulled some strings and is fleeing the country. You're a looney, you know that?" he growled.

Again he fell silent as Ian rattled off details. Marnie would call ahead, arranging his taking temporary custody of Sunny. Then he was to impose on Mrs. Garraty and leave the seven-year-old with her until the trial's end. There were flight times and numbers, the address of where Sunny was staying just outside Vicksburg. It was all too much for a drowsy and foul-humored partner to absorb.

"Mrs. Garraty and I aren't running a nanny service,

you know? And what if the mother's convicted? What'll we do with the child then?''

He held out the phone from his ear, grimacing at Ian's admonishing reply. ''It was a thought, that's all,'' he muttered contritely. ''I'll go,'' he grudgingly agreed. ''I'm not thrilled over making the journey, but I'll do as you ask. I'll get in touch with Mrs. Garraty, then be on my way. Does that suit you?'' he grunted testily, then smiled at Ian's answer. ''Sure 'n' I know you appreciate my obedient nature,'' came the snippy retort before he hung up, yanking back the rumpled covers with a curse and stumbling from his comfy bed.

Somewhere between the kitchen and bathroom, sometime between a cup of hot coffee and a tepid shower, a seedling of a notion became a ''blooming idea'' in the Irishman's head. In all their years of association, Rory had never openly or covertly exercised his senior power or interfered with a case Ian solely represented. But as he drew a first scrape of the razor over his lathered cheek, Rory cast aside ethics along with the razor and marched his foamy-faced self to the phone. Aubrey Hill wasn't the only one with connections in Washington. It so happened that the attorney general of the United States was also a long-standing friend and peer of Connery's. Their comradeship dated back longer than either of them cared to admit. In fact, it was the attorney general who had introduced Rory to his ''darlin' Megan'' and he who had stood at Rory's side when they laid her to eternal rest. From time to time they kept in touch with phone calls and intermittent ''nights on the town.'' So, what was compromising about another spontaneous chat, Rory reasoned, pressing the buttons of the number he knew by heart. Except that his motives weren't exactly pure—that he deliberately intended to mention the matter of pending immunity to his intuitive chum, hoping he'd read between the lines and realize how crucial the timing of a decision in Washington could be to a murder trial under way in Kentucky. His influential friend would know he was asking no special consideration, only an expedient and personal examination of the situation.

At the long-distance whine of, "Attorney general's offices. May I help you?" Rory poured on the charm. "Sure 'n' you already have, Miss Clark. Just the sound of your voice brightens my day."

"It's always nice to hear from you, too, Mr. Connery." The spinster secretary, who'd served the attorney general for longer than *she* cared to admit, recognized Rory immediately.

"Is he in today, Miss Clark?"

"To you, he's always in, Mr. Connery. Hold on and I'll put you through."

Rory experienced a pang of conscience, but then dismissed it. He had no intention of tampering with the legal process; he would merely mention the link between cases in passing. Ian or anyone else would never know that the conversation between old cronies even took place. Discretion was imperative. For should Ian ever discover this one act of intervention, he would never forgive his well-intentioned partner. Rory rolled his eyes heavenward, beseeching divine grace. " 'Tis a small sin. Show a bit o' charity to an old altar boy, if you will."

AT THE SAME TIME as Rory was dashing through the airport terminal to catch a flight to Vicksburg, Aubrey Hill was terminating a phone conversation of his own.

"Then you understand my position on this matter, Earl. Yes, if Charles Copeland was to testify, it most definitely could sway the jury. I think it goes without saying that I'd be displeased should such a miscarriage of justice occur. Mmm...uh-huh...of course I realize you can't overtly interfere. I just wanted to go on record as being adamantly opposed to such a... mm...well, that eases my mind immensely. 'Highly unlikely' is most encouraging. Well then, I'll not detain you any longer. Please give the president my regards, won't you? Yes, always good speaking with you, too, Earl."

Aubrey Hill lowered the receiver, savoring his triumph for a moment. After hours' worth of phone calls to those in high places, he had subtly applied the pressure. By now, his negative feelings on the subject of immunity for Charles Copeland were circulating around Capitol Hill. A.L. was well aware of the jargon that his peers used. A "highly unlikely" was as close to a commitment as he'd get. It would do. They knew he was calling in his political markers, and he was confident they'd use their considerable influence—most discreetly, of course—to deny any chance of immunity for Copeland.

He breathed a bit easier now. Let his daughter-in-law spill tears and profess that his son was a corrupt coward. It was only her word—the word of a Jezebel. Who would believe her? In Aubrey Hill's mind there was only one major rule to live by, and it wasn't the Golden one. He'd built an empire on the principle that what cannot be proven does not exist. Marnie would be sealing her deserved fate by testifying. The jury would most assuredly be convinced of her disloyalty and at last see her as the hypocrite he'd *always* known her to be. He'd succeeded in his vendetta. The woman who'd made a shambles of his life would very shortly be convicted and forfeit what remained of hers. Her sentence of life imprisonment would settle the score at last.

A sardonic smile flitted over his leathery lips. He had only one last phone call to make. Then, since he had no intentions of attending court and subjecting himself to Marnie's vilifying testimony, he'd spend the day surveying the Anderson lands Seth was to have inherited but that would now be passed on to Sunny. He found his granddaughter's company very gratifying these days. There was something rejuvenating about the propagative cycle. Sunny had the Hill flair for persuasion. With a little guidance and exposure she could be molded into.... He caught himself beginning to imagine his granddaughter as she might be years from now, as the assured and vibrant woman he would probably never live to see—perhaps another Jeane Kirkpatrick or Sandra Day O'Connor. He could ensure her destiny. Oh yes, he could begin the process and instill the dream. Sunny would make a superb ambassador or Supreme Court justice. He was convinced of it.

He lifted the phone's receiver and dialed. Some fires could not be smothered. They burn in the heart and heat the blood. Sunny was the spark that could reignite a dream. Did the fools really believe they could keep her from him? That a mere technicality of a passport would stand in his way? He'd secured the proper papers with a mere flex of his influence. As soon as the guilty verdict was pronounced on his daughter-in-law, he and Sunny were departing for Europe. He'd planned it all very carefully. They would fly and make the connection with the cruise ship en route if necessary.

"Hello, princess," he greeted her in an atypically animated voice.

"Are you coming to see me, PawPaw?" the child said expectantly.

"In a few days," he promised. "Then we shall take our trip, Sunny."

"But mama says I must have her permission first," came the pouty reply.

"I've spoken with her," he lied. "Everything's fine. She wishes you to have a wonderful trip. Aren't you even curious where we're going?" He tempted the child as he'd tempted Seth.

"Disney World, I hope," she bubbled.

"Some place even more fanciful. Grandpa's taking you to see Europe. I plan to show you real-life castles and introduce you to an honest-to-goodness queen. Would you like that, princess?"

"But what about mama? I'll miss her. Couldn't she come see the queen with us?"

A.L. didn't even hint at the larceny in his heart. "I'm afraid your mother has previous commitments, Sunny. She will be unable to join us." He hoped Marnie was convicted and incarcerated by the sailing of the cruise ship. "You mustn't worry. Grandpa will be with you. You're my princess and as royal as any European monarch."

"What's a monarch, PawPaw?"

"Power, my sweet. All I hope to pass on to you," he explained with a reminiscent spark in his eyes. "Pack your prettiest things. I'll be coming for you soon."

"Shouldn't I call mama to tell her goodbye?" Sunny asked, a worried note in her voice.

"That's not necessary, princess. I'll tell her for you," he assured her deceitfully.

"Be sure to, PawPaw," she insisted.

"I will. Send me a kiss," A.L. cajoled, waiting for the dutiful little smack to travel the long-distance wire. "That's a sweet one, princess. Bye." He lowered the receiver and smiled. His remaining years might not be as fruitless as he feared. There was still time to prime Sunny for a future he foresaw. A Hill would once again figure prominently among the powerful.

"I HATE HAVING TO BRING SUNNY back to Lexington so near the end of the trial. Connie Hill may despise me, but she adores my daughter. She's guarded her like a hawk from the malicious gossip and news reports." Marnie delayed their entrance into the courtroom, placing an entreating hand upon Ian's arm. "Why are you so alarmed about her welfare? I've a right to know."

"You did place the call and tell Connie Hill to expect Rory, didn't you?" He evaded her question by posing one of his own.

"Of course. But I sense there's more to all of this than a mere precaution, Ian. What's made you so edgy?"

"I met with the old man yesterday evening," he replied in a somber voice. "After spending thirty minutes in his rancid company, I'm convinced that he's utterly obsessed when it comes to you. He'll be satisfied with nothing less than your complete destruction. I'm afraid we've underestimated him. He still has power enough to secure a passport for Sunny without our knowledge. If I guess right, he's merely waiting for judgment to be passed on you before claiming her. I didn't want to chance his reaching Sunny before us. He's very clever and has a fixation about your daughter.''

Marnie paled, the clutch of her fingers on his arm tensing. ''And what if I am found guilty, Ian, and Sunny must be given over to him in the end? Can you imagine his intentions? He'll twist her impressionable mind and bend her to his will...the same as he did with Seth. We can't let that happen, Ian,'' came the panicked plea. ''I couldn't bear it.'' She was dangerously close to becoming hysterical. Sheer terror registered in her eyes.

Ian gripped both her hands tightly, answering in a calm but authoritative tone. ''She'll be safe in Lexington. Only you and I and Rory know she's at Mrs. Garraty's. But you must not fall to pieces, Marnie. Your daughter's future depends on how you conduct yourself in the witness chair today. You've got to tell the truth about Seth and what precipitated the firing of the gun. It's the only way we have any chance at an acquittal.'' His voice softened as he noted the ever-so-slight tremble of her proud chin.

''Sunny will survive the disillusionment about her father. She has your blood, too, Marnie. You have to tell your side of the story or else the jury will never know the real truth of the matter. I'm not going to kid you. Expect Sutter Cane to use every trick in the book to discredit you. But you must not succumb to his pressure. If ever there was a time to take a stand, it's now.''

She swallowed hard, then nodded, gazing trustingly into his sensitive eyes. ''When there's no other alternative, the decision is infinitely easier. Once again, it seems I have no choice.''

"When this is all over, angel, and you are vindicated, I'm taking you and Sunny on a long, leisurely excursion." He smiled confidently. "We'll leave Lexington, Aubrey Hill and all the hurt behind. They say Canada is beautiful this time of year—clear and crisp and far, far away. We'll have time on our hands—time to forget the sorrow and reenergize ourselves. How does that strike your fancy?" He looked around, then brought her fingers to his lips, kissing each one.

"You're a very special person, Ian Dunn," she murmured gratefully. "How could I ever refuse you?"

"Ahh, but will Sunny think me as charming?" he teased. "I plan to launch a major campaign in the hopes of winning her heart."

"You'll succeed, counselor," came the positive reply. "Like her mother, she'll find you irresistible."

He glanced at his watch, then reluctantly released her hands. "It's time. We've got to go in." The smile faded from his lips. "Remember, don't let Cane rattle you. State the facts, refrain from trading barbs, direct your important statements to the jury and positively do not blow kisses at your lawyer during a lull." He grinned encouragingly, opening the courtroom door before she had a chance to regain herself.

In a matter of minutes, the bailrff was calling to order another session. Sutter Cane slanted Marnie a "I'm going to eat you alive" look during the resounding, "All rise!"

Judge Greer took his chair, issuing a bland instruction for the trial to commence. "You may call your next witness, Mr. Dunn," he stated.

"I call the defendant, Marnie Hill, to the stand," Ian declared.

Marnie rose from her seat. The distance to the witness stand seemed infinite. Every dreading heartbeat tolled in her head as she responded to the oath.

Ian positioned himself near the jury before proceeding to question her. He wanted to ensure the direction of her gaze.

"Mrs. Hill," he began. "You are the defendant in this murder trial, wife to the deceased, are you not?"

"Yes," she replied.

"Are you guilty of the charge? Did you intentionally shoot your husband?" His voice resounded like Gabriel's bugle.

"I did not," she stated firmly. "Seth's death was an accident—a terrible, tragic accident."

Ian came a few steps closer. "You were alone with your husband at the time of his death?"

"Yes. We had retired for the night. We were in the bedroom."

"And you were engaged in an argument," he elaborated.

"We were," she said honestly. "As previous witnesses have said, a quarrel erupted between us."

"But you've repeatedly refused to state the cause of the quarrel, Mrs. Hill," he continued. "Since only you and your husband were present and privy to the discordant exchanges, and since he cannot relate the details, it is imperative that you tell the jury what prompted the argument and the ensuing struggle over the Smith & Wesson. Will you tell us now, Mrs. Hill? Will you finally divulge to the jury what really happened that fateful night?"

Marnie's mouth went dry, her eyes drifting to the preying prosecutor, spectators and press. God only knew how much she resented their so obvious lust for the juicy details.

"Mrs. Hill?" Ian commanded her attention. "The court is waiting for an explanation."

She drew a deep breath, lifted her chin, then relented. "As has already been established, my husband was a very sick and troubled man. It's true he suffered from diabetes mellitus, and throughout the last two years of our marriage he was impotent. I emphatically deny that I was unfaithful to him during that difficult time. In fact my socializing, which has been greatly exaggerated throughout this trial, was done on behalf of my husband and with his knowledge. You must understand—" she addressed herself to the jury "—Seth felt he had so little time to achieve his one and only dream—to be president of the United States. He asked for my help. . . whenever, however and with whoever it was possible. The men whom I'm accused of seducing were politically influential. I admit to trying to encourage their support, but I did not go to bed with them in order to gain it."

Ian bestowed a slight smile upon her as he unbuttoned his jacket, then turned his back. "Then it was your husband who solicited support via your behind-the-scenes efforts? And it was at his request that you traveled among the elite as his emissary?"

"Yes. It was a joint decision and done with his approval," she replied.

Sutter Cane leaned forward in his chair, cracking his knuckles, a scowl knitting his brows.

"Then why did he react so hostilely to your excused absences? What made him resent your beneficial association with other men?"

"He was ill and tormented by his impotency. He wanted the presidency but he loved me. He couldn't help being jealous. I thought no one else knew of his condition. Aubrey Hill was correct when he said his son wished not to be pitied. I kept his secret for two years. I bore his tantrums because I knew his torment. Is that so difficult to believe?"

"No, Mrs. Hill," Ian said carefully. "Loyalty is rare, but not unbelievable." He studied the jury. *They* were believing. "Please continue," he urged. "Was it a jealous rage that prompted the shooting?"

"No," she sighed. "I admit we had more than one argument over our arrangement to woo support for his presidential bid, but that night we fought over something much more sensitive."

"Enlighten us, please," Ian prompted.

"My husband's behavior had been very strange for months. I knew something weighed heavily on his mind. He was edgy, afraid of wire taps, of surveillance, of his own shadow," she testified.

"You knew him well. You believed it was something more than the strain of his illness and your absences?" Ian paced as the momentum of her testimony heightened.

Every ear, including Judge Greer's, was cocked. The tension in the courtroom was almost tangible.

"I'd grown accustomed to his moods over ten years. Yes, I knew him probably better than he knew himself. Something very suspicious was going on."

"Did you question your husband about his paranoid behavior?" Ian turned, resting a hand on the jurors' box.

"I object to the phrase 'paranoid behavior,' Your

Honor." Sutter Cane asserted himself. "The defense attorney is not a psychiatrist and is certainly out of line making a layman's diagnosis."

"Sustained," Judge Greer agreed. "But let's not nit-pick, Mr. Cane. These interruptions are tedious and the court wishes to afford the defendant every opportunity to explain without being unduly harassed." At Judge Greer's reprimand, Sutter Cane slouched sulkily back into his chair. "Please rephrase your question, Mr. Dunn," came the request from the bench.

Ian respectfully obliged, though his tone held just a hint of irritation as he rephrased the question. "Did you question your husband about his peculiar behavior, Mrs. Hill?"

"I tried many times," she responded directly to him. "But he evaded the issue, blaming his stress on ill health and the pressures of his office. The tension between us grew because I sensed he was keeping something from me—something that was driving him to distraction," she concluded softly.

Ian approached, lending his silent strength, tele-graphing encouragement through his soulful eyes. "When did the unresolved friction between you and the senator reach a climax, Mrs. Hill?"

She lowered her gaze, her mind flashing back and re-living the pain of Seth's confession. She cleared her throat before answering. "It was the night of the shoot-ing. I insisted that he confide in me. I told him I would tolerate no more excuses or secrets, that this subterfuge could not continue if our marriage was to survive."

"Did your husband react hostilely to your ultima-tum? Perhaps become enraged and...." Ian delib-erately baited her.

Her head snapped up and her expression was exactly as he wished—candid and a bit indignant. "No," she blurted. "You're drawing the wrong conclusion. Seth was not hostile or the least bit threatening toward me."

"But the servants heard him chastise you—loudly and severely." Ian goaded her more. At this point it was hard to distinguish his methods from that of the district attorney. Marnie was stunned by his detached attitude.

"They misinterpreted his meaning," she replied, her body visibly stiffening. "Seth was not chastising me; he was distraught...at his wits' end and...." She turned her head, suddenly afraid of losing her composure and seeking a second to collect herself.

"And?" Ian persisted relentlessly. Even Sutter Cane was astounded by his insensitivity.

"And he was asking my forgiveness," she murmured.

"Please speak up, Mrs. Hill," Judge Greer instructed. "The jury must be able to hear your answers."

She nodded, repeating her answer. "They heard him say that he couldn't live like this anymore. They assumed he was referring to sharing his life with me. He wasn't. He never meant divorce."

"Then what did he mean?" Ian pressed her. "What was he referring to?"

Her chin quivered. For a heart-stopping moment, Ian feared she might revert to her standard reply, sacrifice herself, after all. "Mrs. Hill, you must answer me and tell this court the truth." Ian commanded her compliance, demanded her deliverance.

"My husband spoke those words only minutes after he'd confessed to me that he'd accepted a bribe and couldn't live with the shame of discovery. I didn't realize until too late that at the very same moment he was also reaching for the gun in the nightstand drawer." The truth tumbled from her trembling lips, sending a shock wave over the courtroom.

"Order!" Judge Greer pounded the gavel. "I'll clear this courtroom if there's not immediate order." Even Sutter Cane was stunned, instantly leaning to confer with his associate. The jurors' faces reflected the impact of her statement. Only Ian remained unruffled, risking a rallying smile while everyone's attention was diverted. "You may continue with your examination, Mr. Dunn," Judge Greer said as the commotion ebbed.

"Are you telling this court that the senator was intent on suicide?"

"Yes," came the breathless reply. "He said he feared his indiscretions would soon come to light and that he couldn't bear the humiliation. I tried to dissuade him, begged him to put down the gun. He was beyond listening. He'd been holding the gun at his side. But then he said, 'Understand, Marnie,' and his eyes weren't focusing...." She stared beyond the aghast spectators, unaware of their gawking expressions, instead visualizing the instant of Seth's death. "For some reason I can't forget the look in his eyes... they were so strangely vague...trancelike," she rambled. "I could literally feel his fatalism. I don't know what made me do it, perhaps instinct, but I made a grab for the gun as he began to lift it. Somehow, I guess because I surprised him, I managed to snatch it away. Then, the next second, before I could think or react, he grasped the barrel and lurched me toward him. It was then that the gun went off in my hand and my husband slumped to the floor." A queer, almost disbelieving pensiveness crept over her face.

She paused. The courtroom became oppressively still. "He died so quickly...so unnecessarily," she said in a numb voice. "I meant to save him, not harm him. For better or worse, he was my husband." She blinked, the faces of those in the courtroom coming back into focus.

"And you've been protecting him all along?" Ian said in a reflective tone.

"Yes. I didn't want him to have sacrificed himself in vain. I'd hoped his unethical conduct would not be made public."

"But by your testimony today, it is now a matter of public record. The whole story must be told, Mrs. Hill. Please tell the court what your husband confessed to you before his death."

Marnie glanced at the jury. They were waiting to be convinced. She drew a deep breath, then related verbatim what the senator had admitted, naming Mitsuki International specifically and supplying what details she knew.

At the end of her testimony, Ian asked one last but incisive question, "Did you believe with all your heart that your husband meant to take his life at the instant you intervened?"

She gazed unflinchingly at the paramount twelve, simply answering, "I never doubted his sincerity. I believed. So would you have if you'd been there."

"I have no further questions of this witness, Your Honor," Ian stated.

"You may cross-examine the witness, Mr. Cane," Judge Greer advised.

It was nearly an hour later when Sutter Cane ended his grueling interrogation of Marnie. As Ian had assumed correctly, he attacked her character and veracity at every turn. She withstood his merciless assault like the brave and genteel lady that she was, never deviating from her original statement and refusing to be coerced into detrimental comebacks.

His final remarks were especially vicious. "You must think us very gullible, Mrs. Hill. Do you really expect this court to believe that you're the wronged party in this case? How unfortunate there seems to be no one to corroborate your story. How convenient for you that your dead husband can't dispute your claims of bribes and suicide. I wonder if you have any conscience at all?" Noting from the corner of his eye Ian's indignant burst to his feet, Cane said sarcastically. "Don't bother to object, Mr. Dunn. I'll retract my last statement. I'm through with this witness, Your Honor."

Marnie was excused. She held her head high and her vexation inside as she made her way to the defense table.

"You did well, Marnie," Ian congratulated her as she settled beside him.

Her gaze swept the strangers with whom her fate rested. She offered a silent prayer that they'd believe her and not Sutter Cane. "They don't look convinced," she said with concern.

"Looks can be deceiving," he whispered a second before Judge Greer requested that the defense call its next witness.

"The defense rests, Your Honor," Ian respectfully submitted.

"Mr. Cane?" Judge Greer inquired about the State's resolution.

"The State rests, also, Your Honor," came the emphatic reply.

"Then if there is no further testimony to be given, I will hear final arguments."

It was then that the rear doors of the courtroom burst open, all eyes turning to Justin Hart as he marched up the aisle, motioning for a conference with Ian at the rail.

"See here, Mr. Dunn. What is the meaning of this?" Judge Greer demanded.

"I beg the court's indulgence for only a moment, Your Honor," Ian muttered distractedly while listening to Hart.

"This is highly irregular," Judge Greer huffed.

Ian nodded to Hart, then the latter whisked back up the aisle and disappeared beyond the doors. He flashed Marnie a victory smile, then addressed the court.

"I apologize for the disruption and ask that I be allowed to call one last witness for the defense."

"And why should the court indulge this request?" Judge Greer asked.

"The witness I speak of was only just granted federal immunity minutes ago and was unable to give corroborating testimony until now. It's imperative that this witness be heard, Your Honor," Ian pleaded.

"Does the prosecution wish to voice itself on this matter, Mr. Cane?" the judge asked.

The district attorney was as shocked as everyone else. Aubrey Hill had warned Sutter Cane that Dunn might try to introduce sensationalistic evidence at the last, but he had not mentioned a corroborating witness. He realized that if he objected to the testimony and won the ruling, the nagging doubt instilled in the jurors' minds could possibly be more detrimental than hearing the witness. "I have no objections," he reluctantly acceded.

"You may call your witness, Mr. Dunn," Judge Greer said, granting the unorthodox request.

"The defense calls Charles Copeland to the stand," Ian declared.

And so it happened that fate intervened on Marnie's behalf. Charles Copeland took the stand and, by the matter of his conspiratorial knowledge, verified the senator's complicity in the transit scam and added credence to the suicide theory. Suddenly the roles had reversed, and it was the senator's character that was on trial. The seeds of crucial doubt were sown. The entire courtroom knew it. Final arguments were heard. Judge Greer charged, then retired the jury to deliberate.

A near riot broke out at the dismissal of court, reporters dashing for the exits and fighting over phones to make the late-evening edition with the day's revelations, Sutter Cane and his associate, Marnie and Ian inching their way through the fracas and sidestepping the harassing questions.

"Mr. Cane! Were you surprised by Mrs. Hill's startling disclosures today?" a reporter yelled.

"No comment," came the surly retort.

"Have you a prediction about the verdict, Mr. Dunn?" another newsman shouted.

"I never speculate on the unpredictable," Ian hedged.

The legal battle was over. It had been a brutal skir-

mish. All that remained was an excruciating wait and
the final decision of the paramount twelve.

HOURS AFTER THE CESSATION OF COURT, Aubrey Hill
received an urgent phone call from Sutter Cane.

"I've been trying to reach you for hours." The district attorney's tone was one of exasperation.

"I was inspecting my lands out of town. I had no intentions of suffering through that woman's outrageous lies," came the haughty reply.

"Well, perhaps you should have," Cane snapped.
"It seems her *lies* were substantiated by a surprise witness that Dunn pulled out of his hat at the last minute.
I would've appreciated being forewarned, Judge Hill.
I have a sneaking suspicion you knew of Copeland's
existence and the immunity question for days. Why in
the hell didn't you tell me?"

The old judge's face went ashen, the veins in his
neck distending. "I presumed the immunity matter
was decided and Mr. Copeland posed no threat," he
explained in a tight voice.

"This once you presumed wrong, Judge Hill. Copeland's testimony had quite an impact, I can tell you for
sure. I found myself in the precarious position of being
caught between your and Dunn's cross fire. My object-
ing to Copeland testifying would've been futile."

The force of A.L.'s fist striking the desk rattled
every object upon it. "I want to know your gut feeling.
Will she be convicted?" came the livid snarl.

There was a glaring pause.

"I asked you for an educated opinion, Cane," Hill
shouted.

"Frankly, sir, I have my doubts. But there's always

a chance. It's been my experience that juries can be fickle. The most encouraging thing that could happen is if they reach a quick verdict. A speedy decision usually means they've found for the State and against the defendant."

"Then I shall concentrate all my energy on willing a swift verdict. Good night, Mr. Cane."

The slam of the receiver in his ear sent a humming through Cane's ear.

"Damn them all!" The old man's enraged bellow rumbled like thunder throughout Rosehill. His cry was a sacrilege. Recklessly he plagiarized a power greater than his. Vengeance is mine, sayeth Aubrey Luther Hill.

CHAPTER TWENTY-ONE

THE END OF THE TRIAL seemed to mark the collapse of Marnie's amazing resilience. She was completely drained, borderline catatonic, totally dependent on Ian afterward. As always, he chauffeured her back to the cottage. But then, realizing her near-traumatized state, he took charge of her, catering to her every need. It was dusk by the time he dared to leave her. Assuring himself that she'd finally drifted off into an exhausted sleep, he drove the miles back to Lexington to confer with Rory at the office.

Tired and anxious, Ian entered the dimly lit room without comment, waving away the cloying cigar smoke as he slumped into the chair and shoved the accumulating messages to one side of his desk.

"How is she?" Rory inquired.

"About as you'd expect," came the listless answer.

"Sure 'n' you don't look as if you're holding up well, either," Rory noted.

"It doesn't matter about me. I just wish...." Ian deserted the yearning thought, knowing his voice was about to crack and hating to expose his vulnerability.

Sensing his partner's frustration, Rory wordlessly retrieved the secret stash of bourbon hidden behind the sliding door of the bookcase. "Have a nip. It'll ease the jitters." For perhaps only the second time he poured a generous amount into a water glass and passed it to his young friend.

"I shouldn't. They might call to say the jury's reached a decision."

"It'll be some time." Rory feigned optimism, indulging in a hefty glassful, too.

"Let's hope," Ian sighed, downing the bourbon as if it were mere water.

Rory poured again, then dropped his weary body into a leather armchair. "The little girl's safe. She's a darling, t'be sure. One flash of her minx smile and she had Mrs. Garraty and me twined around her little finger. She's the image of her mother, you know?"

A faint smile curved Ian's lips. "No, I didn't. Then she must look like an angel."

"With a disposition to match," Rory added.

Ian rolled the glass of bourbon between his palms, gazing pensively into the amber liquid. "You heard about Copeland coming forward at the last minute?" he murmured, his tone as flat as his spirits.

Rory nodded, averting his eyes. Blessedly Ian was too distracted to notice the evasive trait or question the stroke of luck. "My first thought was that the Good Lord is smiling upon us," the Irishman lied. Actually his initial reaction had been one of relief that his daring notion had worked and the attorney general had come through.

"I want so much to believe that, Rory." Ian relinquished his grip on the glass, propping his elbows on the desk and running his fingers through his hair. "For the first time in my life, I'm scared," he choked. "I mean, really, truly scared."

"You did a fine job. . . all that could be asked." Rory tried to hearten his discouraged partner.

"Was it enough?" came the agonized question as the distraught young counselor retrieved the bourbon and swallowed needily. "I love her, Rory. I guess I have from the beginning. She's everything to me," he confessed.

"I know, me boy," the Irishman commiserated.

"Can life be so unfair? To give me a few precious moments with Marnie and then snatch her away?" Ian directed the questions to his partner, but they were meant for God alone. Abruptly he stood up from the chair, turning his back and drawing a labored breath. "I wish I believed in justice," he said bitterly. "I've never needed to believe more than at this moment." He walked to the window, his broad shoulders slumped, his head bent.

"Do you remember my saying to you that it wasn't my reputation or her acquittal that worried me?" Rory asked in a serious voice.

There was only a silent nod.

"I said you weren't ready to hear what really disturbed me," the senior partner went on. "It was this moment, Ian—a moment when beliefs are tested. I wish I could tell you that power doesn't count, juries aren't mortal and subject to error, right will prevail." A rueful glimmer shone in the old Irishman's eyes. "I wish, me boy, with all my heart. But I will tell you this. . . ." He gulped from his glass, then set it aside. "I've seen my share of injustices during my decades in a courtroom, but I've also witnessed inspiring instances of equity. Believe in the system, as you believe in her," he urged. "You're a hell of a lawyer. Your defense of Marnie Hill was perhaps the finest of your career. I was proud of you, me boy."

Ian turned to him, genuine gratitude sparkling in his

glistening eyes. "I had a hell of a teacher," he said simply.

"'N' it's pleased I am that you're finally acknowledging the fact," Rory chided. "Go on back to her. I'll leave my number with the exchange and be in touch as soon as the jury reaches a verdict."

Ian needed no more prompting. "Call just as soon as you receive word," he stressed.

"You can be sure," Rory promised him.

Ian paused at the door, turning back to his partner with a tender look. "Thanks for the drink. You'll understand if I tell you I'd prefer not to hear the sound of your voice anytime soon."

"Give the lady my regards." The wise and knowing mentor dismissed the anxious protégé.

MARNIE DID NOT KNOW he lay beside her all night, did not know he cradled her body next to his, breathed in unison, kissed her gently, stroked her adoringly throughout the agonizing wee small hours. If she sighed in fitful sleep, his arms encircled her tighter; if she moaned in unconscious misery, he melded his hard body to her, absorbing her understandable dread and lending his love.

At the precise moment the clock on the nightstand struck 9:00 A.M. the phone beside it jangled. At the shrill ring, Marnie sat up ramrod straight in the bed. Instantly Ian reached out and captured her hand.

She turned to him, stark terror in her eyes. "It can't be.... Dear God! Not so soon." Her anguished whisper echoed his own alarm.

He pulled her against his hammering heart, kissing her forehead, then fumbling for the receiver.

He prayed it was a wrong number. Marnie was trembling all over. He fought to spare her his own panic. "Hello," he managed in a fairly steady voice.

Immediately his heart stilled in his chest. "Yeah, Rory," came the tired sigh. Marnie's whole body went limp against him. Her arm tightened around his neck. "Okay, we'll meet you at the courthouse," was all he answered before hanging up and enfolding her in his arms.

"It's a bad sign, isn't it?" she murmured against his cheek. "They took no time at all to decide that I'm..."

He pressed a fingertip to her lips. "We don't know what they've decided, Marnie." He stubbornly rejected the painful possibility. "At least we won't have to suffer days, maybe even weeks, of agonizing suspense."

"Kiss me," she beseeched him, her lips grazing his bearded cheek and seeking his so sensuously soft mouth. The intensity of his kiss nearly smothered her. Between them, there would never be a sharing more profound.

"I love you so, Marnie," he groaned, burying his head in the silkiness of her hair, a shudder traveling along his muscled back. "You're mine...mine...mine," he vowed.

"Yes, always, dear heart," she crooned, tears escaping from the corners of her closed eyes as she cradled his head and kissed his temple. "Forever..." she murmured, remembering how sweet and terribly fragile was the word.

NEWS SPREAD LIKE WILDFIRE that a decision was in on the Hill case. It was a dismal morning—overcast and drizzling rain. But the gloomy weather didn't deter the crowds that gathered outside the courthouse. Tucked under umbrellas and clad in raincoats, they waited to hear of the widow's fate.

The district attorney arrived first, promptly followed by Judge Aubrey Hill. As the old man seated himself in the gallery, they exchanged smug glances. The jury had been swift. They had every reason to be confident. Aubrey Hill was especially pleased. At long last he would have his revenge. For years she had been like a thorn in his side. Finally he would be done with her! His bags were packed, a plane was chartered. There only remained the pronouncement of a guilty verdict. Then he'd have it all—his daughter-in-law's complete and oh so sweet downfall and undisputed guardianship of his granddaughter. This day perhaps more than any other was a milestone in his life. He gloried in Marnie's impending disgrace.

The gallery hushed as the defendant and her two lawyers entered. Ian looked haggard, Marnie pale and regal, Rory hung over. Hundreds of pairs of eyes singled out the widow; her gaze locked with only one other person's—her father-in-law's. The message he telegraphed was noxiously clear—*rot in hell, Jezebel!*

Ian's hand at the small of her back directed her to the familiar chair. Rory's squeeze of her hand as the jury filed in lent her courage. At the bailiff's "All rise," her stomach churned and she fought the nausea overcoming her.

Judge Greer spared her the humiliation of becoming publicly ill as he expeditiously asked the crucial question. "Has the jury reached a verdict?"

The selected foreman stood. "We have, Your Honor."

"Will the defendant please rise," Judge Greer requested in a solemn tone.

Ian's reassuring hand enveloped hers as he slowly came to his feet, setting the example she must follow. She closed her eyes, rendering a one-word prayer as she clutched the St. Jude medal and forced her body to a standing position. *Mercy!* came the plea. Her knees buckled. Feeling her slight sway, Ian's iron grip clamped around her waist.

Anything. . . I'll sacrifice anything. . . if you'll only just spare her. . . he bargained with the Almighty.

"How say you the jury?" Judge Greer demanded.

"We the jury find the defendant, Marnie Hill—" every heart in the courtroom palpitated as each person anticipated the foreman's next words "*—Not Guilty!*" came the reprieve.

Jubilation erupted at the defense table, Ian embracing Marnie so tight that he pulled her off her feet, Rory jumping up with an undignified thrust of his fist into the air. Sutter Cane dropped his forehead to his palms, shaking his head disbelievingly. Yet his shock was nothing in comparison to Aubrey Hill's. The bitter old man was devastated. He sat paralyzed amid the tumult.

"You're free, Marnie," Ian whispered as Judge Greer struck his gavel, trying to regain some semblance of order.

"I was going to say something trite, like how can I ever thank you?" She smiled the angelic smile he'd come to love.

"I should be gallant and say nothing. . . you owe me nothing. . . ." He cast her a roguish grin. "But the truth is, my fee is going to be astounding." His hazel eyes glinted rascally.

"I thought it might be." She flipped him a saucy look as Judge Greer's call for order was finally obeyed.

She clasped Ian's hand as the presiding judge addressed her. "Marnie Hill, you have been found not guilty. All charges are herewith dismissed. You are free to go!" he declared. "This trial is ended. Case dismissed!" And with a concluding pound of the gavel, the nightmare Marnie had lived for so long was finally, blessedly over.

"Congratulations, me girl." Rory leaned and kissed her cheek. He fairly beamed as she hugged his bear neck.

"Thank you so much, Mr. Connery. I'll never forget your loyalty or kindness," she said sincerely.

The thorny old Irishman was touched. "Sure 'n' it was my pleasure to be representing such a gracious lady." Noting Ian's amused expression, he bristled and thrust out a hand toward him. "If you're as smart as I've always believed, you'll marry her quick and cherish her always."

Ian clasped his partner's hand firmly. "I intend to, Rory," he declared with a broad grin. "Can you handle the practice alone for a month or two?"

"Don't be letting this notable win go to your head, me boy. I'm still the senior member of the firm 'n' was *handling* it long before you cracked your first law book." He winked, then abruptly stepped through the gate and bulldozed his way up the aisle. Neither Ian nor Marnie would ever realize the trump card he'd played in the high-stake legal game.

Ian's adoring gaze lighted back upon Marnie. Gently he took her hands in his own. "Let's get the hell out of here," he suggested in a husky voice. "I've got a lifetime of loving to do."

"*We*, counselor," she corrected him, slipping an arm around his lithe waist as his draped over her shoulder. "You must start thinking in the proper terms," she chided, inching closer to his protective figure as they swung through the gate. "*We* shared the worst times, now *we* are damn well going to savor the good ones."

Aubrey Hill sat motionless as they inched their way through the congratulatory crowd. As his daughter-in-law drew alongside the bench upon which he was seated, the old man's acid eyes snapped in her direction, but neither he nor his fanaticism existed any longer for her. He belonged to a past from which she was walking away.

His arthritic fingers clutched the ivory knob of his walking stick in a stranglehold. *She will suffer yet,* he silently vowed. *She will know years of mental anguish, separated from her child. If she caught the very next commercial flight to Vicksburg, she still would not be in time to spoil my ultimate reprisal. Damn them both! They'll learn a healthy respect for a dinosaur like me! Oh yes, indeed they would!*

As Marnie and Ian emerged onto the courthouse steps, the sun broke through the clouds and a spectacular rainbow appeared in the sky. It was dazzling—an arc of pastels so beautiful that it defied description.

"Look, Ian." Marnie shielded her eyes with a hand, standing and staring up, enthralled by the magnificence she beheld. "It's incredible!" she marveled.

. His arm clasped tighter about her shoulder, drawing her near as he, too, was awed by the splendor. "The Indians used to interpret a rainbow as a good omen, angel," he murmured against her temple. "A blessing of health and happiness, prosperity and peace," he explained.

"Isn't it ironic that it should choose to materialize today?" Marnie leaned her head against his broad shoulder with a wistful sigh.

Ian considered the spectacular sight and her comment for a reflective moment. "Perhaps not, Marnie," he said softly, nestling his cheek in her silky hair. "Somehow I can't shake the feeling that kismet interceded on our behalf. It's silly, I know—" he shrugged, then enfolded her even tighter in his arms "—but nonetheless, I sense our lives were touched in a special way."

It was done! The prophecy had been fulfilled. The wild rose bloomed no more in the valley. It vanished at the exact moment that a miraculous rainbow dissipated from a Kentucky sky. The legend did not reveal if either would appear or divinely choose again. Perhaps the spirit of the wild rose lurks in every heart, its secret of faith lying dormant within us all. Perhaps we need only to be sensitive to hear its message. . . .

HARLEQUIN
PREMIERE AUTHOR EDITIONS

6 EXCITING HARLEQUIN AUTHORS —6 OF THEIR BEST BOOKS!

Daphne Clair
A STREAK OF GOLD

Marjorie Lewty
TO CATCH A BUTTERFLY

Anne Mather
SCORPIONS' DANCE

Jessica Steele
SPRING GIRL

Margaret Way
THE WILD SWAN

Violet Winspear
DESIRE HAS NO MERCY

EYE OF THE STORM

MAURA SEGER

A powerful
portrayal of
the events of
World War II in the
Pacific, *Eye of the Storm* is a riveting story of how love
triumphs over hatred. In this, the first of a three-book
chronicle, Army nurse Maggie Lawrence meets Marine
Sgt. Anthony Gargano. Despite military regulations
against fraternization, they resolve to face together
whatever lies ahead.... Author Maura Seger, also known
to her fans as Laurel Winslow, Sara Jennings, Anne
MacNeil and Jenny Bates, was named 1984's
Most Versatile Romance Author by *The Romantic Times*.

At your favorite bookstore in April.

EYE-D-1

Enter a uniquely exciting new world with

Harlequin American Romance™

Harlequin American Romances are the first romances to explore today's love relationships. These compelling novels reach into the hearts and minds of women across America... probing the most intimate moments of romance, love and desire.

You'll follow romantic heroines and irresistible men as they boldly face confusing choices. Career first, love later? Love without marriage? Long-distance relationships? All the experiences that make love real are captured in the tender, loving pages of **Harlequin American Romances.**

What makes American women so different when it comes to love? Find out with **Harlequin American Romance!**

Send for your introductory FREE book now!

Get this book FREE!

Mail to:
Harlequin Reader Service

In the U.S.	In Canada
2504 West Southern Ave.	P.O. Box 2800, Postal Station A
Tempe, AZ 85282	5170 Yonge St., Willowdale, Ont. M2N 5T5

YES! I want to be one of the first to discover
Harlequin American Romance. Send me FREE and without
obligation *Twice in a Lifetime.* If you do not hear from me after I
have examined my FREE book, please send me the 4 new
Harlequin American Romances each month as soon as they
come off the presses. I understand that I will be billed only $2.25
for each book (total $9.00). There are no shipping or handling
charges. There is no minimum number of books that I have to
purchase. In fact, I may cancel this arrangement at any time.
Twice in a Lifetime is mine to keep as a FREE gift, even if I do not
buy any additional books.

_____

Name   (please print)

_____

Address   Apt. no.

_____

City   State/Prov.   Zip/Postal Code

_____

Signature (If under 18, parent or guardian must sign.)

154-BPA-NAZJ

AMR-SUB-2

WELCOME TO...

SUPERROMANCES

A sensational series of modern love stories
from Worldwide Library.

Written by masters of the genre, these longer,
sensual and dramatic novels are truly in keeping
with today's changing life-styles. Full of intriguing
conflicts, the heartaches and delights of true love,
SUPERROMANCES are absorbing stories —
satisfying and sophisticated reading that lovers
of romance fiction have long been waiting for.

SUPERROMANCES
Contemporary love stories for the woman of today!